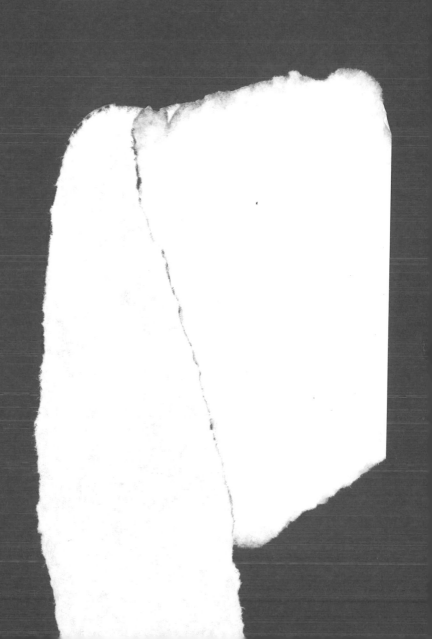

MORTLOCK

MORTLOCK

JON MAYHEW

BLOOMSBURY

LONDON BERLIN NEW YORK

Bloomsbury Publishing, London, Berlin and New York

First published in Great Britain in April 2010 by Bloomsbury Publishing Plc
36 Soho Square, London, W1D 3QY

Epigraphs: traditional folk songs and traditional folk ballads

'Two Old Crows' and 'Babes in the Wood'
included by kind permission of the Copper Family

A CIP catalogue record of this book is available from the British Library

ISBN 978 1 4088 0392 9

FSC
Mixed Sources
Product group from well-managed
forests and other controlled sources

Cert no. SGS - COC - 2061
www.fsc.org
© 1996 Forest Stewardship Council

Typeset by Dorchester Typesetting Group Ltd
Printed in Great Britain by Clays Ltd, St Ives plc, Bungay, Suffolk

1 3 5 7 9 10 8 6 4 2

www.bloomsbury.com/mortlock
www.bloomsbury.com/childrens

For my wife, Lin, and my children, Sally, Alfie,
Frank and even Jack

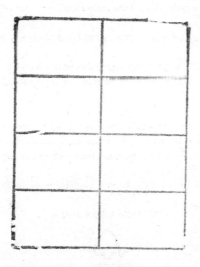

IMMORTAL AMARANT, A FLOW'R WHICH ONCE
IN PARADISE, FAST BY THE TREE OF LIFE
BEGAN TO BLOOM, BUT SOON FOR MAN'S OFFENCE
TO HEAV'N REMOVED WHERE FIRST IT GREW, THERE GROWS,
AND FLOW'RS ALOFT SHADING THE FOUNT OF LIFE

PARADISE LOST, JOHN MILTON

PROLOGUE

ABYSSINIA, 1820

Sebastian Mortlock felt a wriggling invasion between his toes. He glanced down. The ground seethed beneath his torn boots as worms, millipedes, cockroaches and ants twisted over each other. An insect crawled up the arch of his foot. He stamped and grimaced at his two comrades.

Thurlough Corvis grinned and mopped his brow. 'It's a good sign,' he reassured Sebastian. 'This jungle's teeming with life. Even three Englishmen might survive.'

'It's a sign. I'm not sure how good it is,' said Edwin Chrimes, pulling a face and swatting a beetle from his leg. 'There shouldn't even be a jungle here, not in this godforsaken place.'

The jungle, an inexplicable oasis, had brought them to this barren salt desert in the first place. It had pulled them clear of the raised weapons of hostile tribesmen, tugging them past the narrow-eyed gaze of suspicious warlords; dangerous men, who had spent their lives fighting over this hellhole.

The Englishmen were still alive – if oddly dressed. The three of them had long ago abandoned their dark travelling suits for the lighter, cooler local tribal wear. Travelling had stained the white cotton tunics that flowed down to their boots. Turbans enveloped their heads and scarves masked their faces, showing only their eyes.

During their travels, they had become good friends. Corvis had surprised Mortlock. A slight, pale gentleman, more used to the gaming table and the port, he'd found strength in the face of their many hardships – unlike Chrimes. With his red hair and freckles, he had suffered from the scorching sun, his skin blistering in the heat. He never stopped complaining.

'So what now, Sebastian?' Corvis raised an eyebrow, the slanting shadows of the forest canopy exaggerating his dark, pointed features. 'Do we rest or shall we forge ahead?'

'Rest?' Mortlock stretched his powerfully built body, aware of how he towered over his friends. 'We're on the verge of the greatest discovery of all time and you want to rest?'

'You're in charge. I just wondered if you were tired,' Corvis said, raising his hands. 'After all, an old man like you . . .'

'I'm twenty-six, Corvis,' Mortlock objected, though he couldn't disguise the humour in his voice. 'Only a year older than both of you!'

'Well, it takes its toll,' Chrimes chipped in.

Mortlock gave them both a withering glance, then

turned and plunged into the bush.

'If you're so young and fit, you'll have no trouble keeping up!' he called back, throwing down his pack and disappearing into the shadows. He heard Corvis and Chrimes give a yell and then the rustle of foliage as they charged after him.

Mortlock grinned, glancing back only once to gauge the distance between himself and his pursuers. He leapt over fallen tree trunks and dodged around spiny bushes. But the jungle was dense. Vines pulled and snagged at his cotton robes. His laughter died as he panted with the effort of running. Sweat poured down his face. He wrestled through the tangle of vegetation that clung to him, fought against him. It grew darker. He could hear the others still cursing and thrashing about behind him, their voices fainter now. A red glow flickered ahead, enticing him, *like a moth to flame*, he thought. More branches and creepers gripped him as he struggled forward. He fell heavily on to a rotten tree stump and pain lanced up his leg. Mortlock's breath grew more ragged as panic swelled inside him. He felt as if he were drowning in a sea of green. With a bellow of rage he dug his feet into the soft earth and hurled himself forward. The wall of foliage gave way, tearing at his clothing as he fell on to the open ground of a clearing.

Silence.

Trees huddled around the small glade, leaning in as if to protect the small flower that grew in the centre of the clearing. It stood about a foot tall, scarlet petals cupping upwards, like a tulip made from the most exquisite jewels. A pulsing light – reminding Sebastian of the beat of a heart – caused the shades of red to flicker and flow across the surface of the flower's petals.

Now Mortlock could hear Corvis grumbling and snarling as he tore his way through the last few feet of dense jungle. Without looking round, Mortlock heard his friend fall into the clearing, then a second crash as Chrimes followed. The two men appeared beside Mortlock and gazed towards where he was looking. No one spoke.

Birds cried out high above their heads. Distant roars and growls from the undergrowth barely registered in Mortlock's mind. He couldn't take his eyes away from the glowing red flower. He found himself sinking to the ground and was dimly aware of Chrimes and Corvis doing the same. Damp moss cushioned his knees and a humid mist seemed to seep into his bones.

'The Amarant,' Mortlock whispered, glancing at his companions. 'We've found it at last, eh?'

'It's beautiful,' Chrimes murmured, the crimson luminescence making his red hair look aflame. 'So much power in something so fragile.'

'Power over life and death,' Corvis said, ruby light playing across his pale face. 'It's beautiful, yes, but . . . also wrong, somehow.'

Time seemed to slow as Mortlock stared into the red heart of the flower. It pulsed before him, and he felt like he was bathing in its unearthly light as it painted images in his mind.

A twig snapped deep in the forest.

Mortlock stiffened and glanced around. The shadows beyond the flower's pulse shifted as if by a slow, steady movement.

'There's something out there,' Corvis said, his dark eyes burning in the ruby glow. He shivered.

'Like someone's watching us,' Chrimes agreed, staring into the blackness. 'How long have we been here?'

'I don't know,' Mortlock muttered, running his fingers through his matted blond hair. He felt as though he'd just woken up from a deep sleep, drugged and thick-headed. 'Too long. Look at the moon.'

'My God,' Corvis whispered. The bloated moon hung high above their heads. It had been a blazing hot after-noon when they'd run into the oasis.

'Let's go,' Mortlock said, jumping to his feet. His heart pounded.

The undergrowth rustled around them. Vague shapes flitted through the shadows. Whispering voices carried on the breeze like the rustling of dead leaves. The sweet, cloying scent of decay filled the air. An emaciated face grinned out of the undergrowth. Behind it were others.

'What in God's name are they?' Chrimes whispered, sweat beading his forehead.

'I don't think God has much to do with it,' Mortlock replied, his voice shaky and hushed. 'I think they guard the Amarant.' He heard one of his friends give a low moan of fear.

Corvis broke first, his slim frame almost knocking

Chrimes over as he bounded into the bushes. The whispering became a low, angry murmur. Mortlock grabbed Chrimes and dragged him bodily from the clearing.

Thorns and briars snagged and tore at them, ripping flesh and clothes as they fought their way through the vegetation. Mortlock could hear Corvis panting up ahead. He pushed the wide-eyed Chrimes before him, heaving the blade of his machete at branches and creepers. Mortlock snatched a glance into the undergrowth and glimpsed long-dead faces leering out from the shadows. He heard himself scream as the murmur of the dead became a strangled yell of anger. Cold fingers raked his shoulders and snagged at his hair; the sweet stench of decay clogged his nostrils. He slashed at the limbs that tried to snare him, shuddering as his fingers brushed against the dry, icy skin of corpses. His breath shortened as he fell forward. *We're all going to die!* he thought desperately. But suddenly the jungle thinned and Chrimes and Mortlock staggered out into the cold night air of the desert, collapsing on to the shivering Corvis.

Dawn light broke over them, even though night had descended only moments ago. The men stared back into the forest, shivering. Steam rose off the fat leaves of jungle plants.

'Living corpses,' Mortlock panted.

'I had a vision while I sat by it,' Corvis said quietly, looking back into the dark, silent jungle. 'A cold horror clutched my heart. I saw . . . wings, black wings, stabbing beaks, ravens and crows . . .'

'Decay,' Mortlock whispered. 'I saw a death's-head, skulls and charnel houses . . . We can't take the Amarant with us. Those were warnings.' Sweat trickled down his forehead. 'We must leave and never come back.'

'But we've come this far,' Corvis protested, glancing from Chrimes to Mortlock and back. 'Maybe there's a way. If we bring back the Amarant, we'll be famous, rich beyond our wildest dreams.'

'Will we?' Mortlock grunted as he stood up. 'I say we've been given a chance. Let the thing alone.'

'You're right,' Chrimes said, smoothing his thin red beard with trembling fingers. 'We can't take the Amarant. It would destroy us.'

'We must swear that none of us will return to this spot,' Mortlock said. He held out an open palm. He slid his sheath knife from his belt and placed the blade to his hand. He tilted the knife and dragged it across his flesh, scoring a mark on his work-worn skin. Then he offered the handle of the knife to Chrimes. 'A blood pact,' he said simply.

'Agreed.' Chrimes slashed at his palm and held his hand against Mortlock's.

They turned to Corvis. He winced as he made a feeble scratch, only just managing to draw blood. He joined his friends.

'An oath,' he murmured faintly. He failed to meet Mortlock's glance. 'Never to take the Amarant from this place.'

PART THE FIRST

LONDON,
1854

MANY A ONE FOR HIM MAKES MOAN,
BUT NONE SHALL KNOW WHERE HE IS GONE;
O'ER HIS WHITE BONES, WHEN THEY ARE BARE,
THE WIND SHALL BLOW FOR EVERMORE.

'THE TWO RAVENS', TRADITIONAL FOLK BALLAD

CHAPTER ONE
THE KNIFE THROWER

Josie Chrimes levelled the knife, holding it by its blade. She felt its weight shift towards the handle, the cool steel pressing on her forefinger and thumb as she extended her arm. The Great Cardamom stood twenty strides away. *It could be twice as far and I'd still be able to send the blade through him*, she thought. Josie never missed. She reached her arm back, then snapped forward and, with a confident flick of her wrist, sent the knife whirling towards its target.

The sound of the audience's gasp made her smile. The knife flashed across the stage until – with a *thunk!* – it pinned the Great Cardamom's top hat to the cork-board behind him. Knife after knife had described his outline, so close that Josie had seen the front rows of the audience craning forward, wide-eyed, eager to spot a trickle of blood. But now this last knife had hit its mark, Cardamom stepped neatly from under his hat, still pinned to the cork, and smoothed his red hair. With a flourish, he gave a deep bow, looking over at Josie to share a secret wink. The crowd went wild, clapping and cheering.

Josie strode across the stage, narrowing her eyes against the harsh glare of the footlights. Then she took Cardamom's hand and shared the second bow, dipping so low that her nose brushed against her skirt.

As the two of them straightened up, Josie glanced over at Cardamom. She was almost taller than him now. Out in the street, they would have made a curious sight: he stocky, with dyed red hair, clipped moustache and red-lined cloak, she dressed in leggings and a light shift, her long, blonde hair spilling from under a black bow. But onstage, they still made a perfect fit.

Josie took a deep breath, smelling the sweat from the audience and the dust ingrained in the velvet curtains. The music from the orchestra's pit filled the air, vibrating through her bones. *This is where I belong*, she thought, squeezing the hand of her guardian, the Great Cardamom.

'Ladies and gentlemen.' He raised his hand, asking for quiet. 'I give you Artemis the Huntress! Thirteen years of age, a lifetime of talent!'

After a fresh round of applause, their act moved on. Josie watched as Cardamom amazed the audience by producing almost anything they called out from his pockets: pork pies, mousetraps, fruit, coins, doves . . . Even a ferret appeared in his hands. He dragged a bunch of fresh carnations from inside his coat, winked at Josie and threw them to her. Now and then he would release a balloon, and Josie would flick a knife from her hand to burst it. Josie kept her smile fixed but she wondered how Cardamom conjured up all these things. Backstage, she'd often secretly checked his pockets and found them to be ordinary and empty. Her guardian didn't let her in on his secrets. 'That's magic,' he'd say mysteriously. Josie knew it was nothing more than sleight of hand, but that still didn't explain how he knew what the audience was going to ask for.

A levitation act followed the conjuring, then filling a jug from a bottle that never seemed to run dry, rabbits from hats – it was all standard material. Cardamom and Josie often went to the Lyceum up the street to see Professor Anderson, the so-called 'Wizard of the North', perform similar feats. But Cardamom's performance was seamless. As he wove his real magic, Josie would tumble, cartwheel, flip and roll in between tricks or when she brought props on. The collective gasp from the audience when she ran across the stage, then bounced and somersaulted to Cardamom's side, made her grin. She enjoyed herself almost as much as the audience.

Tonight, the clapping and cheers spilled into the wings as Josie and Cardamom squeezed past the dancers who were next on.

'But why Artemis?' Josie asked, pressing herself against the wall and blowing the dancing girls' plumes from her face as they filed by. 'It's such a dull name.'

Cardamom stopped and turned, thrusting his face into Josie's. 'Your talents come from ancient gods,' he hissed,

suddenly sombre. The flush of excitement had faded from
his cheeks. Then he gave a wink. 'And we wouldn't like
to upset them, would we?'

Josie watched her guardian push past the stagehands
and waiting actors, heading out of sight into the dark
interior of the theatre. She frowned. Those moods of his!
Cardamom could shift from maudlin to joking in the
blink of an eye. Onstage he looked demonic with his
pointed red beard and arched eyebrows. And yet, in rare
moments, he could reveal the gentlest of souls. She
hurried after him.

Josie caught up with Cardamom in a storeroom, where
they could talk with no fear of their voices disturbing the
action onstage. It was the place they always went to
when they needed to talk.

'If it makes you happy, Uncle,' Josie sighed, 'I'll keep
the name Artemis.'

Cardamom gave a faint smile. He shrugged his shoulders. 'The audience is going to love you whatever stage
name we choose. As you grow up, the act gets . . . easier.'
Cardamom suddenly looked much older. With a pang of
sadness, Josie noticed that his dyed hair drew attention
to his advancing years.

A short, barrel-chested young man dressed in dark
breeches and a waistcoat emerged from the backstage
shadows beyond the storeroom. A stubby clay pipe
wreathed curls of smoke around his mop of black hair and
his thick moustache. He held a dripping paint brush,
paint speckling his rolled-up shirt sleeves.

'Gimlet!' Josie threw herself at the stocky character and hugged him. She was grateful for the distraction. 'What have you been up to? Have you finished the new backdrop for the Underworld?'

Josie had been watching Gimlet's preparation of the scenery for Cardamom's new act. Her guardian had decided on the theme of Dante's *Inferno*. Dancers would be dressed as imps and demons, while Cardamom would perform tricks that would baffle the Devil himself. Gimlet had set to work on creating the backdrop: flames and furnaces with fearsome, satanic faces staring out from rocky caverns.

'Steady,' Gimlet laughed, holding the wet brush away from Josie's hair. 'I need to put the finishing touches to the scene. I might be living in this theatre for the next few weeks!'

'You already do, Gimlet,' Cardamom teased.

'It beats making coffins,' Gimlet said.

Josie felt herself shudder. Stage sets and funeral boxes. Gimlet had told her he supplied caskets for undertakers when work in the theatre was slack or during an epidemic. *What a life*, she thought. At least her work onstage kept her fed.

Cardamom interrupted her thoughts. 'Come on. Let's get this greasepaint off. It's time to go home.'

Josie shut the dressing-room door behind her and leaned her weight against it for a moment, closing her eyes. Now that she was offstage, she could feel exhaustion seeping through her. She pushed herself forward into the room and tugged off her shift. Then she pulled on the starched blouse and stiff black dress that Cardamom insisted she wear outside the theatre. The fabric made her scratch and wriggle. Cardamom would look at her wearing this dress and always say something hurtful such as, 'I wish you could be more ladylike.'

Josie knew she wasn't a beauty. She didn't need Cardamom to tell her that. When she was younger, she'd watched the dancers with their long, graceful legs.

'Do you want to be a dancer, Josie?' one of them had said, bending down to her and tweaking her nose.

'Oh, yes, please,' she'd replied, but the dancers had giggled and skipped off to their rooms. Now Josie knew why. She was just too plain.

Madame Carla had said she was handsome. Josie knew that 'handsome' wasn't the same as 'pretty'. But then, Madame Carla was the Bearded Lady act in the booth outside the Erato, so she was hardly an expert.

Josie chewed her fingernail and gazed at the pale reflection in the dressing-room mirror. Slowly, with a wad of cotton wool and gentle strokes, she removed her make-up. She sighed as she drew the cotton across her broad nose. *And those eyes*, she thought. *Such a dull brown*. She lifted a hand and twisted a lock of blonde hair round her fingers. She kept it clean and shining, tying it up with a black ribbon. It was the one thing she was proud of.

Josie stood up and smoothed down her dress. Then she hung her costume in the wardrobe and opened the dressing-room door. Cardamom stood in the corridor, a fist raised to rap against the wooden door. His cheeks coloured as he cleared his throat.

'I was just coming for you,' he explained.

Josie looked at him. She'd noticed the faint smell of alcohol on his sour breath. *Not again*, Josie groaned inwardly. He turned and led the way to the stage door. Shaking her head, Josie followed.

Ernie Cumbers, the theatre bouncer, rocked on his heels at the exit. He gave a sharp nod of acknowledgement. 'Evenin', Mr Chrimes. Miss Josie.'

'Evening, Ernie,' Josie said, smiling. Cardamom nodded back. Ernie looked fearsome to anyone who didn't know him: a gorilla of a man with no neck to speak of, a flat nose and tiny eyes in a hammy face. He wore a showy checked suit and a bowler that looked two sizes too small for his head. But Josie had seen him wipe a tear from his eye at some of the sentimental songs performed at the Erato. She'd also seen him throw drunkards halfway across the street when he'd caught them in the dancers' dressing rooms. Ernie caught her eye and tipped his head towards the welcoming committee.

A small group of admirers waited for Cardamom outside the back of the theatre, well-to-do types from what Josie could see of their shiny toppers and smart suits. Some of the ladies present were flanked by coachmen. A gentleman with a long white beard stepped forward and shook Cardamom's hand vigorously.

'Sir, a startling act, so well executed,' the man said, his hand still a blur. 'Where did you learn such wizardry?'

'From ancient fakirs, deep in the hidden valleys of the Himalayas,' Cardamom replied. He drew himself up to his full height and pulled his hand free. 'From the dervishes and witch doctors of darkest Africa. I have travelled the world studying the dark arts, sir.'

Josie heaved a sigh; she'd heard it all before. She stared across the road. A tall, gaunt man, muffled against the winter's night in a long scarf and shabby coat, stared back, making her start. A frizz of grey hair escaped from under his battered top hat. Their eyes locked for a second, then he turned, pushed into the crowds milling along the street and was gone.

Josie blinked and shivered. The man had been watching them, she was sure. The theatre attracted more than its fair share of oddballs. She'd point him out to Ernie if he turned up again. She snapped her attention back to Cardamom's admirers.

'Mr Cardamom, you must come and relate your great exploits to me some time.' A lady in a fur stole handed him a card. Josie pulled a face at the way the woman gazed into his eyes.

'Nothing would give me greater pleasure, madam.' Cardamom bowed low and placed the card in his breast pocket. Josie rolled her eyes. No one addressed her; it was as if she were invisible. They were happy to applaud her onstage – why couldn't they say something now?

Josie stood watching as, after a few more pleasantries, the crowd dispersed. Cardamom half raised his hand to wave but no one looked back as they climbed into their waiting carriages. *He looks so alone*, she thought. He couldn't have looked lonelier if he'd been standing on a windswept moor or a desolate beach. At times like this she understood him. Sometimes she felt the same – alone. No, worse – abandoned.

'Come on. Mrs Yates will be waiting at the door for us,' Cardamom said, turning to Josie. His face had lost all its animation. The show was over. Josie knew that feeling – it was like a paper bag blown full of air one minute, with the air smashed out of it the next. Cardamom led the way down the alley, back to the only home they knew – Bluebell Terrace. As Josie hurried along the cobbles, she watched Cardamom's retreating back. She hoped his darkest mood wouldn't set in again. Not tonight.

O MAKE ME A GRAVE THAT IS LONG, WIDE AND DEEP,
AND COVER ME OVER WITH FLOWERS SO SWEET,
THAT THERE I MAY LIE AND TAKE MY LAST SLEEP,
FOR THAT IS THE WAY TO FORGET HER.

'THE FALSE BRIDE', TRADITIONAL FOLK BALLAD

CHAPTER TWO
THIEF FROM THE PAST

Josie strode alongside Cardamom, her arm linked through his. It was late, but the streets bustled with life beneath the hissing glare of street lamps. Crowds spilled out on clouds of laughter from the brightly lit musical halls and taverns. Hawkers and street salesmen, shifty pickpockets and bluff policemen filled the street. She scanned the faces for the stranger who had been staring at her at the Erato but didn't see him again. Carriages clattered past, forcing Josie to hitch her skirts to avoid splatters of mud. Josie normally loved the clamour. Tonight, though, Cardamom's mood was sinking over both of them like a thick fog.

The noises faded away as they turned into a small street and neared their home, a modest house in a row of identical buildings: a sitting room, a dining room, a downstairs scullery and three bedrooms upstairs. Josie had grown up in this street, happy with her lot. She knew no other life.

Mrs Yates met them at the weather-stained door. Her long face was made all the more severe by the tight bun that she wore, pulling back at her scalp.

'Evening, Mrs Yates. I trust you are well?' Cardamom said, polite as always, but his voice empty of interest.

'It's stew tonight, Mr Chrimes,' Mrs Yates said, ignoring his question. She never used his stage name. Josie stepped over the threshold, glad of the warmth. Mrs Yates gave her a sour look.

'Good evening,' Josie said to the housekeeper, forcing her voice into cheerfulness.

'Stew,' Cardamom sighed, taking his overcoat off. Mrs Yates only had one dish that she cooked: stew, seven days a week. Josie felt any pangs of hunger fading away.

'You've not forgotten my pay's due tomorrow, have you, sir?' Mrs Yates said.

'No, Mrs Yates, I've not forgotten,' Cardamom snapped back, staring angrily at the collar of his coat as he hung it up. He threw his hat on to the table by the door and strode into the sitting room.

'Right then, your stew is on the stove. I'll be off,' she called after him, giving Josie a grimace as she pulled on her overcoat. Under her breath, so that only Josie could hear, she added, 'Going to be one of those nights, m'girl.'

The stew remained bubbling on the stove, hardened around the rim of the pan. Cardamom lay slumped in his chair. Whiskey ran from his upturned tumbler, soaking into his lap.

'I wish you wouldn't drink so much, Uncle,' Josie sighed. Gently, she prised the glass from his grip. 'I wish you could be happy.'

Cardamom stirred and groaned but slept on. Papers slid from his fingers and rustled to the floor. Josie bit her lip. She'd seen them before. He always leafed through them when he was in one of these moods: old letters, a diary, battered and worn, and a small portrait.

He'd shown her the picture before, when she was a little girl. Now, Josie picked it up again. A woman stared out at her. She wore a headscarf, but ebony curls spilled over her shoulders. Her features were fine and delicate. Large golden earrings dangled halfway down her slender neck.

'Mother,' Josie whispered.

'Madame Lilly,' Cardamom had told her the first time he'd shown her the miniature. 'A fortune teller with a circus. So full of life, your mother, a rare beauty.' Cardamom had smiled, his eyes glistening. 'A lady, too. This was such a happy house when you both came to live here. She loved you with all her heart.'

Josie smiled and tried to remember her mother singing lullabies. She had died when Josie was two or three. In her mind's eye, her mother danced around this room, her voice soft and rhythmic. Was it a memory or something her imagination had conjured up because she *wanted* it to be so? And why did she have the feeling that something or someone was missing from this image – a feeling that a third person should be there? Who was it? Her father?

'He passed away when you were but a babe,' Cardamom had said, smiling sadly. 'A performer himself, I believe. We never talked about him . . .'

Josie had no memory of him. She sighed, reaching out for the portrait, about to pick it up.

Cardamom grunted and snorted, shifting in his seat. Josie stared down at the yellowed papers. He had never shared those with her – the portrait, yes. But these . . . Images of past evenings darted through her mind's eye: the drinking, Cardamom throwing the diary across the room or ripping pages from it and hurling them on the fire. She remembered lying in the dark of her bedroom, listening to him shouting downstairs as if arguing with someone. She would go down and find him weeping over the letters.

'Back to bed,' he had snapped when he saw her peeking round the door. The last few weeks had been particularly bad.

But now, here were the papers. And Cardamom was asleep.

She knelt down and picked up the picture and the first letter, turning the page over. Spidery writing crawled across the page, faded and smudged by many years of crumpling and smoothing. Josie began reading.

Thief! You take what is rightfully mine . . . I thought I could count on you as a friend . . . will make you pay . . . Meet me . . . yard. The full power of the Amarant . . .

The name *Sebastian Mortlock* crawled along the bottom of the writing. Josie let the letter and portrait drop back down on to the threadbare rug at her guardian's feet.

'What does it mean?' she murmured. Why would anyone call Cardamom a thief? She looked at him. There was so much she didn't know, had never asked about. He'd taken her mother in out of kindness, looked after them both. When Mother had died of a fever, he had continued to care for Josie, though he was under no obligation to. She owed him her life. In truth, he was the only parent she'd ever known. But what did she really know about him? It was time to find out. With trembling fingers, she reached for the diary.

'Josie?' Cardamom groaned. His eyes snapped open. 'What are you doing? What have you read?'

'Nothing, Uncle!' She scrambled back as he snatched the diary. 'I only . . . the letter . . . Who is Mortlock and why did he call you a thief?'

There. She'd asked the question. It was out now.

Cardamom's bleary eyes widened in disbelief, then anger. 'Nobody. He's gone, d'you hear me? Forget about him.' Cardamom flung himself back in his seat and dragged a hand across his face. But now Josie had started asking questions, she found she couldn't stop.

'Uncle, what is it? Why are you so angry?' She climbed to her feet, ready to face his temper. She felt a sudden and urgent need to know the truth.

'Nothing. For God's sake, girl, stop badgering me!'

'Something's wrong. It has been for years.' Josie felt the

colour rising in her cheeks. 'I'm not a child any more. Tell me.'

'Get to your room!' Cardamom roared, snatching up his glass and throwing it to the floor. Josie leapt back as slivers of glass flew through the air. Broken shards of glass at her feet reflected back the golden flicker from the stove. The doorbell rang.

Cardamom shot a warning glance at Josie. Then he pointed a shaking finger in the direction of the front door.

'Answer it,' he said, his voice tight with tension.

Josie gathered her skirts and ran out into the hall. She dragged the back of her hand across her cheeks, pushing back stray locks of hair from her temples. *Calm down*, she told herself. *Compose yourself*. Then she grasped the heavy brass handle and heaved open the door.

YOU'LL SIT ON HIS WHITE NECK-BONE,
AND I'LL PICK OUT HIS BONNY BLUE EYES;
WITH A LOCK OF HIS GOLDEN HAIR,
WE'LL THATCH OUR NEST WHEN IT GROWS BARE.

'THE TWO RAVENS', TRADITIONAL FOLK BALLAD

CHAPTER THREE
UNWELCOME VISITORS

Three skinny old ladies stood on the doorstep in the deep winter cold, their faces cast in shadow. Josie shivered. Peering through the gloom, she saw that they each had glittering black eyes above long, beak-like noses and small mouths pinched tight. Black ringlets of hair bobbed and shook with every twitch of their heads. Only their different heights told them apart. They wore stiff black dresses of silk and lace that rustled as they stepped closer.

'A charming girl,' croaked the first, leaning over Josie. Josie jerked back as the stranger raked a long talon under her chin. 'How old? Twelve? Thirteen?'

'Such beautiful hair, like spun gold,' said the second, a short woman who swished across the threshold. 'We've come to see your guardian.'

'Is the Great Cardamom in?' asked the third, who was between the other two in height. Josie pressed herself against the wall as the women swept past her.

'I'm Aunt Mag.' The tallest old crone grasped Josie's shoulders in an attempt at a hug. Josie stiffened.

'Aunt Veronica.' The next one gave a rapid curtsy.

'Aunt Jay,' said the smallest, cocking her head to one side. Josie could see her reflection in the woman's dark eyes. 'We are going to get along splendidly, dear!'

The front door slammed shut. Josie was surrounded and found herself lost for words. The closeness of the women was unbearable; their ravenous smiles forced her gaze to the floor. *Three black crows*, she thought. They were eyeing her hungrily, as if she were just enough meat to feast on.

'Forgive me, ladies, but I don't remember asking you in,' Josie said. The three Aunts raised their dark eyebrows and stared at her with their jet-black eyes. Their heads tilted in unison.

'But we're practically family, dear girl.' Aunt Mag stepped forward, forcing Josie to take a step back.

'We need to see the Great Cardamom. He'll be so pleased!' croaked Aunt Veronica, edging nearer. Josie slid away along the wall.

'It's been such a long time!' cackled Aunt Jay. Josie found her back pressed against the door to the sitting room.

'Now, you tell me where he is, sweet girl.' Aunt Mag's breath blew sour in Josie's face. She grimaced, turning her head away from the withered old woman.

Suddenly the door behind her opened and Josie tumbled into the arms of her guardian.

'Josie?' he said, squinting past her at the three old women. 'What's going on? Who are these ladies?'

Josie straightened up, but the Aunts swept her to one side again as they threw themselves at Cardamom.

'You must remember us, Edwin!' croaked Aunt Mag, prodding him with her bony finger. 'Your long-lost aunts!'

'Why haven't you written?' Aunt Jay advanced on him.

'We thought you must be dead,' Aunt Veronica declared, edging Cardamom back into his armchair.

'To neglect us so,' twittered Aunt Mag.

'Aunts? Who are you? What on earth . . . ?' Cardamom began, throwing a startled glance in Josie's direction. A flurry of black enveloped him, obscuring him from view.

'Now don't bother your head with lots of questions!'

'Just relax, we've come to take care of you!'

Panic plunged through Josie. She darted forward just in time to see one of them pinch the back of Cardamom's hand. He let out a cry and Josie saw a black welt as dark as a thundercloud rising through his skin.

'What? What have you . . . ?' Cardamom's eyes rolled back in his head. He swayed as if he were dizzy, shaking his head. He squinted at the fussing crones all around him. Josie bit her knuckles. She wanted to push the Aunts away from him. But they were adults, and frightening ones at that.

When the Aunts stepped back, the Great Cardamom was slumped in his armchair, bewildered and dazed.

Something terrible has just happened, Josie thought. *What is that wound on his hand?*

'There! All settled. I'll make some tea,' said Aunt Jay, smiling. 'Josie will show me where everything is. Won't you, my dear?'

Josie glanced at her guardian, his head lolling on his chest. Then she peered uncertainly at the beaming crone.

Cardamom looked up at her. The expression in his eyes was empty. 'Yes, tea, Josie. That would be ... lovely.'

Tears stung Josie's eyes. Helplessly, she allowed Aunt Jay to shepherd her out into the hall.

Josie couldn't sleep that night – not when she knew those hideous Aunts were hovering by her guardian.

'You go to your room, my dear.' Aunt Mag had wrinkled her hooked nose at Josie. 'We'll look after Edwin.'

'That's all right,' she had protested, giving a tight smile. 'I'll stay with him.' Then she had looked down at her shoes, waiting for the Aunts to leave her alone. There was no way she was going to leave Cardamom on his own with these monsters. Now she sat by the armchair as her guardian continued his deep sleep.

As dawn light illuminated the grimy windowpanes, Josie gazed out into the street. People were starting to move about. She wanted to bang on the glass and scream to the passing neighbours, '*Help us!*' But what would they

do? Just stare or shake their heads and walk away.
Ordinary folk might like to watch the Great Cardamom
on the stage but they didn't mix with him. He kept himself to himself. Hardly anyone even knew he lived here.
She turned back to the room.

'Uncle!' she hissed, shaking his shoulder. He jerked
awake, looking at her with dark, haunted eyes. 'What's
wrong with you?'

Aunt Mag swept in through the sitting-room door. 'Do
be careful, Josie,' she scolded. 'Your guardian looks frail.
Don't bother him with your childish games!'

'But he's not well!' Josie scowled at the old woman.
'What have you done to him?'

'Done to him? Why, my dear, whatever do you mean?'
Aunt Mag's eyes shone brightly. She smirked as she tilted
her head to one side. The two other Aunts stepped into
the room behind her. 'He's just under the weather. That's
all, isn't it, Cardamom?'

The Great Cardamom turned towards Josie. 'Yes . . .
under the weather . . . that's all . . .' His eyes were bleak
and empty.

'We'll soon have him back on his feet!' beamed Aunt
Mag, fussing with the old man's necktie. 'Now, prepare
some tea. Then go to your room. We have important
things to discuss with your lovely guardian – in private!'

Josie looked from Aunt to Aunt. She stared at
Cardamom, silently pleading with him to stand up
to them. But he just stared back dully. She waited,
hoping for something – anything. Then, shoulders

drooping, she turned and left the room.

Josie hurried down to the scullery to make tea. She carried a tray back up the hallway, clattering the china and teapot and scalding her fingers in her haste not to miss anything. Entering the sitting room, she thrust the tray into Aunt Mag's hands. Shutting the door behind her, she paused in the hallway.

Should I? she thought. Then she crouched down at the keyhole.

'There now,' Josie heard Aunt Mag chirp, though she couldn't see much. 'Young Josie has been sent to her room. So, it's just the four of us.'

'What do you want?' Cardamom said. Each word dripped from his mouth like molten lead. Josie winced to hear his voice sound so thick and heavy.

'*We* want? Oh no, Mr Chrimes. We live only to serve. Ours is a humble existence. But if you were to ask what our *master* wants . . .Well, that would be a different story.'

'Your master?' Cardamom repeated. Josie could hear her heart beating loudly in her chest.

'Why, Lord Corvis, of course.' Aunt Mag's voice softened. 'He breathed new life into our broken bodies, made us what we are today.'

'So where is it?' Josie heard Aunt Veronica snap. 'You betrayed your old friend, didn't you?'

'No!' Cardamom protested. 'He brought it upon himself – it wasn't my fault. I never meant to . . .'

'Never meant to what?' Aunt Mag hissed. 'Never meant to steal the Amarant?'

Josie frowned and pressed her face closer to the keyhole. She remembered the Amarant from the letter.

'What?' Cardamom groaned. 'I never stole it. We swore an oath. We all did.'

'Well, somebody didn't keep to their promise,' Aunt Mag said, sounding like a governess chiding a toddler. 'Because when Lord Corvis went to check, the Amarant had been taken. And if it wasn't Lord Corvis, then it must have been you or Mortlock who returned.'

'Why don't we finish him now and be done with it?' whispered Aunt Veronica. 'I despise this place. I hunger!'

'Patience, sister,' Aunt Mag replied. 'You know if we kill him now we may never find the Amarant. Lord Corvis promised that he would use it to make us completely alive if we brought it back for him.'

Josie stifled a gasp. *Finish him?* Who were these hideous crones that they could chat about killing her guardian?

'I know, but –' Aunt Veronica's voice snapped her back to attention.

'Do you want to go back to what you were before? The Amarant will give us full life. That is all that matters. Mortlock can't be found. Only this man is left. He will tell us all we need to know.'

Josie was just able to see Aunt Jay look over her shoulder towards the door. 'Then what about the girl?' she asked. 'She's becoming a liability . . .'

'No,' Aunt Mag retorted. 'She may have value. If this one refuses to talk, we might be able to squeeze some information out of her –'

'My fault,' Cardamom murmured, interrupting. 'No less than I deserve . . .'

Josie bit her lip and straightened up. She wanted to burst in and rescue her guardian but what could she do? With a backward glance towards the door, she tiptoed upstairs.

None of it makes sense, she thought. *They talked about Corvis and Mortlock. Didn't Mortlock write that letter? But he's gone, they say. And what was that about the Amarant?*

Josie couldn't decide what to do next. Should she escape and get help? But she didn't want to leave her guardian with these women. They might look old and frail but they meant to kill him if they didn't get whatever it was they wanted. Maybe the diary and the letter might hold some clues, but they lay on the floor by Cardamom's chair.

There was a knock at the front door.

Josie started back downstairs, but Aunt Jay was at the front door already and, by the time she reached the bottom step, Aunt Mag appeared behind her. She gripped Josie's upper arm, making her wince. She was stronger than any old woman had the right to be and dragged Josie back up the stairs. Josie tried to twist her head round to see who was at the front door, but Aunt Mag's body was in the way. She recognised the voice, though.

It was Mrs Yates: 'Ill, you say?'

Josie opened her mouth to cry out but Aunt Mag's

hand, cold and clammy, slapped down, gagging her.

'Yes, a trifle indisposed,' she heard Aunt Jay croak. 'He hasn't been right since last evening. A touch of fever. I don't think we'll need your services any more.'

'But I'm owed a week's pay,' Mrs Yates grumbled. Josie wriggled and squirmed under Aunt Mag's grasp. She could hear the clink of coins.

'Here, I think you'll find that this more than covers your costs. Now, goodbye.'

The door slammed shut. Aunt Mag steered Josie up the last few steps.

'The housekeeper,' Aunt Jay explained over Josie's head to Aunt Mag. 'Just had to dismiss her, I'm afraid!'

'Let go of me!' Josie cried, pulling away from Aunt Mag and stumbling backwards down the hallway into the sitting room. Aunt Mag's black-button eyes twinkled and sparkled like polished jet as they stared deep into Josie's. Josie felt herself coming to a halt, frozen to the spot by that icy glare.

'It seems we're short of a domestic,' hissed Aunt Mag. 'Maybe the extra activity will keep *you* from interfering.' She gave a syrupy smile that quickly slid from her face. 'Go and fill the copper. Boil some water. Now!'

'I WILL LAY HERE AN' DIE,' HE SAID,
'I WILL LAY HERE AN' DIE;
IN SPITE OF ALL THE DEVILS IN HELL,
I WILL LAY HERE AN' DIE.'

'CLERK COLVILL', TRADITIONAL FOLK BALLAD

CHAPTER FOUR

NIGHT BIRD

Silence hung over the sitting room as Josie tidied up around her guardian. She snatched up the old newspapers from the floor by Cardamom's chair. Aunt Veronica sat close by, glowering at her.

'What are you doing?' she asked, craning her neck to catch a look at the newspapers.

'Just tidying up.' Josie tried to keep her breathing steady. She could feel the pile of papers trembling in her grasp. 'Uncle never tidies after himself.'

'Very well.' Aunt Veronica leaned back in her seat. Josie allowed herself a smile of triumph as she swept out of the room, past the other Aunts. She could feel the thick cover of the diary hidden among the papers. Without looking back, she hurried upstairs to her room and locked herself in.

She sat on her bed and spread the papers out. There it was – the diary. It had seen a lot of harsh treatment. The spine had more or less crumbled away and the two leather-bound covers were kept together with a thick black ribbon. The leather of the covers had been worn to the texture of sandpaper. Loose, yellow pages were sewn together inside.

Josie could just make out the name *Edwin Chrimes* in faded gold lettering on the front. A stab of guilt made her hesitate. *This is private*, she told herself. She bit her lip. Uncle had forbidden her to read this, but if she didn't, then how could she help him? She pulled at the black ribbon, undoing the clumsy bow. The diary sprang open, paper sliding out over her blankets.

The pages resembled the letter she'd read the night before; crumpled and torn, yellowed with age. The writing was faded and hard to make out. She scanned the pages, wishing she'd spent less time on throwing knives and more on her reading and writing. Names, appointments, places: none of them meant anything to Josie. With a sigh, she flicked through the diary, opening some of the folded letters between the pages. And then there it was: the word 'Amarant'. Josie smoothed out the crumpled sheet of paper.

Wednesday, 2 March 1820

We found it. The Amarant. The power over life and death lay within our grasp yet we left it where we found it. Such horrors as I have seen should never travel beyond these treacherous desert lands. I fear our lives may never be the same again . . .

'The power over life and death,' Josie whispered, her finger tracing the faded words. She read on.

My dear friend Mortlock was wise to tell us to abandon it even after all our trials. Corvis worries me, however. Can he ever be trusted to forget the cursed flower?

'Friend?' Josie murmured. But didn't Mortlock send the letter calling Cardamom a thief? And there was that other name, Corvis.

'Josie?' Aunt Jay screeched from the foot of the stairs. 'Where are you, girl?'

'Coming,' Josie called back. She cursed under her breath and bundled the papers beneath her pillow. The diary would have to wait.

*

Josie lay in bed. A thud sounded on the landing outside, as if something were hopping about. It made her wince and mutter, dragging her to half-wakefulness. After the drudgery of the day – polishing, scrubbing and cleaning – even poring over the contents of the diary could not keep her awake. At some point she had fallen into a dark, tormented sleep. Now, something scraped at the other side of her door, ever so gently.

Scratch, scrape.

Knuckling her eyes and pushing her hair back from her face, Josie stumbled out of bed. The cold of the floorboards stung the soles of her feet and she groaned.

Scratch, scrape.

She eased the door open. Darkness filled the landing, but a darker shadow filled the doorway. A huge black crow perched on the banister rail. It was massive, as big as Josie – bigger, with vicious black, beady eyes, a long sabre beak, ragged black feathers. It cocked its head and peered at her, claws *click, click, clicking* as it shifted along the rail towards her.

Josie struggled for breath. Her mouth was dry. She wanted to scream but found she couldn't. She stood, frozen to the spot, her heart hammering at her ribs. The bird edged closer, stretching its neck out. With a gasp, Josie threw herself back into her room, scrabbling at the bolt on the door. Then she buried herself in the bedclothes.

She tried to catch her breath. What *was* that? Some creature of the Aunts, set to guard her? The eyes of the bird looked horribly familiar: black and full of guile. Josie shuddered at the memory.

There was no battering at the door. The creature didn't try to get in. But, every now and then, a gentle scratching made Josie flinch and pull the bedclothes closer round her.

'I can come in whenever I want to,' the noise seemed to gloat. 'You may think you're safe, but I can come in. *Whenever I want.*'

Josie watched the closed door, hardly daring to move. It was going to be a long night.

*

Morning found Josie still bundled in her bed, sweating and shivering. The light made her brave. She listened.

No sound.

She unbolted the door and opened it a crack.

The banister rail was bare.

Had she dreamed it? Was it all just a silly nightmare?

The Aunts sat silently as Josie walked into the sitting room. They stared at her over the rim of their teacups. Cardamom's chair stood empty, one flattened cushion declaring his presence the night before and his absence now.

'Poor man,' Aunt Veronica said, cocking her head. Josie's stomach lurched. What had happened? 'He couldn't get out of bed this morning,' Aunt Veronica continued. 'So very weak.' The final word sounded like an accusation, as if Cardamom were to blame for his own frailty. Josie turned to the door. She had to see him.

'No, don't go rushing upstairs, my dear,' Aunt Jay said, smiling and blocking the door. 'He will need some breakfast. Some toasted bread and a sip of warm milk. Be an angel and go and prepare it for him.'

'And then he'll need a long rest,' Aunt Mag added. Her eyes flashed as she beamed at Josie. 'We've sent word to the Erato theatre. I don't think he'll be performing for quite a while!'

'We said he might have the fever,' Aunt Jay said, inclining her head. 'Strange how a simple word – "fever" – can keep folk from visiting.'

Josie turned towards the kitchen, tears stinging her eyes.

I won't cry in front of these women, she thought, clenching her fists. But she definitely had to get out and find help. As she made Cardamom something to eat, she thought hard.

'Gimlet will know what to do,' she muttered. 'Maybe he'll come to see how Cardamom is. Then he'll see how wrong things are here.' But she knew there was little hope of this. He'd be so absorbed in his scenery-making that he might not even notice Cardamom's absence from the theatre – not until it was too late. If the Aunts had told the theatre managers that Cardamom had some kind of fever, people would stay away for fear of infection. Thousands had died from a cholera outbreak only last August.

But Josie had to get *someone*. A doctor or a policeman – anyone! These women were evil, she knew that much. Something had to be done.

Josie would have to get away and find Gimlet herself. She peered through the grimy kitchen windowpanes at the outside world. Rain pelted down, making the sooty walls of the houses opposite shine. Carriages rattled past and a few passers-by hurried along, bent almost double.

But one figure stood still and upright, just across the road. Josie caught her breath. She recognised the tall, shabby man straight away. He'd been watching them at the theatre door. As if sensing he'd been spotted, he turned suddenly and hurried down the street.

No, don't go! The thought screamed in Josie's head. Whoever he was, he might be able to help.

She rushed down the hallway to the front door and made a grab for the handle. A rustling flurry of crinoline and silk made her turn. Aunt Veronica loomed over her, tall and dark, face tight.

'Are you all right, my dear?' she said, clicking her tongue and bobbing her head.

'Yes,' said Josie. 'Yes, I was just getting some fresh air, that's all.'

'But look at the weather.' Aunt Veronica smiled, stepping forward. 'You'll catch your death . . .'

'I only want to step out for a minute.'

Aunt Veronica was too close now: Josie could feel her breath on her hair, see the liver spots on her hands as the old woman grasped her wrist. Josie winced at the strength of her grip.

'I don't think it would be wise to go outside right now, Josie.' Aunt Veronica's face twisted as she forced Josie's hand away from the door handle. 'What would your guardian think of us if we let you go running about in the pouring rain?' The sugary smile returned once more. Josie staggered back, massaging her wrist. Her stomach tightened as she fought against the tears. The man would be long gone now.

'Quick sticks,' said Aunt Veronica, clapping her hands. 'There are dishes to be done in the kitchen and this floor needs mopping. Half the mud from the street's been walked in!'

With a heavy heart, Josie walked back through the shadowy hall to the kitchen.

*

Scotland Yard
3 November 1844

Sir,

I am writing to inform you that our search for Sebastian Mortlock has proved unsuccessful. Our officers have made enquiries at his lodgings and in the surrounding neighbourhood but with no success. It is very possible that he has gone abroad again, as our detectives understand he has travelled extensively in the past. Should he contact you at any point in the future, we would be grateful if you could inform us.

Your servant,
Chief Inspector T. Mealor

Josie folded the letter, slumping back against her bed-stead. Whoever Mortlock was, he and Cardamom had fallen out over something and then Mortlock had vanished. The other letter had accused Cardamom of being a thief. What could he have taken that would cause the two to fall out? Where was Mortlock now? Josie thought about the man who had been watching them. Could that be him? It might make sense, returning after all these years to get back something Cardamom had stolen. *But Uncle isn't a thief,* she thought, shaking her head.

A shadow fell across Josie. She clutched the letter to her chest as she realised she'd forgotten to lock the door. Aunt Mag glared down at her.

'What have we here?' Aunt Mag snatched at the letter. She gathered up the other papers and the diary and brought her face close to Josie's. 'Some bedtime reading for us.'

'They're private,' Josie protested, trying to grab the papers. Aunt Mag slapped her across the cheek, making her yelp and fall back.

'You should have thought of that before you took them from your guardian,' Aunt Mag hissed. She turned and stalked out of the room.

Josie curled up on the bed, her cheek throbbing. The Aunts were always there whatever she tried to do, one step ahead, waiting for her. Hot tears trickled across her burning face as she buried her head in a pillow. Despair welled up inside her.

How could she ever help Cardamom?

When I am dead and in my grave,
And covered with cold clay,
The nightingale will sit and sing,
And pass the time of day.

'Bedfordshire May Day Carol',
traditional folk ballad

CHAPTER FIVE

A LAST MESSAGE

Josie swept the hair back from her smudged and blackened face and sighed. She heaved the bucket and threw glistening pieces of coal on the kitchen fire. Slumping on to a chair, she leaned heavily on the table. It was hard to keep track of time but Josie was certain that at least five days had passed.

She couldn't get a moment alone with Cardamom. The Aunts always hovered nearby or appeared from nowhere. They flapped and fussed around him, seeing to all his needs, bringing him tea, fluffing his cushions, *killing him with kindness*, Josie thought. It was all fake: the chirpy brightness, the spoon-feeding smiles, the wrinkled squints and sugary words.

Josie had considered trying to creep out at night but the vision still haunted her: the evil-eyed bird crouching by her bedroom door. Josie could only glance in his bedroom doorway to see his exhausted, pallid face propped up against pillows. One of the Aunts would always bustle her away when she tried to get near his bed.

'No place for a child,' Aunt Jay croaked. 'Too much bother for him. Not nice for you, young lady.'

'You'll wear the poor man out!' Aunt Mag had said, grabbing Josie's elbow and steering her back downstairs. But *they* were the ones wearing him down. Cardamom was shrinking by the day.

Now, from a crack in the window, Josie could feel the chill evening air creeping through the streets. She could imagine the people in their homes, stoking up fires and lighting gas lamps. *He* was out there somewhere, too. The watcher. The Aunts huddled around the other end of the kitchen table, pouring tea, observing Josie, who sat at the table corner close by the fire, chilled by their glittering black stares.

Josie stretched and yawned. She stood up and crept towards the door.

'And where do you think you're going, young lady?' Aunt Jay punctuated the question with a clink of her cup in its saucer.

'I'm going to bed early,' Josie muttered, shrugging. 'It's been a long day and I'll need my strength if I'm to black the stove tomorrow.'

'Very well,' Aunt Veronica croaked. 'I shall take you up and tuck you in.'

Doesn't she mean lock me in? Josie thought.

'No need, Veronica,' Aunt Mag said, her cup halfway between saucer and mouth. She didn't even glance in

Josie's direction. 'She's a big girl. She can look after herself.'

'As you wish,' Aunt Veronica grumbled, rustling back to her seat. Josie noticed her eye Aunt Mag suspiciously. 'Goodnight, Josie.'

'Goodnight,' Josie replied. She couldn't believe her luck. This was her chance! She raced up the stairs, careful not to make a noise.

Josie stood in the doorway of Cardamom's room. It smelt stale and fetid. Thick curtains muffled every sound. The wardrobe, Cardamom's desk, the dresser – they all seemed to crowd around, crushing the only occupant of the room. The bed was a mess of twisted sheets and tangled blankets. A candle burned feebly in the corner. Josie could hear Cardamom's breath rattle against his ribs. His cheekbones jutted out and his skin looked parchment yellow.

'Josie, is that you?' he groaned, peering through the dim light. 'Where have you been? I was so worried. I thought –'

'Don't worry, I'm here now. I'm getting you out,' Josie whispered. She ran over and tried to lift him by the shoulders. Cardamom gasped in agony and fell back, panting from the effort. 'You've got to help me, Uncle. I can't lift you on my own.'

'No time,' he wheezed. 'You must escape . . .'

'Not without you!' She pulled at his stick-thin arm but Cardamom slumped down to one side.

'Josie,' he whispered. His eyes softened as he ran a

hand down her tear-stained cheek. 'My beautiful girl. So like your mother . . . There's so much I should have told you and now there's no time.'

'Don't talk like this, Uncle. We can get away —'

'No.' Cardamom shook his head. 'Listen. You must go. You have a brother — he can help. Gimlet knows. Find Gimlet. Destroy the Amarant . . . Find Mortlock. Here . . .'

He reached under a pillow and stuffed a crumpled note into her hand. Josie stared down at it and then back at her guardian.

'A brother? Mortlock? What do you mean? I don't understand.' She hugged Cardamom's frail body. She felt his breathing become more rapid.

'Gimlet . . . will . . . tell . . .' Cardamom panted. 'Keep the note safe. It will . . .' Then he gave a sigh, as if he were sick of the world. Josie felt him become heavy in her arms, still and dead, the last breath groaning from his body.

'Uncle?' Josie laid him back, sobbing and smoothing his hair. 'Don't go, don't —'

A floorboard creaked behind her.

Turning, she saw Aunt Mag framed by the doorway.

'What did he say?' Aunt Mag's voice was low and threatening. She edged forward. 'Did he tell you where the Amarant was?'

Josie flinched at the word, struggling not to cry out. Aunt Mag gave a hiss of triumph.

'He did! He told you! I *knew* if we gave you the chance

to speak, he would tell you.' Aunt Mag's eyes shone as she stepped closer. 'And where is it, my dear?'

Josie straightened up by the side of Cardamom's bed. She turned round, using the movement to disguise the slip of her hand as she hid the note in the waist of her skirt.

'Tell me, Josie, and I *may* spare you.' Aunt Mag gave a crooked, yellow grin and stepped forward again.

As Josie backed away, she found herself pinned against Cardamom's desk. There was nowhere else to go, and Aunt Mag was moving closer. Josie reached behind to steady herself against the desk and felt her fingers graze something cold and hard. Cardamom's paper knife. She clutched it instinctively, testing its weight, judging how easy it would be to throw. She could feel that it did not have a particularly sharp edge but she knew that its point could inflict damage if thrown with force.

'Who are you? Why do you want this . . . this Amarant so badly?' Josie stammered, trying to distract Aunt Mag as she slid the paper knife up her sleeve.

'Who are we?' Aunt Mag gave a twisted leer. She shook herself and lowered her head. Josie stared as Aunt Mag's outline slowly grew and changed.

Feathers, black and glistening, sprouted from her head. Her black dress fluttered and moulded around her body, sweeping up into a wide fantail and revealing scaly clawed legs. Aunt Mag's arms flattened, lengthened and expanded into wings which ended in sharp talons. Hardly able to believe what she was seeing, Josie stared into the same glittering ebony eyes, but now they were set into a monstrous, bird-like face with a long, cruel beak. Black feathers fluttered in the breeze from the open window.

'We are ghuls – ravens of the night, seekers of carrion,' Aunt Mag cackled, lunging forward.

Josie didn't have time to throw the paper knife, only palm it from her sleeve and push it forward. With a scream, Aunt Mag fell upon the point of the blade, then staggered back, the knife lodged in her side.

Josie didn't hesitate. She leapt over the ghul and on to the landing, sending Aunt Veronica, who had just hurried upstairs, sprawling. Josie ran halfway down the stairs as Aunt Jay stepped through the front door. Josie was forced to vault over the banister into the hallway and down towards the scullery. Pausing to grab some steak knives from beside the sink, she crashed through the back door and out into the alleyway that serviced the rear of the houses. Josie panted as she clattered down the narrow passageway and into the street.

Here it was still and calm. The distant sound of rattling carriages, hoofs on cobblestone, echoed in the narrow lane. The houses on either side seemed to huddle together for protection, making the street even darker. A piercing, inhuman scream sliced through the air as a black, feathery silhouette hurled itself out of a window overhead.

The ghul swooped down towards her and Josie launched the first steak knife into the air. The bird screamed with rage, flying out of range, before twisting round to dive at Josie. The second knife missed, forcing the ghul to veer right and circle up again, screeching. Josie steadied herself as, once more, the creature spiralled down.

One knife left. One last chance.

She knew she mustn't fail. The cruel eyes and spiked beak helter-skeltered towards her. She drew a breath. Then she threw.

A shrill, agonised screech tore at Josie's ears. She didn't wait to check the damage she'd done, but ran as fast as she could into the dark night. She felt herself sob with each stumbling step. There were two more birds back there. She knew they would come after her. Every flap and flutter, every dark shape in the shadows, made Josie cry out. Her lungs burned in her chest, but she couldn't stop running until she was out of the alleyway.

The clatter of Josie's shoes echoed off the cobbled side streets that led her closer to the safety and crowds of the main street. Mud splattered her heavy dress. She slipped and stumbled in the gutter as she glanced back.

'Look out there!'

Josie swirled round just in time to see the group of startled gentlemen she was about to run into. She backed away, apologising. Her head ached. She felt sick but the sound of fluttering sent her running on.

The street heaved with people on their way home for dinner. Josie elbowed her way through, hardly caring about her muddy, dishevelled appearance. She ended up crouching in a shop doorway, trying to catch her breath. *I have to think straight*, she told herself. *Stop panicking*.

The Erato theatre.

She had to go there and find Gimlet.

She glanced out into the street and groaned. Aunt Veronica, back in her human form, was pushing towards her, cocking and twitching her head as she scoured the crowds. With an oath, Josie gritted her teeth and staggered to her feet.

A drunken beggar blocked Aunt Veronica's path, waving a tin mug in her face.

'Spare a farthing for an old soldier, ma'am!'

Josie leapt from her hiding place, shouldering people out of the way.

Aunt Veronica's shriek cut through the hubbub: 'Get out of my way, you disgusting vagabond! I'll have you horsewhipped.'

Josie pushed her way past angry faces.

'Stop that girl!' Aunt Veronica screeched. 'Stop her . . . She's stolen my purse!'

Arms snaked out of the throng, trying to grab Josie. She twisted and ducked, dragging herself through the thicket of people. She dropped to the ground and rolled through the feet of strangers, wincing and crying, then pushed herself up again and carried on running. She didn't dare look back.

Ahead of her, she could see the warm lights of the Erato. Josie sprinted down the side of the building. She squeezed through the stage door and ran along the dingy corridor that led to the dressing rooms, weeping with relief.

Josie had made it. She'd escaped!

For now, she thought. Aunt Veronica's shrill cries could still be heard down the street. She had to find Gimlet.

O I shall be as dead, Mother,
As the stones in the wall;
O the stones in the streets, Mother,
Shall mourn for me all.

'The Cherry Tree Carol', traditional folk song

CHAPTER SIX
NO SANCTUARY

There was barely time to acknowledge the familiar smells of damp, mildew, greasepaint, sweat and cheap cigars, no time to listen to the song onstage that the audience was roaring along to. Josie staggered through the narrow backstage passages. *Where is Gimlet?* He seemed to have vanished. She fumbled with the key to the dressing-room door. If she could just get her throwing knives, she'd feel safer.

Distant applause rippled up from the stage as Josie scanned the room, searching for somewhere – anywhere! – to hide, just in case. The room was neat and tidy, just as Cardamom had left it. Combs lay in rows below the mirror, jars of stage make-up beside them. Behind her stood three or four vanishing cabinets, piled up next to the great man's wardrobe. On the back wall, the gaslight from the street lit up a large window, the glass panes covered with paper for privacy.

A heavy thud sounded in the corridor outside. Josie wrenched open the door of one of the vanishing cabinets and groped for the lever. The panel opened and she slid into the concealed rear closet of the box. Closing the panel, Josie pressed her body against the back of the box. The darkness of the tiny rear chamber enfolded her, stifling her; she had never been able to help Cardamom with any of the box tricks because of her terror of suffocation. Now her heart pounded.

Josie held her breath as the dressing-room door creaked open. She closed her eyes and listened. The ghul's talons clicked as it picked up combs and brushes from the dressing table. The wardrobe door shuddered on its hinges, making Josie bite her lip as material swished and hangers rattled. Josie tasted blood in her mouth. The faint sound of applause rippled up from the stage once more. The performers were taking a final bow.

An impatient croak cut over the clapping as boxes were lifted and flung about. Time was running out. The performers would be back soon. Josie tensed every muscle.

The doors of the cabinet crashed open. Josie opened her eyes and saw a thin beading of light around the edges of the panel that concealed her. Silence pressed in. In her mind's eye, Josie could picture the ghul standing inches away from her, head cocked to one side as it puzzled over the empty cabinet, head feathers floating in a ghostly breeze and those dark eyes, like polished jet, sparkling in the gaslight.

A talon scratched gently down the back of the cabinet and the panel that hid Josie. She could almost hear the ghul's mind turning over as it tried to solve the mystery of Josie's disappearance. She braced herself. The talon scratched again. *Scratch, scrape.* Then Josie heard the dressing-room door bang open.

"'Ere, what's going on? Oh my lord . . . No! NO!' a familiar voice screamed. Josie recognised the husky tones of Ernie Cumbers, theatre bouncer. He'd obviously come to investigate the noises in the dressing room.

She screwed her eyes tight shut as the cabinet toppled over with a bone-jarring crash. The false back of the cabinet splintered off, exposing Josie. She could see Ernie lashing out at the flapping ghul. A deep gash lined his scalp and blood streamed down his face, blinding him. His swinging fists could have laid any opponent low in a street brawl but the ghul bobbed and weaved in and out of the blows with ease. Ernie panted heavily, wiping the blood from his forehead. But the pause gave the crow its chance, and it darted its head forward, skewering Ernie with its long sabre of a beak. The big man's eyes bulged and he whimpered as the ghul pulled away. A disgusting squelch accompanied the strings of bloody gut that came away in the ghul's glistening beak. Silence fell as the foul bird jerked the gory load down its gullet. Then Ernie's blood-chilling scream shook the theatre as the ghul fell upon him again, lashing with talons, ripping and tearing with its beak. Blood spattered the walls and mirrors and speckled Josie's face. Something wet slapped against the cabinet and slid down the side. The ghul turned, blood matting its feathers, and fixed its round eyes on Josie.

Footsteps clattered down the passageway. With a scream, Josie stumbled backwards out of the rear of the cabinet, totally at the ghul's mercy. Angry voices filled the corridor. The creature glanced around, uncertain what to do.

'This isn't over, Josie Chrimes. I'll dine on your entrails before long,' screeched the voice of Aunt Veronica, as the ghul launched itself out through the window, sending a shower of glass into the street. 'But another sweet feast awaits me first.' The sounds of her cackling laughter and beating wings drifted back towards Josie as the ghul made its escape.

Gimlet burst into the room carrying a pickaxe. Over his shoulder peered the red and angry faces of three stage-hands, similarly armed.

'Oh my lord,' one of the men said. They stopped and covered their mouths, turning away from the mess that used to be Ernie Cumbers.

'Josie!' Gimlet cried, kneeling beside her.

As Josie's vision swam in and out of focus, she saw the room fill with performers and theatregoers. A policeman elbowed his way in.

'What happened here, miss?' he shouted above the voices of the others.

'Did you see anything?' cried another person.

'Oh god, is that . . . is that Ernie?'

Josie tried to speak but her stomach lurched and

the room began to spin. Her eyelids became heavy and she plunged into darkness as she felt her body slump backwards.

The scent of linseed oil and sawn timber tickled Josie's nose. She felt the weight of warm blankets pressing down on her. She opened her eyes to see that she was sitting in the corner of a huge velvet sofa, which was bald and leaking horsehair. The sound of sawing and hammering echoed from another room. Gimlet's studio. As soon as Josie realised where she was, she felt safe and squirmed down into the nest of blankets.

But then memories of the night before crashed into her mind: the chase, Ernie's dying screams . . . Josie sat up, shivering as the cold air of the studio prickled her shoulders. Cardamom was dead too. Hot tears scalded Josie's cheeks as she remembered the way he had slumped in his bed for the last time.

She dragged her weary body out of the comfort of the makeshift bed. Josie had always loved this cluttered room; the great desk covered in papers, orders, books, plans, charts, cups, glasses and plates. The bare floorboards felt icy on Josie's feet as she wandered over to the doorway that led into Gimlet's workshop.

Gimlet was absorbed in planing the edges of a large trunk. Josie watched the muscles of his brown arms flex and ripple as he moved the plane back and forth over the wood. He reminded her of a circus acrobat, small but wiry, muscles like whipcord. Boxes in various stages of completion lined the room, some brightly painted, some with the names of other stage magicians emblazoned over them. Josie stifled a sniff and Gimlet turned, pushing his mop of black hair away from his thoughtful face and straightening up from his task.

'You're awake,' he said. 'All right?'

Josie nodded.

Gimlet scratched his lamb-chop whiskers. 'You've had quite an adventure. The whole theatre was in uproar. Let's stoke up the fire and you can tell me everything over a hot port.'

Josie's tale came out in fits and starts. Sometimes she had to stop and catch her breath before continuing. Often, tears took over.

'He's dead, Gimlet,' Josie sobbed when she had told him all she could. Gimlet nodded, his face dark with sorrow. 'They said they knew him. They killed him but I don't know why.' She looked at Gimlet. Her eyes felt tired and sore. 'He gave me this.' Josie pulled the note from her sleeve and unfolded the paper, reading it for the first time. As she read, Gimlet gathered her to him in a hug and peered at it over her shoulder. The writing was smudged and scrawling, but Josie recognised her guardian's hand.

There is so much I wanted to tell you, so many regrets that will now lie buried with me. The truth is always at the end of the next sentence we never say. No one knows where the Amarant lies. Forgive my harsh words in the past, Josie, and the times I neglected you. I always loved you. Now think of my last words and don't heed the goodbye. We'll meet again. It is my last wish to be buried in Gorsefields Yard.

Take care, Josie.
Uncle Edwin, your loving guardian

'Poor Edwin,' Gimlet murmured.

'He was delirious at the end,' Josie said, wiping away another tear. 'It's a wonder he could write anything. He was trying to tell me about the past. He said you would know . . .'

Gimlet sighed, taking his pipe out and tapping the bowl on the hearth. 'I know a little of the past, as much as Cardamom would tell me. He was mixed up with a couple of ne'er-do-wells, Corvis and a cove called Mortlock. You've heard these names?'

'Yes.' Josie nodded. 'The Aunts . . . those *things*. They had something to do with Lord Corvis. I saw Uncle's diary, some letters. He fell out with this Mortlock. He called Uncle a thief . . . and Uncle said something about Mortlock just before . . .'

'There, there.' Gimlet put an arm around Josie's shoulders. 'Well, I don't know a great deal about them two. I've heard of them. They travelled the world with Cardamom. He told me some of their tales – far-fetched, I reckon they were. But Mortlock *did* have a fearful reputation. Obsessed with raising the dead, they said. Always seeking ways to do it.'

'The Amarant,' Josie said and gave a shiver. 'It had the power over life and death. Uncle said we had to destroy it. Mortlock mentioned it in the letter I read. The Aunts were after it.'

'The Amarant? Never heard of that before.' Gimlet shook his head. 'What is it?'

'A flower. I think the diary said it was a flower,' Josie replied. 'How could a flower be so strange and terrible?'

'I don't know,' Gimlet said. 'But Cardamom told me that Mortlock did some shocking things. Stole bodies from graves . . . sacrifices . . .'

'Horrible.' Josie shuddered. 'And Mortlock just vanished?'

'Just disappeared, so Cardamom said, never to be seen again. Corvis lived abroad, so Cardamom started his life again. That's when he took in you and your mother.'

'The night it all started and later, too, I saw a man watching us . . . D'you think it could be Mortlock?'

Gimlet shrugged. 'Always possible, I suppose. Secrets from the past have a habit of comin' back to bite you.'

'Like my brother?' The word didn't sound right in her mouth. How could she have had a brother and never known? Or had she always known, deep down, in some strange way? Was he the 'someone' she missed when she imagined her mother?

'Your twin brother? So he told you about him,' Gimlet said quietly. 'He should have done that years ago. Maybe I should have said something, but I didn't think it was my place to do so.'

'I have a *twin*? Why didn't he tell me sooner? How could he have kept that from me?' Josie felt anguished and deeply betrayed. Then she thought of that last argument with Cardamom.

'I don't know why he didn't tell you.' Gimlet looked deep into the fire. 'When your mother died, Cardamom decided he couldn't look after him as well,' Gimlet said, tapping his pipe out on the hearth. He sighed heavily. 'So he split the two of you up. I'm not exactly sure why – he could have afforded to keep you both. I'm so sorry, Josie.'

'Uncle would never have done anything to harm me,' Josie said, putting her head in her hands and fighting back tears. 'He must have had a good reason to separate us.'

'Well.' Gimlet looked troubled. 'Cardamom was like most men, Josie. He's done some good and some bad things, you have to realise that.'

'What did he do with my brother?' Josie asked, struggling to speak calmly. A twin brother, someone like her, someone who would understand how she felt.

'He gave him to an upright and caring man called Wiggins, an undertaker by trade and an old friend.'

'And do you know where we can find Wiggins?' Josie's excitement grew. Her deep-rooted feeling of loneliness began to lift. She was going to meet her brother. He could help.

'He's not too far from here – Seven Dials as I recall,' Gimlet said, nodding his head.

'Then let's not waste any more time.' Josie jumped up. 'Let's go and meet him!'

THE WORMS CRAWL IN, THE WORMS CRAWL OUT,
YOUR BRAINS COME SNIVELLING DOWN YOUR SNOUT.

'THE HEARSE SONG', TRADITIONAL FOLK SONG

CHAPTER SEVEN
THE BOY WITH THE TOAD

The cold nipped and worried at Josie's fingertips and cheeks, making her glad of the scarf and hat that Gimlet had made her put on before following him down the street.

'Can't be too careful if those old Aunts are a-hunting for you,' Gimlet said, and spat into the gutter.

Josie clung to Gimlet's coat-tails to avoid being swallowed up by the heaving, jostling crowds that swarmed up and down the narrow, muddy street. She craned her head back and peered up at the sky. *You wouldn't think it was morning*, she thought. The black buildings overshadowed everything, making the light in the street as dim as twilight.

'We can't be too far away from Mr Wiggins now, Josie,' Gimlet said, pulling her close. 'Stay by me. This area is troublesome and there are a great number of undesirables about.'

Josie knew of the Seven Dials, a rough area littered with ramshackle tenements and flooded cellars, crammed with the poor and hopeless. The buildings seemed to lean in on each other like drunks at a wake. Josie thought that if one fell down, then the whole area would tumble like dominoes in a line.

She and Cardamom had always skirted around the Dials to get to the theatre. Dark alleyways and entrances to courtyards snaked off left and right. She flinched at the ragged crowd that surged around her. These weren't the merrymakers of the Erato. Dubious, unshaven vagabonds leaned against crumbling walls and smoked pipes, assessing Gimlet and his strange, muffled companion. Black-toothed women laughed raucously on the street corners. Here and there Josie heard raised voices, saw scuffles. She fixed her gaze forward.

Wiggins's funeral shop shone like a jewel in a dung heap. Its windows were bright and clean, the paintwork all black and shining, unscathed by the passing multitudes or the mud from the street.

'How does he keep it so clean?' Josie marvelled, staring at the sooty shopfronts that sagged on either side of Mr Wiggins's immaculate shop.

'He's a very particular man is Wiggins,' Gimlet said, smiling. 'He likes everything to be just so.'

'I can see.'

'He applies that to his funeral arranging, too. He's a popular man around here. He doesn't take account of who you are or where you're from. He looks after everything. Sadly, he doesn't make a huge amount of money.'

Josie hung back as Gimlet approached the door. Her

earlier excitement had evaporated and now part of
her didn't want to think about a brother at all. It raised
too many questions about her mother and father.
What would he be like, this brother? Would he be
like her?

They pushed the door and a tinkling bell heralded
their arrival. The inside of the shop matched the outside.
Tidy, almost bare, a long counter stretched across the
back of the shop and various samples of coffin wood and
brass handles stood in regimented lines along its surface.
The smell of wood polish and clean brass hung heavy in
the air.

A young boy, small and pinched-looking, slouched on
the counter. He wore the black suit of an undertaker,
worn at the cuffs and rather too large for him. It threatened to swallow him up. The boy ignored them, his head
to one side as he watched a toad twitching, pinned
beneath his index finger. His hair was cut very short. It
was the same shade of blond as Josie's. His eyes were large
and had a lazy quality that made his whole face look inso-
lent or haughty. Gimlet coughed. The boy continued to
prod the toad, making it squirm. Gimlet gave another
polite 'Ahem'.

'You wanna get something for that, mister,' the boy
observed, not taking his eyes off the toad. 'Seven Dials is
full of quacks who'll cure your cough for a farthing.
Either that or come back in a month when you've turned
up yer toes and we can 'elp.'

'I'm looking for Mr Wiggins,' Gimlet said, casting a

dark glance over to Josie. She could see his jaw tighten as he ground his teeth.

'Well, there's plenty of folks just dyin' to meet 'im,' the boy snorted, poking at the toad's back. Its foreleg jerked up. The boy grinned.

'Could you tell me where I can find him?' Gimlet asked through a fixed smile.

The boy looked up at them for the first time. Josie couldn't help but think that he looked a little toad-like himself, with his wide, turned-down mouth and large eyes. The boy scratched his nose and flicked the toad off the counter. To Josie's surprise and disgust it whirled through the air like a spinning top and bounced off her coat.

'Yeah, I could,' the boy said, jumping off the stool behind the counter and sauntering through a curtain at the back of the shop. 'He's right behind yer.'

The bell tinkled again and a short, pot-bellied old man with pebble-thick spectacles perched on the end of his stubby nose stepped in. His chubby fingers grasped the lapels of his frayed black suit. He rocked on his heels and bent his thin legs as if he were trying to make himself bigger. His tall top hat looked out of all proportion to his body and bore a white ribbon, indicating that he had been to the funeral of a child.

'Can I help you?' he said, squinting through his thick lenses.

'Mr Wiggins?' Gimlet extended a hand. Mr Wiggins inclined his head and fumbled for Gimlet's fingers.

Josie bent down and picked up the toad. She gave a small yelp and dropped it again. It was dead and had been for some time judging by its desiccated state. How on earth could that be?

The two men paused and glanced at her before continuing.

'Yes, hmmm, yes, I *am* Mr Wiggins,' said the frowning man, sounding as if he'd only just realised his identity. 'How may I help you in this hour of deep . . . sadness?' Wiggins breathed the last word out. Josie continued to stare at the dead toad. What sort of boy poked and pawed the mummified remains of amphibians?

'I'm sorry, Mr Wiggins, we aren't here to bury anyone, although we *have* come at a time of great tragedy.' Gimlet gave Josie a sidelong glance and she snapped her attention back to the undertaker, flashing him a stage smile.

'Really?' Wiggins craned his neck further forward, peering harder at Gimlet and then Josie. 'Most irregular. You come to an undertaker but don't require a burying?'

'I'm a friend of the Great Cardamom,' Gimlet said. 'This is Josie – he was her guardian.'

'Ah,' Mr Wiggins said, removing his glasses, polishing them on a sample of shroud and looking up blindly. 'I see.'

'I'm afraid I have some bad news,' Gimlet began.

'I already know about Edwin Chrimes,' Wiggins said, putting his glasses back on. 'News travels fast in this profession, sir. Saddening news, sir, saddening. We were childhood friends.'

'So I believe. Josie knows about her brother ...'
Gimlet began.

'Quite so, yes.' Wiggins gripped his lapels and clicked
his heels. 'I apprised young Alfie of the facts not long ago
myself. Once I'd heard, of course. The truth would out, I
suspected.'

'Indeed. He did make one wish clear,' Gimlet said
quickly before Josie could interject on her guardian's
behalf. 'That was, to be buried in Gorsefields Yard.'

The colour drained from Wiggins's face. Josie thought
he was going to rip his lapels off, his knuckles turned so
white. 'Gorsefie— Well, I . . .'

'Is that a problem?' Gimlet asked.

'I – no ... no. I don't suppose so. Just not one of
the best places. Erm ... full. You wouldn't consider
Highgate Cemetery? It's being extended ... very
respectable –'

'No!' Josie snapped, stepping forward and waving
Cardamom's note under Wiggins's nose. 'It was his last
wish.'

'Josie, why don't you go and get acquainted with your
brother while Mr Wiggins and I talk?' Gimlet said, giving
her a hard stare. 'Where will she find him, sir?' he asked,
turning back to Wiggins.

'Alfie? Why, he's just gone in the back, sir. I do believe
you were talking to him two minutes ago.'

'Oh, joy,' Josie said, giving Gimlet a hard stare. The
toad boy was her brother. Her twin, even! He was meant
to be the one who would understand how she felt. He

was horrible. She paused at the curtain and took a deep breath before stepping through.

The room at the back of the shop matched the front for tidiness. Boxes stood in neat piles and blue, white and green bottles lined themselves up for inspection on the shelves. The smell of carbolic soap mixed with a sweeter, sickly smell that Josie couldn't identify. She thought of Gimlet's messy, chaotic studio. What would Mr Wiggins make of that? Here, four long wooden tables stood in the middle of the room. They were bare and well scrubbed, apart from one, which had something lying on it covered in a white sheet.

Alfie propped himself up against this table, resting his chin on his hands as he gazed at Josie. She could just about see him over the shrouded shape on the table.

'So, you're my brother,' she said. She tried to hide the disappointment in her voice. How could she share the same beautiful gypsy queen of a mother with this street urchin in black?

'So, you're my sister. Wiggins told me about you today when he heard about that magic man dying,' he said with a sneer. 'Could've kept it to 'imself to be honest. Anyway, you don't look like my sister.'

'You don't look like my brother,' Josie retorted. 'You're too small for a start. You look about eight years old!'

'D'you know what this is?' Alfie's wide mouth broke into a grin as he pointed to the shrouded object on the table. Josie shook her head. 'It's a dead body. D'you want to have a look?'

Josie shook her head again and took a step back towards the curtain.

'Go on. Wiggins is always tellin' me to have a look. Most folks just keep their dead at home until they're buried.' Alfie's eyes seemed to glow as he fixed his gaze on Josie and began folding the sheet back. 'But Wiggins offers a special service for those as want to pay.'

Josie watched, hypnotised, as Alfie exposed a wispy mass of white hair and a pale wrinkled brow. She wanted to look away but a grim fascination made her stare.

'What he does is drain all the blood from the veins,' Alfie murmured, revealing the white face of an old woman. She looked like she was in pain. Her mouth and eyes were shut tight, making her whole face wrinkle. The jawbones protruded through stretched skin as thin as parchment. 'Then he pumps them with arsenic. You've heard of arsenic, haven't you?'

Josie nodded, chewing her thumbnail.

'It's a deadly poison. Sometimes they sit up when he does it!' Alfie giggled, twisting his finger in the corpse's hair. 'He says it's only the fluid pumpin' through the veins but it looks proper peculiar!'

'Don't!' Josie protested, clenching her fists at her sides. How could she be related to this nasty little creature?

'Y'see, when a body passes away, so to speak,' Alfie's voice became a whisper, 'it begins to rot. Flies get in through the mouth, nose . . . and other ways.'

'Stop it,' Josie hissed.

'The eggs can hatch within a day if it's warm enough . . . All them maggots.'

'That's horrible. How can you talk this way?' Josie looked away in disgust.

'It comes to us all in the end,' Alfie said, rolling his eyes to heaven, 'but a bit of arsenic in the veins soon puts a stop to any of that unfortunate decay. Mark my words, folks'll be clammerin' for this in years to come. Embalmin', they call it.'

'Is that what you do?' She risked a glance back at the boy.

'Not exactly.' Alfie coughed and looked crestfallen. 'Wiggins won't let me touch the chemicals. I'm a mute.'

'A what?'

'A mute. I stump along after the coffins lookin' all mournful. Like I'm sorry that the deceased has kicked the bucket.'

'And that's it?' Josie said. To her it sounded ridiculous. Surely he must have other duties than following a coffin?

'It's an important job. I help out carryin' and fetchin' stuff, too.' Alfie sniffed and looked defensive. 'There's a lot to see to at a funeral.'

'Sounds dull,' Josie muttered.

Alfie gave her a sneer and leaned forward, pressing his elbows on the body's middle. The corpse's chest rose and its head fell back, emitting a low groan that rattled from the dead woman's jaws. Josie screamed and leapt back, her heart hammering. Alfie gave a howl of laughter.

'That livened you up a bit, then!' He sniggered as he

released the pressure on the corpse, allowing it to settle once more. 'Don't worry. Nuthin' more than a few gases lettin' themselves out the old lady's throat. It could be worse!'

'Hideous! How can *you* be my brother? I hate you.'

'Well, I wasn't exactly clappin' me hands with glee when old Wiggins told me about you,' Alfie snarled. 'Bad enough bein' an orphan and never knowin' your ma or pa, but then to get lumbered with a stupid sister, too.'

'Stupid?' Josie spat, snatching up a small, empty bottle that lay on the table nearest her. 'Stupid?' She sent it whirling across the room. Time slowed. She watched the blue glass catch the light as it travelled. She bit her lip as Alfie threw himself behind the table – too late. The bottle bounced off his forehead with a hollow clunk and shattered on the tiled floor. He slumped behind the table, groaning.

Josie turned on her heel and pushed her way out through the curtain, nearly ripping it down in her anger.

'I don't care if I've killed him. I want to go now,' she snapped at Wiggins and Gimlet, who stood gaping at her, wide-mouthed. 'He *can't* be my brother. He's too odious!'

Her coffin, it was brought; in it she was laid,
And took to the churchyard, this sorry young maid,
No father, no mother, nor friend, I am told,
Came to see that poor creature put under the mould.

'The Poor Murdered Woman', traditional folk ballad

CHAPTER EIGHT

THE GHUL AT THE WINDOW

Gimlet seemed amused at Josie's outburst, which made her even more furious. She stamped around his cluttered studio, kicking offcuts of wood across the floor, hammering her fists on the arm of the sofa so hard that dust and horsehair flew out of the seams.

'He was hideous, Gimlet!' she cried. 'How could a toady little boy like that help us find this Amarant?'

'You got on like brother and sister, then?' Gimlet said, smiling. 'Don't be too harsh on him, Josie. He's had a difficult life. Wiggins is a kindly soul but not strong on discipline and Alfie's grown up in a notorious area.'

'Don't be too harsh?' Josie stared, clenching her fists. 'He threw a dead toad at me and then frightened me half to death with an old woman's corpse! And you're telling me not to be too harsh?'

Gimlet opened his mouth to reply but the bell on the workshop door gave a muffled tinkle. He darted a glance at Josie, put a finger to his lips and padded over to the door.

'Two old crones,' he whispered, peering round the doorway. 'Looks like those Aunts of yours. Didn't you say there were three?'

Josie nodded. The anger drained from her and she could feel her face paling. A cold draught prickled her spine.

'Better stay hidden. Crouch below the window there. If another one's lurking about, she won't see you.' Gimlet stepped through into his workshop, clicking the door shut behind him.

'Can I help you, ladies?' said Gimlet. Josie could hear his voice through the door. He sounded cheerful and relaxed but she knew he wasn't.

'Mr Gimlet?' Aunt Mag's cracked voice drifted into the studio. Josie's knees felt weak. She glanced around, wanting to run, hide – anything to escape the horror of that voice. 'We are so sorry to bother you but we are relatives of the late Great Cardamom.'

'My word. Cardamom? Passed away, you say?' replied Gimlet. Josie shrank further below the window. 'A great sadness. He was a good friend.'

A shadow caught Josie's eye. She pressed herself against the cold wall. Above her was the dark shape of Aunt Jay at the window, her eyes glittering as she scanned Gimlet's studio through the pane of glass. Josie bit her lip, trembling. The ghul was so close.

'Which is why we knew that you'd share our tremendous concern,' came the voice of Aunt Veronica through the door as Aunt Jay's shadow, black and ugly, stretched across the opposite wall. 'Sadly, the young girl for whom our late brother was guardian has gone missing.'

'We are eager to find her.' Aunt Mag's voice grated on Josie's ears. She froze as she saw Aunt Jay's hooked nose and long fingernails scraping the windowpane, searching for an opening. 'To fulfil our . . . *obligations* to her.'

'She has some strange fancies and I fear that the burden of grief has quite turned her poor mind,' continued Aunt Veronica. Josie screwed her eyes shut and tried to become one with the plaster of the wall. 'She fled the house with no belongings and we wondered if she'd come to you.'

'I'm sorry to say I can't help you, ladies,' said Gimlet. Aunt Jay rattled at the window frame, testing it. Josie stifled her sobs of terror. 'I know Josie well and it concerns me that she may be out on the streets unprotected. I will make enquiries myself and if I hear anything I'll contact you. Are you staying at Cardamom's house?'

'No,' said Aunt Mag. 'We will be in touch, Mr Gimlet. We'll send word of where we are staying once we have made arrangements.'

The doorbell rattled again as they bustled out of the workshop. Aunt Jay's dark shadow slid off the wall, leaving Josie shuddering on the floor.

Gimlet looked a shade paler when he returned. 'I don't think they were too convinced, Josie. That was a bit close for comfort,' he said, sitting down heavily in his chair.

'Aunt Jay, she was outside the window,' Josie

stammered. 'I thought she was going to come in!'

'Don't worry, girl,' said Gimlet. She ran to him and he put an arm round her. 'I'll keep you safe, but I think we'd better move you.'

'Move me? Where to?' Josie said, grabbing Gimlet's sleeve. She saw Gimlet give a sly grin and she backed away. 'Oh no! Not back to that bumbling old man. And as for that awful boy . . . The only way you'll get me back there is in a box!'

'Just what I had in mind,' Gimlet said, starting forward.

'No, Gimlet, I can't! I hate boxes,' Josie said, staring at the coffin that lay on Gimlet's handcart.

'Look outside,' Gimlet said, laying a hand on her shoulder. The grey sky was hardening, the brief twilight silhouetting the rooftops. But clearly visible in the gloom were rooks, ravens and crows thronging the slates, all bickering and flapping for space. Josie could hardly see the roof tiles for feathers. 'Now it might just be me, but I reckon those birds are keeping watch on us for the Aunts. We were lucky this morning, but what better cover than Gimlet taking a few caskets to an undertaker's?'

Josie grimaced, and reluctantly clambered into the rough wooden box and lay down. Gimlet lowered the lid. The darkness and closeness of the rough wooden sides pressed in on her. There were a couple of bumps as Gimlet placed some other boxes on top and then her stomach gave a lurch as the handcart jolted into movement.

The air in the box became colder. Josie could hear the noises of the street: costermongers selling off the last of their goods before the end of the day, snatches of conversation between passers-by. She bumped and rolled around, scraping knees and elbows as the handcart bounced over cobble and kerbstone. Josie crossed her hands over her chest to stop them from banging against the sides.

She tried to distract herself from the crushing prison of the box. Thoughts and images tumbled over in her head – Alfie sneering at her, the corpse rearing up . . . Cardamom had said Alfie could help her but he seemed beyond awful. *I wasn't exactly friendly*, she admitted to herself. *But then, he* was *rude to me!* Perhaps she'd been too hard on him. If he could help her, then maybe she needed to give him a second chance.

The bone-numbing ride trundled on. Josie squeezed her eyes tight shut. Her breathing became shallower. She wanted to scream and kick her way out of the box. She whimpered and curled up as best she could, trying to remember how long it had taken her to get to Seven Dials last time.

'We're here,' Gimlet's muffled voice broke through the darkness. 'Wait until we're inside before you make a move.'

More bumping and the cart tipped, sending Josie rolling to the side. She heard Gimlet grunt and then she flew to the other side of the box, banging her head. *Just wait until I get out*, she thought angrily.

'Mr Gimlet, again,' Josie heard Wiggins say in surprise. 'I don't remember ordering any caskets . . .'

'Forgive me, Mr Wiggins,' Gimlet said. Josie heard the other boxes on top of hers being lifted. 'You can have these, but I have a favour to ask of you.'

Even the yellow gaslight of Wiggins's shop dazzled Josie as she raised the lid, sat up and peered about.

'That is the last time I do that, Gimlet.' Josie rubbed her temples and winced. 'Did you have to be so rough?'

Wiggins pressed his spectacles to his face and craned his neck forward. 'Well, I never,' he began. But Gimlet took his elbow and manoeuvred him to one side as Josie climbed out of the box and leapt to the floor.

'I do apologise, sir. We find ourselves in a dire situation.' Gimlet lowered his voice and began to explain. Josie stood massaging life back into her arms and legs. Every now and then, Wiggins would turn round from his conspiratorial huddle with Gimlet and frown at Josie. She gave a tight smile and looked at the floor.

'It's very irregular.' Wiggins stared back at Josie. 'But it seems that the poor girl is a victim of Cardamom's past sins. Not her fault, sir, not her fault.'

Josie pursed her lips. What right did he have to criticise her guardian? *Let he who is without sin cast the first stone*, she thought, wondering what secrets *he* had buried away. And where was toad boy?

Alfie appeared through the curtain to the back room.

When he saw Josie his eyes widened and his lip curled.

'What's she doin' 'ere?' he snapped.

Josie tensed and folded her arms. *Remember to give him a chance*, she told herself.

'It seems, young man, that your . . . hmmm, yes, your sister is staying with us for a while,' Wiggins said, pushing his spectacles up on to his forehead.

'Over my dead body!' Alfie snarled, whirling back through the doorway.

Josie couldn't stand it any longer. 'Do we have to stay here, Gimlet?' she pleaded.

'Sorry, Josie, but I have to go back to the studio.' Gimlet came over and placed a hand on her shoulder. 'You'll be fine here. I'll be back in the morning.'

'But what about the Aunts?'

'They'll be more suspicious if I don't return,' Gimlet said. 'Don't worry, I'll be careful.'

He hugged her and Josie watched helplessly as Gimlet disappeared into the foggy night. She wondered if she would ever see her friend again.

A HANDKERCHIEF SHE SAID SHE TIED
ABOUT HIS HEAD, AND THAT THEY TRIED;
THE SEXTON THEY DID SPEAK UNTO,
THAT HE THE GRAVE WOULD THEN UNDO.

AFFRIGHTED THEN THEY DID BEHOLD
HIS BODY TURNING INTO MOULD,
AND THOUGH HE HAD A MONTH BEEN DEAD,
THIS 'KERCHIEF WAS ABOUT HIS HEAD.

'THE SUFFOLK MIRACLE', TRADITIONAL FOLK BALLAD

CHAPTER NINE
NIGHT VISITING

Josie sat up in her makeshift bed in Wiggins's parlour. Squeezed on to the sofa, she surveyed the tiny room: one armchair, a small table, an aspidistra by the window. Wiggins had set a fire in the grate and a few feeble flames cast deep shadows.

Josie felt as if a huge hole filled her stomach. Tears forced their way out between her eyelashes. She read over the note in the half-light, even though the words were already ingrained in her memory. Something about it teased at her – like when she couldn't remember a name, even though she could feel it there, just out of reach.

She stuffed the note down the side of the sofa and stood up, padding over to the door that led down to the shop. A faint light glimmered from below. Someone was downstairs. Josie looked at Wiggins's bedroom door. He hadn't come out; she'd have known if he had. It must be

Alfie. Josie took a breath and placed a tentative foot on the top step. Then she ran down the stairs.

The shop lay empty. Moonlight gave a silver silhouette to the counter and the coffin lids that leaned against it. But a stronger glow of candlelight shone from behind the curtain to the back room. Josie crept forward and peered in.

The room looked the same as it had that afternoon, only now shadows danced on the walls, so that the potion bottles and instruments seemed to jump about on the shelves.

But Josie's eyes were drawn to the figure in the centre of the room.

Alfie stood over the corpse, his skin glowing in the candlelight. His eyes had rolled back in their sockets, showing only the whites, and his mouth was set in a snarl. His whole body shook as he pointed a finger at the woman's corpse. Josie's eyes widened. She could feel the blood pumping through her temples as, slowly, the corpse's hand began to rise. Josie wanted to scream out loud, to run away – anything but watch as the dead woman's arm lifted. Then Alfie gave a violent shudder and collapsed. The arm flopped back on to the table. Alfie lay still on the floor.

Josie leapt through the curtain to her brother as he lay groaning.

'Did you . . . see?' Alfie croaked.

'What in heaven's name were you doing?' Josie asked, frowning. Alfie looked feverish, his forehead glistening with sweat, but his shivering had subsided.

'Raisin' the dead.' Alfie gave a snigger that turned into a wracking cough. 'Did you see? Her arm lifted.'

'If this is another one of your ridiculous pranks . . .'

'No!' Alfie said. 'No, it's not a trick. I can do it.'

'But how . . . why?' Josie felt certain now that this was no joke. Alfie looked spent, exhausted and terrified by what he'd done.

'I don't know.' He climbed to his feet and dropped into a chair. 'It's a curse . . . somethin' that just happens. Always has but, as I get older, it happens more often.'

'That toad in the shop this afternoon.' Josie squirmed, remembering the desiccated fragment that Alfie had been jabbing with his finger. 'It moved.'

'I know.' Alfie nodded. 'That toad was a bit dried up, like – only his leg would move. There just needs to be a scrap of somethin' to bring it back, skin or bone, y'know. Small things are easy but a whole cadaver takes some effort.'

'It's horrible.' Josie stared at her brother.

'I don't do it for laughs.' Alfie frowned back. 'I'm only tryin' to understand it. I just want to know why it happens and if . . . if I can control it.'

'Control it?' she repeated. Her heart was pounding.

'Sometimes, when I'm walkin' past a body, I can feel it drawin' on me, pullin' the strength from me. It'll start to twitch or groan.' Alfie's face was deathly pale. 'I tried tellin' Wiggins about it but he's never noticed. Blind as a bat that one. He just says it's all gases and muscle tension.

But I know different. It's 'orrible and I don't know why it happens. I thought if I could learn more about it, maybe I could stop it happenin'.'

'That's terrible.' Josie laid a hand on his shoulder. Here in this dingy back room, Alfie looked small and pathetic.

'I don't need no pity,' Alfie spat, jerking his shoulder away. 'Life's hard but death can be worse from what I've seen.'

'I only meant it must be awful to have that happening all the time,' Josie snapped back. 'I've got enough to worry about without wasting pity on *you*.'

'Yeah, well, I can look after meself,' Alfie murmured, staring at the floor. There was an awkward silence and then Alfie coughed. 'Look, I'm sorry I was rotten to you this morning. There was no call for it.'

'That's all right.' Josie gave a tight smile. 'I expect it was as much of a shock for you as it was for me. I'm sorry I threw that bottle at you. Did it hurt? Must have given you quite a bruise.' Josie frowned and stared at his forehead where the bottle had struck him. She would have expected a dark bruise to be blooming there, but it was clear and pale as if it had never been touched.

'It did.' Alfie gave her a hard stare and rubbed his head. 'Black as Wiggins's hat it was . . . but I heal quick.'

'In an afternoon?' Josie was surprised.

'I always 'ave, don't you?' Alfie asked.

'I don't know,' Josie said. She'd never really thought about it. She'd had falls when she tumbled across the stage, she'd nicked herself on knives, pinched her fingers in box lids and ropes . . . but there had never been any lasting marks. Some of the acrobats and contortionists she saw backstage bore horrible bruises and scars.

'I had a fight with Edgy Taylor and we split each other's lips,' Alfie said, drawing a knuckle across his mouth as if he could still feel it. 'Mine was fine in a day; he looked like a codfish for a week! We laughed about it later.'

Josie gave a short laugh, and then felt her frown return. She'd never had a fight like that. She didn't have any friends to speak of – not ones her own age. The folk at the Erato were nice to her, but they were all much older.

'It's very strange,' Josie mumbled, shaking her head.

'You're right there and no mistake,' Alfie said.

'Not just that. So much has happened to me over the last few days,' Josie said, sitting down on a tall-legged stool.

Alfie listened, wide-eyed, as Josie related all that had passed. She ran to retrieve the note stuffed down the side of the sofa, and held it out for Alfie to read.

'Funny the way he says things,' he remarked, pulling a face as he handed the note back. 'Sounds a bit . . . dunno . . . odd.'

'Gimlet said that, too,' Josie said, frowning at the scrawl on the page. 'He tried to tell me something about the note . . . but couldn't . . .'

She carried on telling her story, pausing every now and then to regain her composure. Alfie looked on, occasionally clearing his throat and trying not to catch her eye.

'Blimey, you 'ave been through the mill,' he said after Josie had finished. 'And you 'ad a picture . . . of my mother?'

'*Our* mother. She was beautiful, a gypsy queen.' Josie smiled.

'I wouldn't mind 'avin' a peek at that . . .'

'It's at the house still,' she said, wishing she could get it to show Alfie. 'Cardamom said that our father died when we were babes. I've no idea what he looked like, or even his name.'

Alfie shrugged. 'No skin off my nose. Never really thought about it before, much.'

Josie nodded. It was true. She thought more about her mother. Was that because Cardamom had talked about her more or because she had a portrait? Josie didn't know. 'Before he died, Cardamom said you could help.'

'I dunno how.' Alfie pouted and stared past Josie into the shadows. 'But blood's thicker than water, I s'pose. He sounds like he . . . well, y'know . . . thought a lot of you, this Cardamom.'

'He was like a father to me.' Josie felt her face crumple and she bit her lip. She stifled another sob. 'I left him lying there with those . . . *things*. What I wouldn't give to see him one last time.'

'Well.' Alfie pushed his bottom lip out as he thought aloud. 'Maybe that's one way I can help.'

'What do you mean?' Josie asked.

Alfie gave a broad smile. 'He's here!'

You crave one kiss of my clay-cold lips,
But my breath smells earthy strong;
If you have one kiss of my clay-cold lips,
Your time will not be long.

'The Unquiet Grave', traditional folk ballad

CHAPTER TEN
THE WHISPERING CORPSE

'After you visited this mornin', we went to collect your uncle,' Alfie said. 'The house was open – ransacked it was, turned upside down, and he was just left layin' there in the bedroom. Well, Wiggins was proper outraged and we brought him back, meanin' to give him the right send-off tomorrow. Wiggins is particular about these things, y'know.'

'Can I see him?' Josie said, her stomach tightening. But did she really want to see her guardian cold and lifeless?

Alfie nodded. 'Come on,' he said. Josie slid off the stool and followed her brother to the back of the room.

Alfie fidgeted beside the shrouded body of Cardamom. 'Before I uncover him, well, you need to know . . . not to put too fine a point on it, Josie, but he wasn't in the best condition when we brought him in.'

Josie's head swam as she steadied herself, holding on to the edge of the table. 'I want to see.'

'We tried to tidy him up as best we could. Wiggins is a bit of a maestro at it, but this one was difficult.' Alfie gently pulled back the rough cotton shroud. Josie drew a deep breath.

Cardamom's body lay there, his skin marbled and pale. His eyes gaped red and empty; a bloody trail wept down his grey cheeks. His teeth were clenched tight in a snarl and his back seemed arched and tense. He was dressed in his best suit, the one he wore when he and Josie took Sunday walks through town in happier times. But he didn't fill it. The mid section of his body seemed flat, empty.

'We considered packin' him with somethin' but Wiggins wasn't sure if that would be dignified.'

'Packing him?' Josie whispered.

'Yeah.' Alfie fiddled with the button on his coat. 'Well, there's no easy way to say this . . . His whole stomach was . . . ripped out. We don't know what happened to him.'

Josie felt the blood run cold in her veins. The ghul's words on the night at the Erato came back to her. It said it was going to a 'sweet feast'.

'I know what happened to him. It was those frightful creatures. I swear I will avenge him.' As she spoke, Josie felt different – stronger. Her body shook, but she didn't feel scared. 'Can you wake him?'

'What?' Alfie stared at her, his mouth wide in astonishment.

'Wake him,' Josie said again, cold determination

flooding her. 'He was trying to tell me something. I'm sure it was about the Amarant. You have to try and bring him back.'

'Well, I dunno.' Alfie scratched his head with a trembling hand. 'I've only ever made arms or legs move or got corpses to groan a bit . . .'

'Try it,' Josie ordered. She folded her arms, blotting out any thoughts of her guardian as he was now, focusing on her hatred of the ghuls. 'Bring him back.'

'I'll 'ave a go,' Alfie murmured, shuffling his feet. 'But I can't say as I like it.'

He stood next to the Great Cardamom's ravaged corpse and held his hands over the body, palms down. Alfie's eyes closed and his brow furrowed as his breathing deepened and slowed. Josie's stomach fluttered as she watched her brother shake and tremble. But Cardamom remained prone on the table. Not a twitch. Alfie threw his arms down with an exasperated gasp.

'It's no good,' he said. 'I'm spent after movin' that old lady. I can't do this, too!'

'Just try again,' Josie snapped. 'Don't give up so easily.'

Alfie assumed his stance once more and breathed deeply. Josie watched intently as her brother's eyes rolled back in their sockets and his hands trembled again. Long minutes passed. Alfie's breathing grew faster. Josie noticed Cardamom's little finger twitch. Josie wondered if she'd imagined it – but then his hand curled into a fist. She backed away from the table, her newfound courage lost for a moment. Alfie drew a huge breath and

Cardamom started up from the table, lifting his shoulders and head. Air whistled from his mouth and the vacant, bloody pits of his eyes stared at the ceiling.

'Josie,' Cardamom said, his voice thick and rasping. Each syllable dragged as if it was an effort to pronounce.

'Uncle,' Josie said, grabbing his cold, clammy hand. 'Tell us what to do. Help us – we need you!'

'Destroy . . . the . . . Amarant,' hissed the dead magician, red tears of blood trickling down each cheek.

'But we can't, Uncle. We don't know where it is!' Josie cried.

'Destroy it,' Cardamom's voice grated.

'Tell us how, Great Cardamom,' Alfie whispered huskily, his eyes still rolled back in his sockets. He looked like a corpse himself.

'Sacrifice . . . and . . . a tender heart,' Cardamom's voice rumbled. 'But beware . . .'

'What do you mean? Beware what, Uncle?' Josie gripped his hand tightly.

'Mortlock . . .' Cardamom jerked forward, then fell back on the table with a heavy thud. In the same moment, Alfie twirled round in a tight pirouette and crashed to the ground. 'Beware Mortlock,' Cardamom hissed with a last breath. Then his body lay still on the table once again.

For a moment, Josie couldn't move. Now, in the dim light, the expression on Cardamom's face looked peaceful. His teeth were no longer clenched, the frown lines on his brow had smoothed. His whole body seemed slack and loose. Josie covered her face with her hands and wept, shaking with grief.

Alfie hauled himself to his feet, using the edge of the table for support. He looked dishevelled and exhausted.

'Bloody 'ell,' he panted. 'I feel like a coach and four has run over me. Erm . . . You all right?'

'Yes, yes,' Josie said, scrubbing roughly at her eyes. 'What did he mean, "sacrifice and a tender heart"?'

'How should I know?' Alfie said, leaning against the table and wiping the sweat from his brow. 'And who's this Mortlock cove?'

'An old friend of my uncle's.' Josie shook her head. 'They had a bitter dispute over something. He vanished years ago, apparently.'

'But if your uncle's tellin' us to beware of 'im . . . doesn't that mean he might 'ave come back?' Alfie said, shivering.

'A strange man's been following me . . . maybe it's him.'

A footstep at the door made Josie turn with a start. Mr Wiggins stood, fully clothed for the day, blinking at them.

'Ah, there you are,' he said. 'I wondered where you'd got to. Getting acquainted, I see?'

'Yes, Mr Wiggins,' Alfie said respectfully. Josie noticed the difference in his tone when Wiggins was about. Wiggins was like a father to him, she supposed. Cardamom had given Alfie into the care of Wiggins. He must have trusted the old undertaker to give him responsibility for a child's welfare.

'Mr Wiggins,' Josie said, 'you knew my uncle quite well . . .'

'Hmmm. I should like to think so, Josie, yes.' The old man nodded, polishing his glasses. 'A good man essentially, but fell in with some rum sorts.'

'Like Mortlock?' Josie said.

Wiggins stopped polishing. Then he carried on rubbing at the lenses.

'That particular individual vanished from our lives some years ago, thankfully,' Wiggins said, his voice very quiet. Josie thought he was going to snap his spectacles in two. 'You are young and don't know the hurt that man caused. I'll make allowances this time but I'll not have his name mentioned again.'

'What –' Josie began to ask, but Alfie placed a hand on her arm and shook his head. Why had Wiggins clammed up like that?

'Anyway,' Wiggins continued. 'We need to get ready, Alfie. We have a grave to dig and a funeral to conduct. Come!'

THE LID OF THE COFFIN HE OPENED UP,
THE SHROUD HE FOLDED DOWN,
AND THEN HE KISSED HER PALE, PALE LIPS,
AND THE TEARS CAME TRICKLING DOWN.

'LORD LOVEL', TRADITIONAL FOLK BALLAD

CHAPTER ELEVEN
GORSEFIELDS YARD

Alfie and Wiggins stood in the doorway, shovels in hand, wrapped up against the dawning winter day. Outside, shopkeepers set out stalls and the first customers picked their way along the frosty pavements.

'Right, Josie, we won't be too long.' Wiggins scratched his head and stared at the spade. 'It's a while since I've dug a grave personally, but I want to make sure it is deep enough for Edwin.'

'Deep enough?' Josie said, frowning at Alfie. 'What do you mean?'

'A city-centre burial ground,' Alfie said, flashing Wiggins a knowing look. 'Pretty much full these days.'

'Forgive me, miss, but I did tell Mr Gimlet. Gorsefields is no place to bury your guardian,' the old undertaker said, shaking his head. 'The minister for Gorsefields should close it but they keep taking new burials. Once it was a fine place, fresh and respectable. But now? Not so.

Overcrowded. Do you know, I was talking to a gravedigger the other day who accidentally dug up his own father because the graves were so close together. It's not right.'

'Oh my!' Josie brought a hand to her mouth. She wondered whether Cardamom had been in his right mind when he wrote the note. *Perhaps I should ask Wiggins to bury him somewhere else*, she thought. But before she could open her mouth, Alfie spoke up.

'Well, I've seen the note, Mr Wiggins, and it's plain as day. Gorsefields, it says. He must have had his reasons.'

'So, Gorsefields it is.' Wiggins grimaced and shook the spade. 'We'll make the grave good and deep. The sexton won't like it but that's hard luck for him.'

'You should tell him you're diggin' under the old yew tree. That'd make his day, Mr W.' Alfie grinned but Wiggins shook his head.

'No,' he snapped, frowning at Alfie. 'That wouldn't do at all.'

'The old yew tree?' Josie said, struggling to keep up with the conversation.

'An old wives' tale,' Alfie snorted. 'They reckon the ground under the tree is cursed. There ain't a sexton for miles around who'll dig in that patch of earth, nor anyone who wants buryin' there. Load of nonsense if you ask me.'

'Yes, well, we aren't asking you, young man, and I'll thank you to keep such tales to yourself. That's hallowed ground you're talking about,' Wiggins said, jabbing his finger at Alfie. 'As it is, we'll be close enough to the yew, which I'm not happy about.'

The bell jingled and Gimlet peered around the door. Josie dashed forward to hug him.

'See?' he said, grinning. 'Told you I'd be fine.'

'The Aunts?' Josie asked. Gimlet looked troubled.

'They were lurking around outside, I'm sure. I can't say I got much sleep, but they were gone by morning.'

'Perfect timing, Mr Gimlet.' Wiggins shook his hand. 'We are deep in preparations for Edwin's funeral. I'm sure Josie would like to get ready for what will be a difficult day. If you could stay with her?'

Alfie and Wiggins stamped out into the cold street, each with a shovel over his shoulder, leaving Josie to relate the night's events to Gimlet.

Josie clambered out of the cab and frowned at the hordes of people congregated around the gates to Gorsefields Yard. Gimlet paid the driver and ran after her, scanning the sky. Josie looked up, too, terrified by what she might see there. She pulled up the cowl of the cloak Wiggins had lent to her, covering her face.

'If Cardamom's funeral is meant to be a quiet affair, then it's failed,' whispered Gimlet as they approached the churchyard.

Josie smiled weakly at the crowds that milled around them: women with dark, painted eyes and feathers pluming from their hats, men with magnificent waxed moustaches and tall hats. They all stopped talking to stare at the hearse as it rolled into the yard. Mr Wiggins sat at the front of the black cart, his top hat shining in the cold morning sun. The hearse looked like a large coffin on wheels. Josie assumed that the real coffin lay inside the box of the cart. Alfie marched alongside it, ignoring Josie. He gazed ahead, carrying a strange wand covered in black cloth.

Josie recognised most of the mourners as they paraded past, shaking her hand, murmuring their regret: chorus girls, strongmen, comedians and puppeteers. Even in their black clothes, they looked glamorous.

'Anything we can do, Miss Josie,' muttered a muscular stagehand. 'You only have to call on us, you know that.'

Josie hugged the giant. She remembered Ernie's twisted body and sighed. Even with all his strength, he was no match for the ghuls.

Gorsefields Yard was a dingy, dismal burial ground squeezed between slum dwellings that threatened to burst their ragged edges. Two leafless silver birch trees stood sentry at the gates of the yard, their skeletal branches waving over the monuments and mounds. A small chapel squatted in the corner of the yard, blackened by soot and smog. Josie shivered at the huge gnarled yew tree crouched next to the chapel, its twisted branches casting a shadow over half the yard.

The hearse stopped and Alfie and Wiggins stepped to the side of the carriage as a number of burly showmen in tight-fitting suits prepared to bear the coffin. The rollers at the back of the hearse rumbled as the casket emerged. Josie watched, numb, as the theatre folk carried the coffin towards the deep, muddy hole that was to be Cardamom's final resting place. She watched Wiggins fussing at ribbons and polishing his hat with his forearm and she felt a glow of gratitude. He'd laboured hard to ensure Cardamom had the right send-off. She could see why folk respected him.

A familiar face appeared beyond the graveside crowd, keeping his distance. Josie took a breath and froze.

He stood, tall and gaunt, behind a weathered Celtic cross. His mass of fluffy grey hair billowed from under his hat, threatening to push it off, and a wispy grey beard framed his wide drooping mouth. Thick brows sat like giant caterpillars above his large, sad eyes.

Josie raised her hand, glancing around for Alfie or Gimlet, but Wiggins took her elbow to usher her into the service. When she looked back, the man had disappeared again.

The chapel was as dingy and cramped as the yard it stood in. The minister's voice droned on through the service. Would Cardamom find a place in heaven? Was he a good man? Josie would never criticise him aloud but what she'd heard made her wonder. She thought of her guardian, doves flying from his opened hands on the stage, smiling as he produced a penny from a small boy's ear. Tears sprang to her eyes. Then she remembered him pale and wizened, trapped in his bedroom. He was no thief and he didn't deserve such an end, she was certain.

Outside once more, Josie watched the coffin being lowered into the ground. He was gone. She threw a handful of earth into the grave. The funeral congregation filed past, rattling a thin scattering of soil over the casket lid.

Most of the crowd had dispersed when an impressive black carriage rolled into the yard, behind the funeral hearse. The red crow on the coat of arms flashed boldly in the winter sun. A stony-faced driver leapt down from his seat and opened the door.

Josie shivered as she watched a tall female figure step out of the carriage. The figure was swathed in a long black coat with a deep hood. Gimlet stepped up beside Josie as the woman approached and paused on the other side of the grave. Her features were lost in the shadows of the hood.

'Lord Corvis has sent me with a command not to harm you,' the shrouded figure said. Josie recognised the voice of Aunt Mag. 'He offers you a chance. Tell us where the Amarant is and you can go free.'

'You can tell his lordship that –' Gimlet began angrily, but Josie held her hand up.

'Tell Lord Corvis,' she began, feeling her face flush, 'that I will not rest until the Amarant, and your hideous selves, are destroyed. At my guardian's graveside, I swear this.'

Aunt Mag stood motionless and silent. Then she inclined her head.

'You have declared war, Josie Chrimes, and war you shall have,' she hissed.

Josie caught a flash of Aunt Mag's black eyes. Then the ghul turned and strode back to the coach. Josie kept watching the creature until the coach door slammed shut.

HERE'S A PIECE OF GOOD ADVICE
I GOT FROM AN OLD FISHMONGER:
'IF THE FOOD IS SCARCE
AND YOU SEE THE HEARSE,
THEN YOU KNOW THAT YOU'VE DIED OF HUNGER.'

'WAXIES' DARGLE', TRADITIONAL FOLK SONG

CHAPTER TWELVE

THE STRANGER IN THE STREET

Wiggins insisted on bringing the funeral party back to his shop for 'light refreshments'. Josie hadn't felt hungry but Wiggins's offer had touched her and so she and Gimlet agreed.

Now they stood in silence, chewing cuts of pork pie and sipping tea.

'So,' Mr Wiggins said at last. 'In addition to making the odd casket, you work in the theatre, Mr Gimlet.'

'I make stage props, sir. I believe my grand title is "engineer", but I'm really a humble carpenter.'

'Wasn't the good Lord himself?' Wiggins set his cup down and pulled off his glasses to polish them. 'Where would we poor undertakers be if there was nobody to make our coffins for us?'

'I've made a few caskets and coffins in my time,' Gimlet said. 'Sowerberry was always a good customer, sadly no more.'

'You knew Sowerberry, then?' Wiggins nodded with approval. 'A fine undertaker, a fine fellow all round . . .'

Josie gave Alfie a despairing glance as Gimlet and Wiggins compared business contacts.

'What's up with you?' Alfie said through a mouthful of pork pie. A shower of crumbs fell from his lips.

'Weren't you taught any manners?' Josie hissed, flicking a piece of pastry from her shoulder. The image of the stranger still stuck in her mind. 'I saw him . . . at the funeral. The stranger!'

'It's those Aunts of yours I'd be worried about.' Alfie sprayed again.

'Cardamom said to destroy the Amarant. If that man *is* Mortlock, we have to speak to him.'

'Yeah, he also said to *beware* of Mortlock. Anyway, why don't you just tell Wiggins we've got to go?' Alfie said. 'You're too lah-di-dah with yer manners and affectations sometimes.'

'Too what?' Josie clenched her fists. 'Anyway, who says *you're* coming?'

'I do,' Alfie said. 'I'm kind of involved, you bein' my sister an' all. You didn't complain when I helped you last night. Besides, your uncle said I could help, remember?'

Josie narrowed her eyes at him. He was right. By coming to find him and telling him what had happened, she had dragged him into it. And he was right about Cardamom, too, but that didn't make it any easier to accept this strange boy pushing his way into her life.

She turned to Mr Wiggins, who was still holding forth.

'Of course, Mr Mould was a fine undertaker but always had a tendency to look a little self-satisfied . . .'

Josie put down her teacup and said, 'Mr Wiggins, I'm very grateful for everything you've done for us.'

'The least I could do.' Wiggins beamed. 'Attention to detail, that's the key. I've always believed that a good send-off is the last right of an Englishman. If you don't mind, I've taken the liberty of ordering a headstone – a simple affair but dignified. The stonemason owed me a favour.'

'Thank you, Mr Wiggins, you are too kind,' Josie began. A dark figure scurried past the shop window, making Josie stop. 'It's him again,' she gasped. 'Mortlock.'

Knocking the tea tray from the table, Josie charged out of the shop into the cold, barging through the crowd as the man hurried ahead of her. She could see his head sailing away above the sea of tattered hats and bonnets.

'Wait! I want to talk to you!' she yelled, pushing and elbowing through the grumbling pedestrians. She was closing on him!

The stranger glanced back, wide-eyed, and broke into a clumsy jog. His coat-tails flickered inches from her grasp. Josie snatched at the velvet of his jacket pocket, her fingers gripping on something smooth, then she was suddenly thrown backwards on to the muddy street. A dull pain spread across her stomach and she gasped for breath. Apples, pears and a rather heavy cabbage bounced off her head. Dazed and winded, she looked up at a fruit and vegetable barrow blocking her view.

'You all right, miss?' a round, red-faced fruit seller said, peering down at her. 'You wanna watch where yer goin'. Walked right into me barrow. Look at me lovely apples . . . ruined. Someone'll 'ave to pay for them, y'know . . .'

But Josie had stopped listening. She grinned in triumph at the business card she'd snagged from the man's pocket. A small crowd gathered around her as she sat up, muddy water oozing through her skirts, her breath returning. Dirt smeared the name at the top, but Josie could read the address quite clearly:

The Emporium
of
Archaic Antiquities

ANTIQUARIAN BOOKS
OBSCURE MAPS
ARCANE ARTEFACTS

13 JESMOND STREET

Gimlet and Alfie appeared, panting and pushing their way through the onlookers. They helped Josie to her feet as Mr Wiggins came puffing into the circle.

'Mr Gimlet, I'm quite happy to put the girl up for as long as you want, providing she doesn't insist on making a habit of smashing my best china and sitting in puddles in the street,' he said, sliding his spectacles up his nose. 'But I will not have her under my roof if she utters that man's name in my presence again!'

'But I'm sure it was him –' Josie began to protest.

Gimlet raised a hand, silencing her. 'I'm sorry, Mr Wiggins, she can be quite . . . *high-spirited*. Come on, Josie,' Gimlet muttered. 'Let's get you in and cleaned up.'

Back in Wiggins's parlour, Josie dried herself off and changed her muddy clothes, then went down into the shop to the others. Wiggins had taken himself off to the back room to tidy up.

'I presume there was a reason for that pantomime in the street,' Gimlet murmured, raising one eyebrow at Josie.

'It was the man who's been watching me. I got this from him.' Josie showed him the card. 'We should pay this place a visit.'

'Archaic . . . Anti . . . what?' Alfie said, squinting at the card. 'What kind of a place is that?'

'The Emporium,' Gimlet snorted, snatching the card. 'Belongs to Evenyule Scrabsnitch, another charlatan. Sells "curiosities" to gullible country squires. So-called "ancient tomes" and stuffed "quirks of nature" – rabbits with six legs, two-headed piglets and the like. A total quack.'

'Well, whoever that man was, he's been there,' Josie said. 'Maybe this Scrabsnitch knows him. We need to start somewhere.'

'Josie, Scrabsnitch is a crook. You can't trust a word he says,' Gimlet pleaded.

'You seem very familiar with him.' Alfie frowned, tucking his thumbs into his braces. Josie thought he looked a bit like Mr Wiggins.

'I made some cabinets for him.' Gimlet said, looking shamefaced. 'A glass case that magnified some specimens, made them look more impressive than they were.'

'Well, Mr Gimlet, it seems to me that you can't go around callin' people fake when it was you as helped them in the fakery!' Alfie said, pointing an imperious finger.

Gimlet started to say something but then pursed his lips and folded his arms.

'Very well,' he said, the corners of his mouth turning down. 'But take *anything* Mr Scrabsnitch says with a sackful of salt, that's all. We'll get the pony and trap though. It's a fair way to his shop in Jesmond Street.'

A half-hour ride brought them near to their destination. Or as near as they could get to Jesmond Street. The busy day was in full swing now and carriages and carts clogged the roadway. Horses whinnied, stamping and kicking up mud. Drivers cursed each other, trying to back up so that others could pass. The steam from the horses and the breath of the drivers mingled with the light mist left from the previous night's thick fog. A peddler's cart and a grand coach had become entangled, their wheels buckled together. A constant swarm of pedestrians edged around the vehicles, weaving in and out, tiptoeing over horse droppings and worse.

'The city gets more and more clogged up,' Gimlet said, jumping down and backing the trap up before it became mired in the crush. They found a quiet side street and tied up the pony.

'It'll take some time to untangle that mess,' Josie said as they entered Jesmond Street on foot.

'Mr Wiggins says that one day we'll all travel in tunnels under the streets. There's a man in Parliament who wants to make underground railways,' Alfie said.

'I doubt that'll happen,' Gimlet called back. 'The city would be choked with the smoke from the engines below.'

'Something's got to be done.' Josie frowned as she forced herself between two portly gents. 'Number thirteen, there it is.'

Scrabsnitch's Emporium of Archaic Antiquities stood out of the row of shops like a tramp at a society wedding. The other shopfronts were polished and well kept, produce hanging in the windows in uniform rows. The emporium wedged itself between them, paint peeling from the window frames, the panes of glass grimed and opaque. Its pointed frontage poked up higher than the other buildings and leaned forward alarmingly, as if it might crash into the seething street below. Josie wrinkled her nose.

'I told you,' Gimlet said, rolling his eyes heavenward. 'Don't expect too much here.'

A dull metallic clank heralded their arrival as they heaved open the door. Josie looked up to see a rusty bell. She caught Alfie's eye. It was a far cry from the polished professionalism of Wiggins the Undertaker.

The inside of the shop was vast; it reminded Josie of a church or maybe a library. Bookshelves lined the walls, disappearing up into the shadows near the ceiling. Display cases stood in rows and piles of books and papers, stuffed animals and various articles of junk cluttered every surface. Old chairs and dull suits of armour were dotted about the room. A thick layer of dust coated everything. A few dim gaslights illuminated parts of the space and a feeble light struggled through the begrimed windows.

'There's the old faker,' Gimlet said, nodding across the cavernous room.

In a far corner, a high-backed armchair housed a grey old man. He was dressed in a silk smoking jacket and a matching pillbox hat. The gown had once been a deep crimson, Josie could tell, but it had faded with age. Blossoming trees swirled across the painted silk and colourful parrots sat on their branches. The old man's face was shrouded in the frizzy grey beard and grey hair that exploded from under his hat. But Josie recognised his eyes. It was the watcher.

'Mr Gimlet,' he said, pointing at them with his long-stemmed pipe. 'And the two youngsters. I've been expecting you.'

AMARANTUS FLOS, SYM'BOLUM EST IMMORTALITATIS.

CLEMENT OF ALEXANDRIA

CHAPTER THIRTEEN
EVENYULE SCRABSNITCH

Josie frowned at the stranger in the fancy smoking jacket. 'You're not Sebastian Mortlock?' She couldn't help but feel a little disappointed. That would have been one piece of this puzzle in place. Now she had a new piece to fit.

He flinched at the name, looking nonplussed, then gave an embarrassed cough. 'My name is Scrabsnitch, Evenyule Scrabsnitch, purveyor of mystery and antiquity –'

'Give over, Ted,' Gimlet snorted, but the man's expression did not change.

'Ted?' Josie repeated, frowning.

'Don't be fooled by that Evenyule nonsense. He uses a false name to impress the village idiots who visit this place,' Gimlet murmured. 'His real name is Ted, Ted Oliver, and he wasn't expecting us.'

'Believe what you want, Gimlet.' Scrabsnitch waved a bony hand. 'I *was* expecting you, once I realised the young lady had snatched a card from my pocket.'

'Hardly second sight, then, Ted,' Gimlet said, folding his arms. 'Now, perhaps you can explain why you've been following Josie all this time.'

'I've been trying to pluck up the courage to approach you,' Scrabsnitch said, peering up at her through bushy eyebrows, his shoulders slumping, 'and your guardian before . . . he passed away. But I was wary of the company you've been keeping.'

Gimlet strode forward, grabbed the old man's lapels and pulled him up out of the chair. Josie thought he was going to hit him. The old man hung from Gimlet's powerful grasp, dropping his pipe.

'What do you know about them?' Gimlet snarled.

'No more than I've observed! Put me down.' Scrabsnitch waved his arms and kicked his feet in the air as Gimlet lowered him to the ground.

'Gimlet! You're too rough,' Josie said and laid a reassuring hand on Scrabsnitch's arm. 'You must forgive my friend, Mr Scrabsnitch. He's had a difficult time recently, as have we all.'

'Here you are, mister.' Alfie rescued the man's pipe from the floor, while stamping out a smouldering fire that had struck up on the dry carpet.

'I knew your guardian well, Josie Chrimes,' Scrabsnitch said, his voice shaky as he settled himself back into the chair. 'Besides, I used to visit the Erato every night. I loved your act and Cardamom was *such* a magician.'

Josie couldn't help smiling. It seemed like an eternity
since she'd last performed onstage. It had been in
another world, another time.

'He used to frequent my shop often in the old days,
with Sebastian Mortlock.' Scrabsnitch seemed to shiver.
'Cardamom and Mortlock came here, spending Lord
Corvis's money.' He gave a hollow laugh. 'I could never
pass any fakes off on them. More recently, I received this
from your guardian. He gave it to me for safe keeping, he
said.'

Scrabsnitch swept aside piles of papers with his skinny
arm, and a vase shattered on the floor as he thumped a
large package down. Josie, Alfie and Gimlet coughed
and spluttered on the dust that mushroomed up from the
documents.

'Gave it to *you*?' Gimlet snorted.

'*He* trusted me, Gimlet. Cardamom was never one to
stand in judgement against people. He knew he could
rely on me as serious scholar of the arcane. A kindred
spirit almost.'

'*Serious scholar.*' Gimlet sneered once more.

'Judge for yourself, Josie,' Scrabsnitch said, ignoring
Gimlet. 'Is the packaging tampered with? Are any seals
broken? Once he left the package, he stopped coming to
the shop. I was worried about him but whenever I
approached him, he had company . . .'

'I saw you at the theatre.' Josie nodded. 'And then at
the house.'

'I didn't know Edwin was in quite such mortal danger

or I'd have acted differently. When I heard he had died, I knew I had to let you know about this parcel, but again, finding the right time was difficult.' He looked over at Gimlet. 'Some folk don't trust me the way your guardian did.'

Gimlet gave another snort and sauntered over to the window to look out at the chaos in the street. 'I'll keep a close eye out here, Josie – watch out for any unwelcome visitors.'

Josie looked at the brown paper parcel. It seemed intact. She ripped into the packaging and drew a breath.

Letters, maps and charts spilled on to the table. Beneath them lay a leather-bound book. She picked it up and ran her finger across the gold lettering on the cover: *Sebastian Mortlock's Journal.*

'They've all got Mortlock's name on them,' Josie said, her voice faint as she turned over envelopes and sheets of paper. 'They must've belonged to him . . .'

'Your guardian acquired these around the time of Mortlock's disappearance, it seems. For some reason, he moved them here a matter of weeks ago,' Scrabsnitch said. 'He must have felt they were important.'

Josie sat down at the table and opened the book. Before she could start reading, Alfie unrolled a map, its corner poking over the book.

'Do you mind?' she hissed, flicking the map aside.

'But look, it says AB-YSS-IN-IA . . . Abyssinia.' Alfie's eyes widened. 'And look at that.'

Josie leaned over the hand-drawn map, scanning over

the foreign names, the pale blue splodges for waterholes and confusing lines and numbers. But right in the centre lay a green mass and, at the heart of that, a red spot with the word *Amarant* printed in shaky script beside it.

'Then they did find it,' Josie whispered. It made sense. Why else would they have this map?

'This Amarant, have you heard of it?' Alfie said, perching himself on the edge of a rickety table and staring boldly at Scrabsnitch.

'There *is* a plant called the Amarant. It exists. An ordinary flower, but the ancient Greeks believed it blossomed for ever.' Evenyule Scrabsnitch ran bony fingers through his tangle of hair. 'They associated it with Artemis and Diana, the Greek and Roman goddesses of the hunt.'

'Artemis, that's the stage name Cardamom gave me,' Josie said.

'Maybe the Amarant was in his mind, young lady. Your uncanny accuracy with all manner of missiles would make you a queen of the hunt. The link would not be lost on Cardamom, I assure you. Milton also mentions the Amarant in his epic poem *Paradise Lost* – a strange and dangerous bloom indeed.'

Josie sat forward and listened intently. 'Tell me about it.'

'The Flower of Life.' Scrabsnitch's voice had fallen to a whisper. 'The first flower in the Garden of Eden, blessed by the Lord to give any who held it power over life and death. Many men have died searching for it.'

'And because of it,' Josie sighed, looking back to the journal.

It is agreed. We depart for Abyssinia on 20 July 1819. Corvis is generously funding the expedition. Chrimes complains about the heat before we have even embarked! Imagine: to find the Flower of Life. To have the power over life and death itself!

I am fortunate to have such good travelling companions. Corvis has a dark sense of humour but doesn't let his wealth or high birth stop him from enjoying the company of commoners. Chrimes has been a dear friend for several years now . . .

Josie paused. They all sounded such good friends. What had gone wrong? She glanced down at an irregular-sized piece of paper. She pulled it out of the pile. It was a flyer advertising 'Lorenzo's Incredible Circus'. A tall ring-master stood at one edge of the paper, half framing the list of acts. A lion pawed the air from a corner of the sheet.

'*Madame Lilly,*' she read aloud, '*tells the fortunes of the brave. The Flying Gambinis, trapeze artists to royalty. Ulrico the Clown. Cardamom the Great, magician and conjurer . . .*'

'*And Professor Necros,*' Alfie continued, '*Communicator with the Spirit World, Master of the Ghostly . . .*'

'Uncle never told me he worked in a circus,' Josie said, frowning. Part of his life had suddenly been revealed to her, a hidden part. She couldn't understand why he had never told her about it. 'Maybe that's where he met Mother.'

'Madame Lilly, this her, then?' Alfie said. He sounded casual but Josie thought she caught a note of emotion in his voice. He touched the cameo picture of the fortune teller on the poster.

'What d'you think?'

'Dunno what to think really,' he murmured. 'Very beautiful . . .'

'Cardamom didn't tell me much about her. She was a fortune teller, a dancer, she loved life . . .'

'There are many things that Cardamom didn't tell anyone about,' Gimlet said, drawn from the window by the conversation. 'Many things he wanted to keep secret, buried. Too shameful to remember.'

'Uncle would never do anything shameful,' Josie said, folding her arms.

'Not the Cardamom you knew, Josie, but he had his dark moments, his depressions when painful memories swamped him. From what I know, he started life humbly enough, trying to scrape a living in sideshows and funfairs. He was, by his own admission, a pretty poor conjurer.'

'Well, he wasn't when I knew him,' muttered Josie, staring down at the journal again. How could Gimlet say such things? She'd known Cardamom most of her life, and, despite his moods, she'd loved him and trusted him. And he'd been the only family she had.

'Blimey!' Alfie said out loud, shoving a letter under Josie's nose. She recognised the handwriting, and the address at the top.

Bluebell Terrace
7 July 1844

Mortlock, my dearest friend,

I write to you one last time for the sake of our friendship and all the difficulties we have been through together. If it is true that you possess the Amarant then I beg of you, destroy it. No good can come of it. I know the ill will you bear towards me and can understand, but it is the cursed flower that has brought this upon you, not me. If you cannot bring yourself to destroy it, then let me help you. We agreed many years ago that bringing the Amarant here would result in disaster. Can you not see what is happening?

Your ever-faithful friend,
Edwin

'Mortlock had the Amarant,' Josie said. The letter at home had called Cardamom a thief. Had he managed to take the flower from Mortlock?

'Looks like Mortlock was up to no good with it,' Alfie said, whipping the letter back. Josie flicked through the journal, looking for the same date as the letter.

'There's something here, written a few days before Mortlock sent that letter to Uncle accusing him of theft,' Josie said, dragging her finger down the page.

1 July

My research has confirmed my greatest hope: the Amarant gives great power. Of the three corpses I have had delivered, I was able to awaken one on my own but at great physical cost. I was exhausted. I've known of this ability since I returned from Abyssinia. A parlour trick. But, with the Amarant, I could animate all three, make them walk, carry out simple tasks, and with no strain to myself. Think of the possibilities of such power! How can this be a curse?

'He could wake the dead,' Alfie murmured, staring at Josie.

'From my own research, I understand that the Amarant is said to give power to anyone who comes into contact with it,' Scrabsnitch said, appearing at Josie's shoulder. 'But as well as leaving some vestige of power, the Amarant will curse the recipients.'

'Curse?' Alfie pulled a face.

'In the hands of the divine, the Amarant could only do good. In the hands of flawed humanity, it draws on the darkness that lurks in us all. I watched Cardamom perform and his act baffled me. I've seen other conjurers and magicians and know a little about the mechanics of artifice. It is hard to fool me, but your guardian's skills were of a different order. He foxed me every time. That is all I will say.'

'I could never guess how he accomplished some of his tricks,' Gimlet added, nodding slowly. 'If he found the Amarant, do you think its power helped him?'

Scrabsnitch shrugged. 'It's possible if, as you say, he has been in the presence of the Amarant.'

'Maybe Uncle took it from Mortlock and hid it,' Josie said, 'to stop him from doing any more bad things.'

'That might explain why Mortlock's not about now,' Alfie added. 'He could still be lookin' for it.'

'We've got to find a way to destroy it,' Josie said, frowning at the journal. She turned the pages. 'Sacrifice, he said to us, Alfie. That, and a tender heart.'

'Got to find the bloomin' thing ourselves first,' Alfie muttered, shaking his head.

'And you aren't the only ones interested, by the way.' Scrabsnitch glanced at them over the top of his spectacles. 'Your three old ladies came in asking about Cardamom and the Amarant only last week . . .'

'The Aunts,' Josie spat. 'They are searching for the Amarant, too.'

'Aunts?' Scrabsnitch looked from Alfie to Josie. 'I wouldn't be so happy to claim them as relatives.'

'What d'yer mean by that?' Alfie frowned.

'I don't know.' Scrabsnitch shook his head. 'Just something about them. They didn't seem natural and when I saw them at your house . . . well, I was fearful of calling.'

'Ghuls,' Josie said. 'They aren't human.'

'Ghuls?' Scrabsnitch paled beneath his fuzz of beard.

'You've heard of them?' Josie asked.

'In my line of work you get to hear of – and see – all manner of strangeness,' Scrabsnitch said, scratching his beard. 'The word "ghul" means demon. They appear in most traditions. Ghuls are usually associated with the dead and they devour the newly deceased. You're in trouble if they're involved.'

'We're in trouble if they get the Amarant, from what I've heard,' Gimlet said, shaking his head.

'They'll kill us all,' Alfie muttered.

'Worse, they could trap you between life and death, neither fully alive nor resting,' Scrabsnitch added. 'They could create whole armies of the dead to ravage the world of the living.'

'Whatever they have in mind, it ain't good,' Alfie groaned.

'It would be hell on earth,' Evenyule Scrabsnitch said.

'Does that sound so bad?' came a grating voice.

The blood drained from Josie's face, as she and her companions turned round. The Aunts stood by the door, their throats ruffled in black silk and lace, heads cocked. Thin smiles split their hatchet faces.

'We could make our own little hell in here, right now,' Aunt Jay said. Then she spread her arms wide.

O MOTHER, MOTHER, MAKE MY BED,
O MAKE IT SOFT AND NARROW,
SINCE MY LOVE DIED FOR ME TODAY,
I'LL DIE FOR HIM TOMORROW.

'BARBARA ALLEN', TRADITIONAL FOLK BALLAD

CHAPTER FOURTEEN
GIMLET'S CHOICE

Bodies twisted and feathers burst forth. Josie had seen the Aunts transform before, but it didn't make the moment any less shocking now. Aunt Veronica and Aunt Jay shook out their glossy feathers and snapped their sharp beaks. They flanked their sister, Aunt Mag, who kept her human form.

Josie glanced around for a weapon and found her hand resting on a pile of pewter plates. She snatched the first one and sent it whirling across the room at Aunt Mag. It would have been a direct hit, but Aunt Jay darted her head forward and her long beak snatched the plate out of the air, inches from Aunt Mag's head.

'You'll have to do better than that, young lady,' Aunt Mag said. She gestured to Aunt Veronica, who launched herself into the air, sending clouds of dust billowing across the room.

Josie grabbed a plate in each hand and sent both

spinning at once, followed by two more. Aunt Veronica twisted and spiralled, dodging one plate. Josie feinted with another, then sent it hurtling in a different direction. The plate spun in a perfect arc and hit Aunt Mag on the temple with a metallic clang. Aunt Mag wobbled, then fell to the floor, dragging half the contents of a display case on top of her.

But Aunt Veronica was closing in. Josie cartwheeled out of the ghul's way while Gimlet grabbed a pikestaff that leaned against a suit of armour. He jabbed it at the snapping ghul, forcing it to beat its massive wings in a hasty retreat. The air filled with dust and fluttering papers, as ornaments and artefacts smashed to the floor.

'We've got to get out! Is there a back door?' he yelled at Scrabsnitch, but the old man stood transfixed by the sight of the creatures.

'Here,' Alfie called, pushing open a door. 'Mr Scrabsnitch, come on!'

But Evenyule remained frozen to the spot as Aunt Jay hurtled across the shop towards him. Suddenly, he turned and looked straight into Josie's eyes.

'I wish you luck, Josie,' the old man said. Then he threw himself under a display cabinet. Aunt Jay landed in a shower of glass and dust on top of the case. Scrabsnitch crawled under the next cabinet, moving with surprising speed.

Josie threw another plate at Aunt Jay as Gimlet backed towards the door, parrying Aunt Veronica's razor beak with his pikestaff. Aunt Jay wheeled about and fixed Josie with her beady eye. Beyond her, Josie spotted Scrabsnitch's head bob up as he scurried through a door on the other side of the room.

Alfie's hand clamped on to Josie's arm and she felt herself being dragged into the back room. Gimlet gave a final vicious jab at Aunt Veronica before leaping back, and Alfie slammed the door against the scrabbling, screeching ghul.

The clutter in the back room was even worse than the front. Chairs were piled on top of each other, leaning at crazy angles. Alfie shoved chairs and boxes to one side and managed to drag another door open. It squealed on rusted hinges but opened just wide enough for them to squeeze out.

They pushed their way into a dingy yard, stacked with crates and old planks. Beyond the yard was a narrow alley, with walls that ran with black putrid slime. Josie wrinkled her nose and pulled a face at the smell.

'If we can get to the street at the front of the shop, we'll be safer,' Gimlet said. 'The crowds there might put the ghuls off.'

Slipping and cursing, they sprinted up the muddy alley back into Jesmond Street and the chaos of the traffic jam. Gimlet elbowed his way through the crowds, as more people spilled out from stranded carriages and coaches.

Josie glanced back and saw Aunt Mag, a livid bruise on her brow, pushing her way towards them. Just as they passed the front of the Emporium, its filthy windows exploded out into the street. Glass rained down on the packed crowds. Horses whinnied and women screamed as two giant crows burst out of the windows, swooping down on the three fugitives. The frozen winter sky blackened as thousands of crows, rooks and jackdaws swept on to the crush of people, pecking ears and eyes and pulling at hair.

The crowds pushed forward, the surge of bodies squeezing the breath out of Josie. She felt their heat and closeness, the rough fabric of their clothes, their elbows and knees digging into her. She forced her body forward, trying to ignore the curses and yells around her. People began to stumble and fall, and were trampled upon as others fled. Josie grabbed Alfie and Gimlet and ducked into the middle of the street, under the huge wheels of a coach. They picked their way between the wedged carts and carriages, keeping their heads down as Aunt Jay and Aunt Veronica hovered above the seething crowds, snapping and pecking, unable to get near their quarry.

The world became a mass of stamping hoofs, screeching birds and screams of fear. Josie wove down the street, her heavy skirts snagging on the close-pressed wheels. The crowds pushed, overturning a trap and pinning the horse, which kicked out in terror.

Finally, she dragged herself out of the tangled mass. Gimlet grabbed her hand and, followed by Alfie, they sprinted up the street towards their trap. Josie cursed the stiff dress that swished against her legs. They turned into the narrow alley and clambered aboard.

'Josie, look!' Alfie yelled, his voice shrill.

'Going somewhere?' croaked Aunt Mag, now in her crow form.

The three ghuls had landed in the alleyway, blocking their exit. Gimlet snapped the reins, making the pony set off at a gallop towards them. Aunt Jay and Aunt Veronica threw themselves aside, but Aunt Mag flew into the air above them. She hovered, beating the air with her huge black wings, claws outstretched. She was waiting for the trap to bring them to her.

'Don't look back,' Gimlet called as they raced towards the ghul's talons. Giving a final snap on the reins, he leapt up and caught Aunt Mag's scaly legs, dragging her down to the cobbles as he fell.

'Gimlet, no!' Josie screamed. But the trap was already leaving him behind as the pony bolted. Josie stared back at the rapidly receding figures struggling in the alley behind them. She saw Gimlet grab hold of Aunt Mag's beak and force her head back. His clothes hung in blood-soaked rags where the ghul had slashed at him with her claws.

'We have to help him!' Josie cried. She clambered to the front of the trap and groped for the reins to stop the pony, but they were being dragged along the street, far out of reach. She watched helplessly as Aunt Jay launched herself after them with terrifying speed, leaping on to the back of the trap and making it tip and lurch.

Snatching up the whip, Josie lashed out at her. She struggled to keep her balance as the pony continued to bolt through the crowds. Aunt Jay swung her talons at them. But it all seemed to happen so slowly, like a dance. Josie threw herself to one side. Alfie crouched in the seat, desperately trying to fend off the ghul, but it still managed to slice his face. He pivoted and slumped down into the trap, a long red gash running down his cheek.

Josie cowered, hiding her head in her hands, as Aunt Jay reared up to deliver another blow. Instead, the sound of tinkling glass and a metallic clang made Josie look out from between her fingers. Aunt Jay was gone, entangled in a tall gaslight, her legs dangling.

But the trap was gaining speed. The pony, foaming at the mouth, raced across the cobbles. Josie's heart hammered, keeping time with the pounding of the horse's hoofs. Crowds flashed by, diving aside to avoid being crushed. Yells of anger and fear were snatched away by the wind as the trap rocked and pitched along the street. Alfie started to roll over the side and Josie just managed to catch him and pin him in the seat, leaning her weight against him. The cut on his ashen face was turning a livid blue.

The pony grew more frantic as a chestnut seller's brazier crashed over. Josie glanced down at the reins, which were flicking and bucking off the cobbles. The body of the trap swayed and bounced. She made a stretch for the reins, leaning dangerously far out as the clatter of the steel-rimmed wheel reverberated through her head. The trap lurched again and Josie dragged herself back up as Alfie slid to the floor, pinning her now. She pushed him upright, nearly spilling out of the trap again as the pony careered around some brave onlookers who were trying to slow it down. She gritted her teeth and leaned down a second time.

'Come on,' Josie muttered. The cobbles rushed by, hard and grey, sparks crackling from the horse's hoofs. She wedged her leg beneath the seat and reached out perilously far for the dancing reins.

A distant ringing filled Josie's ears. She looked up. Thundering straight towards her was a fire cart with a team of horses. Even from this unlikely angle, Josie could see the look of horror on the driver's face. She glanced down as the reins flicked along the sparking cobbles, and snatched them up. Thighs, stomach and back all seemed about to snap. Bile rose to fill her throat as she righted herself and yanked on the reins.

The trap veered left, scraping along the length of the fire cart. Josie ducked as buckets and ropes bounced and rattled overhead, torn free in the collision. An axe sliced through the air above Josie's head, clanging on to the street on the other side of the trap.

The ringing of the bell disappeared as the pony thundered on. Josie had lost all sense of direction but the stench of sewers told her the river wasn't far away. More faces sped past in a blur. Josie jerked on the reins, pulling from side to side, anything to get the horse to come back to its senses. Something clattered against the left wheel of the trap and the whole thing began to pitch even more wildly and unevenly.

A stabbing pain exploded in Josie's head. She was

knocked back into the trap and lifted her fingers to her forehead. It felt warm and wet. When she pulled her hand away it was slick with blood. She glanced back at a swinging shop sign.

Josie's vision blurred; shadows filled her eyes. Her stomach lurched and she suddenly felt weightless. The trap had come to a stop and Josie's body was flying through the air. She could hear the trap smashing into the side of the street. Rough cobbles smacked against her elbows and shoulder.

Then everything was still.

Josie could hear a wheel clicking as it whirled on its axle. Alfie groaned, somewhere off to her left. She tried to stand but her legs buckled and she fell to the ground, looking up at the dark sky, blood pulsing in her head.

A cold breeze blew against her face. The black silhouettes of ragged birds flitted across the moonlit clouds and Aunt Mag's triumphant, grinning face filled the night above her.

Gimlet was dead, of that she was sure. *And now I'll join him*, she thought. It was all over.

PART THE SECOND
ROOKERY HEIGHTS

The cock does crow, the day does dawn,
The worrying worm does chide;
And if we're missed from where we came
Sore pain we must abide.

'The Wife of Usher's Well', traditional folk ballad

CHAPTER FIFTEEN
THE LIGHTS ON THE MARSH

Warm blankets swaddled Josie, hugging her. She twisted and stretched, screwing her eyes tight. For a moment she thought she was on Gimlet's sofa, but the stabbing ache in her temple brought her back to reality. Josie's body pulsed with a dull pain that reminded her of the previous night's horrors. Gimlet's bleeding face, his screaming at her to flee, the rattling, bone-shaking ride. After that, she had vague memories of being lifted higher and higher, of vomiting into the freezing black air as sharp talons dug into her shoulders and whisked her into the night sky.

She opened her eyes. Josie lay in a huge four-poster bed, old and carved with vines and birds. It dominated the room, leaving a small area to her left for a dressing table, a chair and a mirror. These matched the bed – heavy, dark and crusted with carving. To Josie's right, the narrowest of gaps separated the bed from a bay window that let the grey light of a winter's afternoon stream into the dusty room. Outside, Josie could see flat, washed-out marshland. In front of her, two chairs and a small table stood before a crackling fire that leapt in the small hearth. Josie touched her head gingerly – it was swathed in a large bandage.

A girl a few years older than Josie sat in one of the chairs. Dressed in plain black with a white apron, her red hair tied back in a tight bun, she looked like a maid or servant. Her thin, angular face was pale and freckled, but her blue eyes were soft and her mouth held the faintest trace of a smile as she returned Josie's stare.

'Where am I?' Josie said, sitting up and shivering as the blankets fell away. The chill of the room caressed her neck and shoulders. She looked down at the thick night-gown she was wearing. 'What day is it? Where are my clothes? Where's Alfie?'

'Settle down,' the smiling girl said, coming over to the bedside. 'My name's Arabella. You've had a nasty accident. It was lucky we found you out on the marsh road there or you'd be dead with the cold for sure . . .'

Panic washed over Josie. 'I need to see Alfie,' she said, throwing back the blankets and swinging her legs out of the bed. Immediately her head began to spin. She fell back on the pillows, groaning.

'There, there, don't worry. You're safe now,' said Arabella, easing the covers over her. 'You're at Rookery Heights. Alfie must be the boy what was with you. He's down the corridor. You can see him soon enough but you

must take it steady. Your head's badly cut and you're
covered in bruises. I'll get you some soup.'

Arabella left the room. Josie tried to sit up but slumped
back again. Alfie was safe. But Gimlet? She covered her
face with trembling hands. Tears trickled through her
fingers. Gimlet was her one connection with Cardamom.
Apart from Alfie, he was all she'd had left. Losing him
was more than she could bear.

When she looked up again, Arabella was stood by the
bed with a steaming bowl of soup and chunks of bread on
a tray.

'Come on. Get some of this down you and get your
strength up.' She gave a sad smile and placed the tray on
Josie's lap as she sat up and wiped the tears away.

'How did I get here?' Josie asked, blowing on the
surface of the soup to cool it. The smell of chicken and
vegetables made her mouth water. How long had it been
since she had eaten? She felt guilty for feeling so hungry.
Gimlet was beyond hunger now.

'The ladies of the house found you as they returned
from London,' Arabella said, glancing out of the darkening window. 'Your trap had gone off into a ditch.
Thought you was dead at first. You've been out cold all
day – it's nearly night-time again.'

Josie sipped at the soup. She could guess who the
ladies of the house were. Part of her screamed to escape
but she had to stay calm. She had to find out as much as
possible if she were to stand any chance of escaping.
Arabella was right: she'd need all her strength.

'Who owns Rookery Heights?' she asked between mouthfuls of soup.

'Lord Corvis.' Arabella lowered her voice. 'The new lord, the son. He's not long taken over . . .'

'And you work for him?' Josie said.

'My family have worked on this estate for years and years but . . .' Arabella stopped and glanced at the door.

'But?' Josie leaned forward, wincing a little as she moved.

'Things have changed lately.' Arabella's voice had fallen to a whisper. 'Since the ladies came and Lord Thurlough took over. I mean, things were never perfect. The Corvis family have always been cold fish – but they were fair. Now the rents have gone up, our houses don't get repaired and the crows –'

'Crows?'

'Everywhere.' Arabella pulled a disgusted face. 'Hundreds of 'em. Peckin' at crops, stealing our eels. Mrs Sullivan in the village even had to shoo one off her baby's cradle last week. Lord knows what would've happened if she hadn't heard the crying.'

'Where do they come from?' Josie asked, though she could guess. She'd seen how the Aunts attracted crows, using them for their evil ends.

'Crows 'ave always lived in and around Rookery Heights. That's how it got its name, so they say.' Arabella sniffed. 'But never so many and Lord Corvis made it worse, that's for sure, when he dismissed the gamekeeper after he killed a score of them. And there's other things, too . . .'

'What do you mean?' Josie said. Her soup bowl was abandoned as she listened to the girl. A movement distracted her and Josie glanced over to the window. An enormous raven perched on the sill outside. Its feathers glistened with blues and greens, like oil on water, and from between the feathers speared the longest and cruellest of beaks.

Arabella had also seen it. 'Oh, look at me, scarin' you with my chatter,' she chirped, her voice overly bright. 'Don't you pay me any heed, miss. I just get carried away with myself. Drink yer soup up and get some more rest . . .'

'But I want to see my brother. I want to see Alfie.' Josie pulled herself up, groaning with the effort. Her whole body ached and her head felt as though it might burst out of the tight bandage. She glared at the raven as it ruffled its feathers and grazed the tip of its enormous beak across the glass of the window. It had unnerved Arabella. Josie wished she had something to throw.

'All in good time, miss. Look, you're spillin' what's left of yer soup there.' Arabella frowned and snatched the bowl away. She eased a hand against Josie's shoulder, pushing her back into the pillow. After all she'd been through, Josie felt too weak to resist. 'It'll be dark soon and your brother needs his rest, too. Nasty gash he had across his face. You can't go disturbin' him now.'

Arabella bustled off with the soup bowl. The rattle of a bolt as Arabella left told Josie she was locked in. Exhaustion weighed down her eyelids but jabs of pain snapped her to attention again. She rolled to her side, struggling to find a comfortable position. Her thoughts gave her no peace either. Cardamom had told her to find the Amarant. Had he hidden it? She racked her brain, trying to think of places they had visited. How secretive he had been! He'd told her virtually nothing about his past. Their lives had moved between the theatre and Bluebell Terrace. And what about Mortlock? Was he out there now, searching? Hunting for the Amarant just as the hideous ghuls were? If he had vanished years ago, why did she feel his presence lurking in every shadow? Why did his name crop up time and again?

Time dragged on. Evening shadows crept up the bedroom wall, darkening the room. Josie was staring out of the window, still lost in thought, as Arabella returned with a lit paraffin lamp. Something glowed feebly in the distance, a light punctuating the flat line of the horizon. Josie had to squint to be sure it wasn't a reflection of the lamp.

'Is that another house?' Josie said, catching Arabella's elbow. The girl glanced over and gave a gasp.

'Oh, that,' she said, forcing a laugh. 'No, probably just the gamekeeper after some poachers . . .'

'You said Corvis dismissed the gamekeeper,' Josie said, narrowing her eyes.

'Did I?' Arabella gave another foolish giggle and almost ran for the window. 'Maybe a barge out to sea, then. Could be anything really. You get some sleep. I'll draw them curtains; it's cold out there.'

And with that she had gone. Josie sat up in bed for a while with the lamp turned down, wondering about the dim glow out across the darkness. If it wasn't another house, what could it be? And why had Arabella reacted so nervously when Josie asked about it? If only she could talk to Alfie. She shivered and huddled under the covers. She had no idea what the night might hold.

'WHAT WILL YE LEAVE TO YOUR SISTER ANNE?'
'MY SILKEN SCARF AND MY GOLDEN FAN.'
'WHAT WILL YE LEAVE TO YOUR SISTER GRACE?'
'MY BLOODY CLOTHES TO WASH AND DRESS.'
'WHAT WILL YE LEAVE TO YOUR BROTHER JOHN?'
'THE GALLOWS TREE TO HANG HIM ON.'

'THE CRUEL BROTHER', TRADITIONAL FOLK BALLAD

CHAPTER SIXTEEN
LORD CORVIS

Josie's night passed miserably. Her lamp sputtered and died, leaving her in total darkness, her nerves prey to every scratch at the window, every rustle. Floorboards creaked, the wind moaned across the marshes and rattled her window in its frame. Josie was used to the sounds of the city: carriages clattering on cobbled streets, costermongers crying out to attract custom. The noises here were alien to her.

Cackling magpies and crows brought the first feeble suggestions of dawn. Josie limped out of bed to the window and looked out across the flat grey landscape. It was empty but for a few scrubby trees, a dilapidated windmill and a hangman's gibbet standing stark and black against the washed-out marshland. The house stood on raised ground and looked down on the marshes as they spilled out towards the sea. Rust-red squares dotted the distant waterline, the sails of Thames barges plying their trade along the coast. Josie remembered seeing them at the docks in the city once. But they were far from London now. A tumbledown brick wall marked a perimeter of sorts around the house and a pitted drive led to its front door.

Few plants bothered to grow in the land surrounding the house. But rooks, ravens and crows of all descriptions lined the ledges and roofs of outlying houses, huddling and bickering together in the cold dawn. Wherever a bird roosted, smears of white crusted the surfaces and dripped down the walls. Josie pulled a face and peered over to where she thought the light had been in the night. Nothing interrupted the grey line of the horizon.

She hobbled to the door and turned the handle. It was bolted from the outside. Josie cursed under her breath. Not that she had any intention of escaping; she wasn't fit enough yet. But she needed to see Alfie, to know he was safe and well. When Arabella finally arrived with breakfast on a tray, Josie was pleased to see her and straightened up in bed, wincing with each bend of a limb or twist of the body.

But Arabella looked pale and drawn.

'Breakfast, miss,' she murmured, placing the tray down. Josie frowned. Where was the smiling girl from yesterday? She looked like a hunted mouse, shoulders slumped, head to one side, staring at the carpet.

'Can I see Alfie today?'

'Couldn't say, miss,' Arabella said, stepping back and giving a sidelong glance to the door. Josie's stomach lurched.

Aunt Mag leered from the threshold, hands clasped in

front of her, dark eyes twinkling with triumph. She took a step forward.

'I trust you're comfortable, Josie Chrimes,' Aunt Mag hissed with a yellow-toothed grin. 'Don't get used to it. Lord Corvis is *interested* in the pair of you for now, but it is the Amarant he truly wants. Come with me.'

Josie caught a glimpse of Alfie's face behind Aunt Mag, a livid scar coursing across his white cheek. His eyes met hers and widened. Josie threw herself forward, sending the breakfast tray crashing to the floor. 'Alfie,' she cried, hobbling to the door and hugging him, ignoring Aunt Mag's sneer.

'Owww,' Alfie groaned. 'Steady on.'

Josie stood back, grimacing at her complaining joints and her smile dropped. 'You look terrible,' she said.

It was true, the gash across his cheek stood out blue and angry. He swayed and gave a feeble grin.

'Thanks, yer no oil painting yerself,' he said, wincing and grabbing her shoulder for support. He looked like a little old man, so frail and colourless.

'Enough! His lordship is waiting,' Aunt Mag snapped. She led them along dusty passageways. Even though it was morning, the house was dark and shuttered. Aunt Mag's oil lamp cast a globe of light in the shadows.

'It reminds me of a mausoleum,' Alfie whispered. Every now and then a cracked oil painting of a lady in silks or a tarnished suit of armour would pass through their little illuminated bubble.

'Everything here needs a good dusting down,' Josie

whispered back. Dull unpolished tables supported vases of brown desiccated flowers, which in turn supported a tangle of thick, dusty cobwebs. 'Uncle may not have been too fussy about housework, but at least Bluebell Terrace was clean.'

'Got a strange taste in ornaments, too,' Alfie murmured. Here and there, hideous statues and carvings snarled out of the gloom: ancient gods with many arms, tusks and fearsome scowling faces, weapons raised, frozen in mid blow.

'Horrible,' Josie said.

Aunt Mag pushed on the large double doors into the dining room and there at the end of a long polished table sat Lord Corvis. Aunt Mag swept past them and stood at Corvis's shoulder, her black eyes locked on to Josie, cold and steely. Josie slipped her hand around Alfie's and gave a squeeze. His skin felt cold and clammy. He squeezed back.

'Welcome,' Corvis said. Josie had never seen such a neat, well-groomed man. He sat very tall in his chair, regarding them with imperious, ice-cold eyes. His pointed features were tanned brown, a clear indication that he'd been away from the grimy winter streets of London for many years. His coal-black hair shone. The creases of his suit were pressed razor sharp, from the lapels of his tailcoat to the hem of his dark trousers. A single diamond sparkled on the end of the pin in his black silk tie. Corvis smoothed his pencil moustache. 'You've led me a merry dance. Sit down.'

Josie and Alfie edged into the room, both of them

eyeing Aunt Mag nervously. They sat at the end of the table, on either side of Corvis's seat. Corvis turned to them, leaning his elbows on the table.

'I'm not going to burden you with questions just yet, children,' Corvis began, reaching for a china teapot. 'You've been through quite an ordeal and need time to recover.' He stopped pouring his tea and peered at Alfie. 'Though not that much time, it would appear. If I didn't know better, I'd say you were healing before my very eyes. Remarkable.'

'What do you want with us?' Josie said, glaring at Corvis.

'We'll discuss all that once you're feeling better, my dear,' Corvis said, stirring the tea slowly. 'For now you are our guests. Isn't that right, Mag?'

Aunt Mag said nothing, but Josie noticed her bony knuckles whiten as they gripped the back of Corvis's chair.

'Feel free to move around the house,' he said and took a sip from the china cup. 'But please don't try to leave. I have forbidden the ladies from harming you, but you've seen what they can do. I wonder how much restraint they would exercise should they have to . . . *apprehend* you.' Corvis gave a tight smile and put down his cup. The audience was over, Josie could tell. 'Mag, take them back to their rooms.'

Arabella stood waiting in Josie's room with some bread and cheese on a tray to replace the ruined breakfast. 'You've met him, then. What d'you think?' she said, putting the tray down.

'Gave me the bloomin' creeps,' Alfie grumbled, cutting a corner off the cheese.

'His eyes reminded me of the ghuls,' Josie said. 'To think he was Uncle's friend once. I wonder what changed him . . .'

'I can't imagine his lordship bein' anyone's friend,' Arabella said in a low voice.

Josie knew from her manner that she held no love for her master or the ladies. *But does that make her an ally?* Josie wondered. The girl was clearly frightened of the Aunts. Did she know what they really were?

'Thanks, Arabella,' Alfie said, smiling at her and waving a crust.

'That's all right.' Arabella blushed. She shook herself. 'Anyway, I can't stand round here gossipin' to you two. Make sure you rest and if you want anything ring the bell. I'll hear it.' She bustled out of the room and Josie eased herself on to the end of her bed.

'How do you feel now?' she asked.

'Like death,' Alfie replied. 'Gettin' better by the minute, though, I can feel it. I can't remember much after the ghul slashed me. Gimlet – is he . . . ?'

'He must be. I saw him covered in blood.' Josie nodded and stifled her tears.

'Why didn't they see *us* off?' Alfie said, looking down at his hands.

'Corvis still thinks we know where the Amarant is,' Josie whispered, fiddling with her bandage.

'I wish we did. We could work out how to destroy it and

that'd be an end to it.'

'Whatever they want, we'll play along,' Josie replied, winking at Alfie. 'Until we're feeling better and we've worked out how to escape – and then we'll burn this place to its foundations and get back to London!'

'Don't think I can sleep with those things under the same roof as me,' Alfie said.

'I know what you mean, but we're safe for now,' Josie said, not quite believing herself.

They talked and dozed through the afternoon, skirting around any further mention of Gimlet or the horrors of that night. Neither felt strong enough to move beyond the confines of the room. Arabella breezed in and out with hot soup.

'At least the bloomin' Aunts or Lord Corvis 'aven't stuck their ugly mugs through the door,' said Alfie. Daylight succumbed to darkness and, once more, the weird glimmer of light appeared across the marshes.

'Can you see that?' Josie pointed to it.

'Lights.' Alfie shrugged. 'Maybe it's a house or some-thin'.'

'No, I asked Arabella about it and she wouldn't say.'

'Hmm, too far out on the marshes to be a house.' Alfie nodded. He fell silent for a moment and then said, 'There's somethin' about the light, too. Like it's callin' yer to go out into the dark and find it. But that'd be stupid and dangerous . . .'

'Like a moth to a candle,' Josie whispered, pressing her nose to the cold glass.

'AND WHOSE BLOOD IS THIS,' HE SAYS,
'THAT LIES IN MY HALL?'
'IT IS YOUR YOUNG SON'S HEART'S BLOOD,
'TIS THE CLEAREST OF ALL.'

'LAMKIN', TRADITIONAL FOLK SONG

CHAPTER SEVENTEEN
THE DELIVERY

Josie was woken the following morning by fluttering and scratching at her window. Pulling on a dressing gown, she clambered across the bed and drew back the curtains, gritting her teeth at the stabbing pains in her joints.

A square, bulky man pushed a large sack in a wheelbarrow up the front path towards the house. Crows and ravens swooped and veered around him, making him wobble and tip the barrow as he waved his shovel hands to shoo them away. They seemed very excited. Josie hurried to the door, wincing with each step but eager to find out what was going on. She slipped out into the shadows of the house. The sound of the Aunts, every bit as excited as the crows on the roof, drifted up from the hall.

Josie crept past the cobwebs and withered plants towards the stairs. A flurry of activity below made her duck behind the thick banister rails. She peered down through the spindles at the scrum in the hall.

The Aunts must have got to the door before the delivery man even had a chance to ring the bell, and now they crowded round him. The sack was now on his broad shoulder and quivered with his every move. The Aunts reached out and stroked the heavy bag. The man tried to keep his eyes on them all, glancing nervously from woman to woman as they scuttled about him.

'You're early, Mr Carr,' crowed Aunt Veronica, hopping from foot to foot. Aunt Jay inhaled deeply, as if scenting the bag.

Josie made out a nasty, over-ripe, meaty aroma. What could be in that bag? She had never seen the Aunts so animated.

'Bring it through, young man,' croaked Aunt Mag, clapping her hands together. 'And put it on the table.'

'We'll deal with it from there!' cackled Aunt Veronica.

The sound of screeching and chuckling faded, following the group as they shuffled out of the hall and disappeared from Josie's view into a side room. She crept down the stairs a step at a time, until she stood in the hall.

Oak panelling darkened the place. There were more dusty aspidistra plants, an umbrella stand and a dinner gong by the door. A huge tiger-skin rug snarled silently at her from the black-and-white floor tiles. The delivery man's empty wheelbarrow propped the front door open, letting the cold air of the grey morning seep into the house. Josie thought about making a run for it now, taking her chance, going for help in the village. She couldn't leave Alfie, though. What would the Aunts do to him once they found out she had escaped? Josie shuddered.

The delivery man reappeared from the side room, a disdainful look on his face. He glanced sidelong at Josie as he stalked past her and touched the peak of his cap. Then he stopped, staring back at her with piercing blue eyes.

'You visiting, miss?' His voice sounded so soft after the harsh cawing of the Aunts. 'Look a bit out of place 'ere, if I may say.'

'Y-yes,' Josie said, stepping forward. *Can I trust him?* she thought. He might call Corvis if she asked for help. 'I don't want to be here . . .'

'I don't blame you.' The man rubbed his beard and regarded Josie closely.

'I want to leave . . . but my brother isn't well enough yet . . .' Josie tried to choose her words carefully. Maybe he thought she was some strange young relative of Corvis's, playing a game.

'This is a rum old place and no mistake.' The man smiled, glanced back at the side room and stooped close to Josie. 'Listen, I come 'ere every other day, more or less. If you and your brother need any assistance, then let me know . . .'

Josie's heart lifted. A way out, a chance to escape! 'Thank you, Mr . . . ?'

'Carr – Jacob Carr, miss.' Josie's hand became lost in his huge grasp.

'Josie,' she said, returning the shake.

'Pleased to meet yer, Miss Josie,' he replied. Josie heard him call back as he picked up the barrow, 'Now, I'm not hangin' round here a minute longer, but remember what I said . . .'

Jacob vanished into the frozen morning. Josie's smile faded as she glanced across the hall. She wasn't free yet. The side-room door stood ajar. A sickening smell of offal, rotten eggs and something putrefied made Josie gag. She should have crept away but she couldn't stop herself from peering in. The Aunts were hunched over a table. Josie had to crane her neck to see. She held her breath, conscious that they might turn round at any moment.

The sack lay split open and its contents slithered in all directions. At first Josie thought she saw a bright red-and-purple blancmange. But the stench told her something different. Liver, lungs and intestines – all manner of offal slipped out of the sack in a shivering, bloody pile. Josie hardly recognised the Aunts. They were bent over the table, tearing chunks from the heap with their teeth, swallowing and gulping them down. Blood smeared their hands, their clothes, their faces. It dripped from their lips and down their pointed chins. Their black eyes burned fiercely as they gobbled up the stinking mass. They glugged and gargled as each gory gobbet was jerked down their throats.

Josie wanted to scream, to close her eyes and wake up somewhere else. Her stomach lurched as she staggered away from the door, stumbling over the tiger-skin rug, and ran back up the stairs. Her feet thudded on each step, but she didn't care about stealth now. She imagined the Aunts, smeared in blood, clattering after her as she sprinted along the landing towards Alfie's room.

Alfie was sat up in bed, his breakfast on a tray, when Josie burst in on him. Arabella, busy laying out his clothes on the end of the bed, looked up, startled.

'Wass goin' on?' Alfie mumbled through a mouthful of egg.

Josie couldn't speak. She leaned on her knees, gasping for breath. She felt sick and dizzy.

Arabella hurried to her, steadying her. 'Josie, what is it? What's upset you so?'

'The delivery,' she panted, dropping heavily on to a chair. 'Horrible . . .'

'Delivery? What you on about, Josie?' Alfie frowned.

'There's a delivery here almost every other day,' Arabella said, looking grimly at Josie. 'A barge comes up from London, ties up at the quay down by the village and a man brings the sack up. Smells somethin' awful. Never went near it meself – the ladies always deal with it . . .'

'They deal with it all right,' Josie said. In between gasps for breath she told them what she had seen. At the mention of Jacob Carr, Arabella turned and went back to smoothing Alfie's clothes.

'That man's trouble,' she sniffed. 'Comes down from London with his wayward ideas, turnin' country folks' heads. Leadin' them astray . . .'

'At least he's trying to help us,' Josie said, glaring at Arabella's back. 'We're in trouble here. You know your 'ladies' aren't all they seem.'

'None of my business,' Arabella said, shaking Alfie's shirt a little too vigorously. Alfie sat mute, a forkful of egg frozen between plate and mouth.

'Be honest, I bet you've seen all kinds of things that you couldn't explain,' Josie said, stamping over to her.

'I don't 'ave to explain,' Arabella spat. 'I just do me job and keep me head down. I'm just a servant here and I'd like to keep me position if it's all the same to you.' She barged past Josie and hurried out of the room.

'What was all that about?' Alfie said, clattering his fork to the plate.

'She knows things aren't right here – why does she just ignore them? She could be trying to help us, too,' Josie said.

'Well, you've a funny way of gettin' her on our side,' Alfie murmured. 'D'you hear what she said about the barge? It comes from London. That's our ticket out, I reckon.'

'From what Jacob said there'll be another delivery the day after tomorrow.'

'Then we'll need Arabella to get a message to this Mr Carr.' Alfie raised his eyebrows. Guilt flushed Josie's cheeks and neck. Alfie was right: she shouldn't have snapped at Arabella like that. She had nothing to do with the search for the Amarant or Josie's feud with the ghuls; she was just a servant girl trying to keep her living in the crumbling mansion.

'Let's get dressed and go and find her,' Josie said,

shutting out the thought of the ghuls devouring their rancid feast. 'I'll apologise.'

Josie peered out of her bedroom door into the dark corridor. Excitement and curiosity had driven her down to the hall last time. But seeing the Aunts feasting together brought their true nature back into clear focus. Did Corvis have total control over them? Josie doubted it, somehow.

'You ready, then?' Alfie appeared at her side. She jumped back, banging her head on the door frame.

'D'you have to sneak up on me like that?' she snapped. He looked so much better – in such a short time. Lord Corvis was right: he was remarkable. *Maybe I am, too*, she thought, twisting her neck and stretching her arms out. She'd disposed of the head bandage and felt stronger than she had just yesterday.

They wandered in silence through the house. The air hung thick and heavy. Windows needed throwing open, carpets beating, spiders and beetles chasing out of dark corners.

'This place is bloomin' massive,' Alfie muttered, glancing round.

'Yes,' Josie whispered back. 'If we head downstairs, the kitchen and laundry should be there somewhere . . .'

'Let's just hope Arabella is, too.' Alfie hugged his arms round himself. 'This gloomy old dump's givin' me the shivers.'

They crept across the hall, eyeing the Aunts' side room cautiously. Alfie tripped over the tiger-skin rug, cursing, his shoes clattering on the tiles, but nothing stirred in the room.

Carpets replaced the cold stone floors as they edged deeper into the house. Thick tapestries covered the wood panelling.

'Think we missed the servants' quarters,' Josie snorted. But Alfie didn't reply. Josie glanced round just in time to see him vanish through a door. She dashed after him and found herself standing in a room lined with bookshelves. A large desk covered in papers squatted in the centre.

'Must be his lordship's study,' Alfie said, pulling a book down and squinting at the cover. '*Practical Daemonology* by Professor Envry Janus. Sounds lovely.'

A book lay open on the desk. Josie stepped over and flicked through the pages. 'This one's written by hand,' she said, running her finger along the date at the top. She gave a gasp. 'I think it's his journal . . . Look – yesterday's date.'

Alfie craned his neck over her shoulder. '*I admire their spirit,*' he read. '*It is still a mystery to me how they recover so quickly . . . the boy should be dead after the wound inflicted by the ghul . . .*'

Josie flicked back through weeks and months and read aloud: '*All those years of wandering the world, chasing any thrill and excitement, engaging in any vice that would blot out the memory of that hideously beautiful flower . . . I punished myself for wanting to betray my friends and take the flower.*

When I finally succumbed to the temptation to return to Abyssinia, I found the Amarant had gone. It was I who had been betrayed . . .'

'He sounds proper bitter,' Alfie muttered, following the words with his finger.

'Just making excuses for himself,' Josie spat. She continued reading. 'Look, here, four weeks ago: *Sent message to Chrimes at his theatre . . . demanded a meeting . . . rebuffed me . . . told me to stay away from him . . .* See, Uncle was a good man – he wanted nothing to do with Corvis or the Amarant.'

'I know, Josie, I know,' Alfie said, soothing her. 'Hey, d'you think that's why he gave Mortlock's papers to Scrabsnitch – cos he thought Corvis might get hold of 'em?'

'He must have known that Corvis would come looking for him.' Josie lowered the book for a moment. Had Cardamom known that Corvis would be so ruthless? No wonder he had seemed preoccupied in those last few weeks.

'If he'd known about the Aunts,' Alfie whispered, placing a hand on Josie's shoulder, 'he'd have got you to safety, Josie, I'm sure he would.'

Josie gave a smile and stifled her tears. She coughed and focused on flicking further back through the book. 'Listen to this,' she said, her voice faint and horrified. '*Found three specimens yesterday: a magpie, a raven and a jay. Dead but fresh, shot full of pellets and hanging on a wire fence . . . The powers gifted me by the Amarant have brought them to new, if imperfect, life . . .'*

'Is he talkin' about the Aunts?' Alfie said, staring in horror at the page.

The door creaked open, making Josie start and drop the book on to the desk. Alfie gave a startled yell. Aunt Veronica stood at the threshold, her eyes twinkling, the lace-work of her black dress caked brown with dried blood. Josie felt her throat tighten at the sight.

'Lord Corvis found us stiff and cold, swinging bloody in the icy breeze,' she hissed, with an evil grin. She paced towards them. 'He brought us to new life. To what we are now . . .' She leaned over the desk, her face close to Josie's.

'L-Lord Corvis has commanded you not to h-harm us,' Josie stammered. Her knees felt weak and her head throbbed as Aunt Veronica eased closer, glaring at them.

'Don't worry.' Aunt Veronica's voice had fallen to a whisper. 'Our time will come, Josie Chrimes. You can't escape. Our crow brethren are very efficient guards. They count people out and they count people back in. They are everywhere and they would know in an instant if you left.'

Arabella appeared behind her and politely cleared her throat. 'I'd better take them back to their rooms now, miss,' she said, giving a curtsy, her face stony and pale, eyes downcast.

'Take them, then,' Aunt Veronica hissed. 'But remember, Josie, we'll choose our moment well.'

I'LL DO AS MUCH FOR MY TRUE LOVE
AS OTHER MAIDENS MAY;
I'LL DANCE AND SING ON MY LOVE'S GRAVE
A WHOLE TWELVEMONTH AND A DAY.

'THE BROWN GIRL', TRADITIONAL FOLK BALLAD

CHAPTER EIGHTEEN
ARABELLA'S TALE

Josie, Arabella and Alfie walked back through the house in silence. The angry exchanges in the bedroom hung over them. *Just say sorry*, Josie told herself. *Why can't I just say I was wrong?* Alfie obviously had the same thoughts as he kept raising his eyebrows and nodding in Arabella's direction.

Finally, as they entered Josie's room, he coughed and said, 'Josie has somethin' to say to yer, Arabella.'

Josie glared at her brother. What a nerve, speaking for her. But he was right, she knew that much. 'I'm sorry,' she said, looking at the floor. 'I shouldn't have snapped at you earlier. It wasn't fair . . .'

'No, Josie,' Arabella said, blushing and giving a smile. 'It's me as owes you an apology.'

'How much did you hear just now in Lord Corvis's study, Arabella?' Alfie asked, his voice soft.

'Enough to know the ladies don't mean you no good,'

she said. Her voice dropped to an angry whisper. 'But I suppose I knew that the minute you arrived. They talk over me as if I'm brainless or deaf. I know things ain't right here – known it since his lordship come back . . . What could I do, though? Hearing your story, Josie, well, it kind of woke me up . . .' She closed her eyes, took a deep breath, suddenly gabbling, 'Which is why I've resolved to go an' talk to Jacob about takin' a couple of stowaways back to London day after tomorrow.'

'You . . . what?' Josie leapt up, hugging Arabella. 'Oh, how can we ever thank you?'

'S'all right, just get away safely.' Arabella smiled, then frowned at Alfie, who stood morose and deep in thought.

'That's all very well,' he murmured. 'But how are we gonna get out of the house?'

'What's to stop yer from just walkin' out when the ladies are . . . y'know, with their delivery?' Arabella shuddered.

'The birds,' Alfie said. 'You heard what the old crow said: they count people in and out.'

'D'you think that's true?' Arabella said, pulling a dubious face. 'I mean, they're only old crows.'

'We've seen 'em in action,' Alfie said.

Josie thought of the cloud of chaos outside Scrabsnitch's shop. 'Alfie's right,' she said. 'It's hard to believe, Arabella, but they serve his lordship and the ladies. I'm sure they can be deceived, though . . .'

'What if Arabella were to meet Mr Carr at the gate, walk up the path with 'im and then keep 'im occupied inside somehow?' Alfie thought aloud.

'While we slipped out,' Josie finished.

'Easy.' Alfie grinned. 'Two people in, two people out.'

'Then you could get to the barge and you'd be off to London – they don't hang around here long at all, believe me,' Arabella added.

'But Jacob would be stuck in the house,' Josie said, her shoulders sinking. 'And the barge can't leave without him . . .'

They sank into silence. Josie chewed her nails. Her head felt as if it would burst at any minute. Jacob would have to come with them, that would make three. *How can we get three out and only two in?* she thought. Alfie paced the room.

'The only way,' Arabella said at last, 'is if the delivery man stays in the house. I might be able to get one of the boys from the village to bring the delivery up instead of Jacob – the ladies don't care who brings the package.'

'You're takin' a big risk 'ere,' Alfie said. 'You sure you'll be all right?'

'Don't think his lordship'll suspect nothin' if I just play dumb,' Arabella said, trying to sound casual but twisting her fingers together. 'He might punish me for bein' stupid and lettin' you get out, but what choice do we 'ave?'

Despite having a plan, the room seemed even more claustrophobic and gloomy when Arabella left them to do her work.

'Lord Corvis might get suspicious if I spend too much time up here,' she said, winking as she left the room. 'I'll go an' check if one of the village boys is available for delivery service . . .'

There's so much that could go wrong, Josie thought, watching the door close. She stared at the diluted colours of the marsh and listened to the mournful cackling of their crow guards. Were the crows clever enough to tell people apart? What would happen to Arabella if Corvis suspected that she had helped them? Josie shook her head.

'Maybe we should try to think of a plan that doesn't involve Arabella,' she said, running a finger down the windowpane. She turned and stared at Alfie. 'What *are* you doing?'

Alfie had his palms outstretched around a small swarm of flies. They buzzed and wove in and out of each other. He coughed and lowered his hands. The flies fell to the floor, dead and desiccated.

'Oh, Alfie, that's disgusting!' Josie gazed at him. She remembered the toad boy she'd met in the shop. A lot had happened since then. Alfie blushed and looked at his feet.

'Well, I thought I might as well keep tryin'. They're only small but I'm learnin' to concentrate and it's gettin' easier. I can control 'em. Maybe it'll come in handy some time.'

'Yes, if we need an army of dead flies,' Josie muttered, giving him a withering stare. A flurry of panic rose up in her stomach and she threw herself on the bed. 'What if it all goes wrong, Alfie? And we've still got to find the Amarant. We'll never do it.'

'We've got to 'ave a go,' Alfie said softly. 'Corvis is gonna start askin' questions soon. He wants that Amarant an' he thinks we know where it is. We've gotta get away and find it before he does.'

All afternoon, Josie struggled to come up with a different escape plan, fretting about the details of the one they had. Could they rely on the boy Arabella would find? How long would the Aunts spend on their feast? Josie cursed herself for not being more level-headed this morning. She could have timed them.

'I keep thinkin' about that note, the one your uncle gave you,' Alfie said, interrupting her thoughts. 'It didn't sound right. More like a riddle or somethin' . . .'

'How d'you mean?' Josie chewed the ends of her hair. What was he thinking about that for now? They needed to escape before anything else.

'Well, that "think of my last words . . . don't heed the goodbye" business. It sounds like a puzzle.'

'Can't you just concentrate on one thing at a time, such as how to get out of here?' Josie snapped. Her nerves were frayed.

'Suit yerself,' Alfie grunted and took himself off into a corner to reanimate his fly swarm. Daylight succumbed to darkness and, once more, the weird glimmer of light appeared across the marshes.

'That light again,' Josie said, pressing her forehead against the cold glass.

'Wonder what it is,' Alfie murmured, leaning over her shoulder.

There was a knock at the door and Arabella stepped inside, bringing more soup. She seemed excited and nervous.

'Right, I nipped down to the village and saw Sammy Nichols. He said he didn't mind bringin' the delivery – very keen to show me how brave he was.' She grinned, blushing. 'I left a letter for him to give to Jacob Carr, too, explainin' that Sammy would be comin' to pick up the delivery instead this time . . . and that Jacob is to expect two passengers for his journey back to London.'

'Thank you, Arabella, I know you're taking a risk.' Josie hugged her. 'I just wish there was another way . . .'

'Oh, don't you worry about me,' Arabella said. Josie detected that same brittle cheerfulness she had heard when she first met her. 'I can look after meself.'

'Arabella,' Alfie said, leaning closer. 'I was lookin' at that light out there on the marshes. Do you know what it is?'

'No.' Arabella pursed her lips, then sighed. 'Well, I know what they say it is but . . .' She shook her head and looked away from the window.

'Why, what is it?' Josie said, her eyes wide.

'It's a horrible story,' the servant girl said. 'It don't do no good to talk of such things.'

'Go on,' said Alfie, sitting on the bed and looking out through the window.

Arabella chewed her knuckles, staring out of the window herself. 'We've enough to think of, what with the ladies an' all.'

'Please,' Josie said. 'There's something about the light that draws you in.'

'I know, that's what's bad about it. That light shines way out there on the marshes towards the estuary,' Arabella said. 'Has done every night as long as I can remember.'

'Tell us, Arabella, please.' Alfie pulled at her sleeve.

'They say every year a travellin' circus used to come to the Corvis estate to over-winter and repair equipment, like. A powerful magician performed with them. Some say he'd got his powers from the Devil himself. He was in love with the most beautiful gypsy woman you ever saw. One winter he had to travel – to meet with Satan, they say – and when he came back, the gypsy woman had died . . .'

Josie stared out at the light. It seemed to glow stronger as the story unfolded.

'The circus had burned her body and her caravan with her. The magician was furious. He reckoned he could've stolen her back from Death 'imself. In a blind rage, he cursed the whole circus to a livin' death, there and then. It's said that they perform out there on the marshes every night, hoping to draw an audience. Anyone who goes there never comes back.'

'Do you know anyone who's tried to go?' Josie said in a hushed voice.

'Over the years there's been a few boys from villages nearby who've wandered into that part of the marsh and never returned.' Arabella stared, frightened by her own

story. 'A few travellers have been lured from safe paths by
the light, their belongings found floatin' in one of the
gullies the next morning. Never a body.'

'They drown in the marsh?' Josie said, biting her lip.

'You're near the sea out there towards the estuary. Tide
doesn't come rollin' across the marsh; it bubbles up
through the gullies and pits, through the marsh grass,
too. You can easily get caught if you're in the wrong
place at the wrong time. But nobody knows exactly why
they never find a corpse,' the frightened servant girl went
on. 'There's a saying round here for them what go
missing. They say they've "gone to see the circus of the
dead".'

Alone in her room again, another long night stretched
ahead of Josie. Strange notions tumbled around her head
and she climbed out of bed to gaze at the faint glow in
the dark. There was definitely something oddly mes-
merising about the light. Like Alfie had said, it was
almost as if it were calling to her. Surely it couldn't be
anything dangerous. It looked warm and inviting – a safe
haven. Somewhere to run to.

A stealthy footfall made a floorboard creak outside on
the landing. Something scratched and clawed at her
door. The Aunts were becoming impatient. Lord Corvis
wouldn't wait for ever.

Josie climbed back into bed and buried herself under
the blankets, trying to blot out the sigh of the wind, the

creak of the house and the disturbing scratching at her bedroom door. Huddled under the covers, she fell into another haunted night of broken sleep.

WHO'LL DIG HIS GRAVE?
'I,' SAYS THE OWL, 'WITH MY SPADE AND SHOVEL.'

WHO'LL BE THE PARSON?
'I,' SAYS THE ROOK, 'WITH MY LITTLE BOOK.'

WHO'LL CARRY HIM TO THE GRAVE?
'I,' SAYS THE KITE, 'IF IT'S NOT AT NIGHT.'

'WHO KILLED COCK ROBIN?', TRADITIONAL NURSERY RHYME

CHAPTER NINETEEN
THE CELLAR

Morning finally arrived, bringing bad news with it. Alfie arrived at Josie's bedroom door with his breakfast tray. Arabella hurried close behind him.

'Thought I'd eat with you if it's all the same.' He grinned, settling into the armchair by the fire and stabbing a fork into his egg. There was something wrong, Josie could tell even if Alfie was oblivious to it. Arabella stood silently wringing her apron in her fists.

'What is it, Arabella?' Josie asked, sitting her on the end of the bed.

Alfie clattered his fork to the plate. 'Is somethin' wrong?'

Josie shook her head. 'Can't you tell? Look at her – she's shaking!'

'It's his lordship,' Arabella said, twisting her apron even tighter. 'He's told me to take yer to the cellar . . .'

'What for?' Josie's stomach turned. 'You don't think

he's found out about Jacob somehow?'

'I don't think so,' Arabella said, shaking her head. 'But that cellar . . . Well, I've never been in, but the noises that come from there sometimes – screamin' and such – makes me blood run cold.'

'Blimey, what are we gonna do?' Alfie moaned.

'Not much we can do.' Josie shrugged but her voice quavered. 'We can't escape yet. We just have to go along with it and hope he's not going to lock us down there.'

'Well, finish yer breakfasts first,' Arabella said, but Josie pushed her plate away and shook her head.

'I think we've finished,' she said, looking at Alfie, who had gone a sickly pale shade.

Arabella led them through the dusty, shadowy house once more. Josie stayed silent. She felt trapped. What was Corvis going to do? He wanted to know the whereabouts of the Amarant. How far would he go to get that information? She shuddered.

They came into the entrance hall and Arabella took them to a small door beneath the stairs. 'He said to go in there an' wait for him,' she said, her voice faint.

Josie pushed the door open. The groan of the hinges echoed into the dark emptiness beyond.

'Doesn't sound very cosy,' Alfie muttered behind her.

'Be careful,' Arabella said, as Josie led Alfie through the door and to the top of a flight of narrow stone stairs that ran far down into the shadows.

They wandered down the steps. The sound of their footfalls echoing in the dark void made Josie feel small and insignificant. Looking down made her dizzy; four lamps burned distantly at floor level below.

'This room must be almost as big as the house itself,' she whispered.

'Bigger, I'd say,' Alfie replied, peering over the edge of the steps. 'I can see benches and tables down there. Looks like some kind of workshop.'

'Or a torture chamber.' Josie shivered.

Strange objects cluttered the edges of the room, including cages of all sizes, some big enough to imprison a man. Chains and manacles lay on top of barrels and boxes. The piles of junk stretched off into the shadows that masked the cellar walls. Three benches formed a 'U' in the centre of the room. One had scalpels, knives and bottles of chemicals on it, and another lay bare.

'Look at these.' Alfie leaned over the third bench and poked at a line of small black feathery bundles that lay in a row there. Josie joined him. The smell of decay made her wrinkle her nose in disgust.

'Dead birds,' she said, pulling back. 'Why would Corvis have all these dead birds down here?'

'Dead crows. D'you remember his journal?' Alfie said, staring at the table. 'He's been experimentin' on them. He wanted to make an army of ghuls, just like the Aunts.'

'But what for?'

'Dunno.' Alfie shrugged. 'But he reckoned he needed the Amarant to do it . . .'

'And now you can tell me where it is.' Corvis stood

at the top of the stairs, gazing down on them. Behind him, Josie could see the black outlines of the Aunts. He started down the steps. 'I understand you've been exploring the house. I assume that must mean you have recovered.'

Josie and Alfie remained mute, watching as Corvis and the Aunts descended towards them.

'I only wish we'd caught them trying to escape,' Aunt Mag croaked as she followed Lord Corvis over to the children. Aunt Veronica and Aunt Jay gave a grating snigger behind her.

'Now then, Mag,' Corvis said, lifting one of the rotten bundles from the bench. 'Alfie and Josie might help us yet. Let's not be unkind.'

Corvis slammed the dead crow on to the centre of the bare table and gave Alfie a grim smile. 'I'll show you something.' He took a long, vicious-looking knife from the bench behind him and opened his palm. 'I did this once to swear an oath – with your precious guardian and Sebastian Mortlock.' He drew the edge across his hand, tracing a red furrow, then closed his hand into a fist. 'Now watch . . .'

He held his fist over the bird on the bench and squeezed. A tear of blood dripped down on to the bird. Josie stepped back, eyes watering at the foul-smelling vapour that bubbled up from the carcass. The three Aunts huddled together behind Corvis, grinning and twitching at the scene.

'You see, I have been in the presence of the Amarant,'

Corvis drawled, squeezing another droplet of blood on to the carcass. 'My father suppressed the crows of Rookery Heights. My gift from the Amarant was to be able to bring them to a new and enhanced existence.' He pulled a silken handkerchief from his pocket and wrapped it around his hand. 'My blood flows in their veins. That power came from just a brief encounter with the Amarant.' The dead crow began to writhe and flap on the bench, its eyes glowing red. 'They're quite weak to begin with, for the first few hours. Easily despatched . . .'

'Why're you doin' this?' Alfie said, staring at the crow as it twisted about on the table. Josie stood up and backed away. It was growing, changing. Josie gave a squeal of disgust.

'A demonstration,' Corvis said, smiling still. He placed the knife on the bench in front of Josie. 'I know where my gifts came from and what they are. What are yours? I wonder. Mag, the boy – should he be alive now?'

'He should be crow's meat,' Aunt Mag spat, fixing her eyes on Alfie.

The crow on the bench was the size of a small dog now, but Josie recognised the familiar long beak, the vicious talons growing before her eyes. It screeched in agony as bones cracked and reformed, joints popped and realigned. Bare flesh bubbled from under old feathers, bursting with fresh quills and glossy black plumage as it swelled like some hideous balloon.

'Remarkable healing powers, the pair of you,' Corvis said, ignoring the monstrous changes right under his nose. 'That wound on your head, Josie, would have laid a normal person low for weeks, possibly killed them, and yet you've recovered in a couple of days. How do you explain that?'

Josie said nothing. She looked distractedly from Alfie to the quickly developing monster on the bench. Finally it stopped flapping and perched, glaring down on Josie with glowing eyes. It ruffled its spiky feathers and scraped its claws along the wood of the table. The Aunts clapped their hands and grinned at each other.

'Magnificent, isn't it? Hungry, too,' Corvis said. His voice sounded slightly weaker. Black shadows ringed his eyes. Josie thought he looked so much like the Aunts: eyes cold and glittering, nose pointed and long. He paused and clicked his fingers as if he had forgotten someone's name and was trying to recall it. 'So where did you say the Amarant was, Josie?'

'I didn't,' Josie said.

The crow on the table gave a hiss, snapping its beak at her. She pulled her head back and stumbled away. Alfie stood frozen in horror at the sight of the newly born ghul.

'Don't underestimate me, girl,' Corvis said, his face twisted into a snarl. 'I only need one of you to tell me where the Amarant is . . . The other is expendable. Now, my beauty.' The hatchling ghul swivelled its head round to stare at him. Corvis grinned at Josie. 'Kill the boy.'

THE GRAVE'S THE MARKETPLACE WHERE ALL MUST MEET,
BOTH RICH AND POOR, BOTH SMALL AND GREAT,
IF LIFE WERE MERCHANDISE THAT GOLD COULD BUY,
THE RICH WOULD LIVE – ONLY THE POOR WOULD DIE.

'DEATH AND THE LADY', TRADITIONAL FOLK BALLAD

CHAPTER TWENTY
THE FLEDGLING GHUL

The ghul reared up on the bench, sending Alfie stumbling on to his back as it flapped its massive wings. It cocked its head and craned its neck, peering first at Josie and then at Alfie. Lord Corvis closed his eyes, rubbed his temples and shook his head.

'THE BOY,' he snapped, raising his voice as though the ghul were hard of hearing. He glanced over at Josie. 'They're newly made, not too bright yet – vulnerable, as I said.' His tone was casual, as if he were discussing the weather. He turned his attention back to the crow, pointing at Alfie and clicking his fingers impatiently. 'The boy! That one! Him!'

The creature swivelled its head round, gave a low croak of menacing realisation and glared at Alfie. Aunt Jay clapped her clenched fists together and jumped up and down. The fledgling gave a low croak as Alfie lay on his back. He scrabbled away from it.

'Josie, what'll I do?' he said, his voice quavering.

'Stop it,' Josie hissed at Corvis. She glanced down at the knife on the bench, instantly weighing up its sharp point and solid bone handle.

Corvis caught her eye. 'You can save him. Show me what you can do.' He grinned, looking more ghul than human. 'Or you could sacrifice Alfie and kill me . . .'

'Josie . . .' Alfie called as his head bumped against the back wall of the cellar. The ghul hopped closer, its cackling mingling with shrieks of laughter from the Aunts.

Leaping forward, Josie snatched the knife from the bench. It felt heavy, the bone handle cold on her palm as she aimed it at the creature.

The ghul hissed, taking a few more hesitant stalking steps towards Alfie, lowering its head and stretching its neck out as it prepared to bound forward. Josie could see the sinews in its legs stretch and flex, the glossy feathers rippling. Alfie's pleading eyes stared at her over the ghul's hunched body. The bird's back faced Josie, making it a tough shot. But there was no more time to breathe or balance, no more time to take stock.

'Josie, it's gonna –' Alfie squeaked. A hoarse croak drowned him out as the ghul leapt into the air.

Josie flicked her hand, hurling the knife. It twisted and spiralled towards the ghul. She watched the light play on the vicious blade as it cut through the air. It whistled past the ghul's head. Alfie gave a yell of horror but then, with a satisfying metallic *ping*, the knife bounced off the wall of the cellar and struck the ghul right between the eyes.

Blood spattered the dusty floor as the ghul's feet swung up and it fell flat on its back. It lay thrashing and flapping in agony as its life blood pooled and congealed around it.

Only the sounds of the knife quivering in the ghul's skull and Alfie's ragged breathing broke the silence that followed. Alfie lay staring at the twitching, feathery heap. The Aunts clung to each other, glowering in dismay at Josie. Then Corvis's slow handclap echoed around the cellar.

'Bravo,' he said. 'I'd heard you could throw but that was simply amazing . . . almost unbelievable, in fact.'

'I wish I had a second knife,' Josie spat, glowering at Corvis. Anger boiled inside her. What he'd done was evil. He would have quite happily watched Alfie die merely to put her to the test.

'Your talent intrigues me, that and your miraculous healing ability.' Corvis pulled the bloody handkerchief from his hand and held up a clean palm. No sign of the cut remained. 'You have the power of the Amarant flowing through your veins, children. You've been near it. Now tell me where it is.'

'Why should I?' Josie sidled around the twitching body to where Alfie struggled to his feet.

Corvis stared into the distance, as if reliving a dream. 'It is mine . . . taken from me . . .' He paced the length of the bench. 'And if you won't help me . . .' he said, and his face darkened. Again, Josie thought she saw something of the Aunts in his sharp features. 'Then I will leave you to the tender mercies of my ladies.'

The Aunts inched forward, bobbing and chuckling. Corvis stopped beside them, smoothing his hair down with a hand and frowning as something downy appeared between his fingertips. Josie felt a jolt of shock run through her. *Feathers?* He hastily shook his hand, sending the fluff drifting to the ground, where Aunt Mag snatched and wafted the small feathers away.

'Give me the Amarant and I'll keep them away from you for ever,' he said.

Josie thought of Cardamom wasting away, Gimlet struggling in the street, Ernie at the Erato. She frowned and glanced over at Alfie, who looked three shades paler again.

'Mr Scrabsnitch said that the Amarant could only do evil in the hands of men,' Josie said, trying to conceal the tremor in her voice. 'What would you do with it?'

'What would I do?' Corvis gave a laugh, as if he couldn't believe that a child was questioning him. 'I'd bring order to the world.'

'You'd just kill people, like your "ladies" have,' Alfie said, leaning heavily against the cellar wall, exhausted by his brush with the ghul.

'But what is death, boy?' Corvis shook his head. 'With the Amarant, we can make all that right.' He turned to Josie. 'Death has no meaning when you have total control over it. We can bring them back.'

'Bring who back?' She eyed Corvis and her frown deepened.

'The world is a chaotic and unhappy place,' Corvis

said, stepping over the dead ghul and coming close to Josie. His tone had become intimate. 'With the Amarant, *we* can choose whether to live for ever or die. *We* can bring our lost loved ones back to life . . .'

For a moment, Josie forgot her hatred of this man. Could he bring Cardamom back? And what about Gimlet? She imagined them beside her once more, laughing, sharing a joke and teasing her. She thought about the mother she'd never really known, and imagined having a real family. *Maybe Corvis would help me*, she thought, hesitating. He had once been Cardamom's friend, after all. Mortlock had taken the Amarant, not her uncle – she was sure of it.

'But we can't all live for ever,' Alfie piped up again, breaking into Josie's daydream. 'There'd be no room. Mr Wiggins says that death is nature's way of keepin' the population from gettin' too big.'

'Ah, a devotee of the Reverend Malthus and his so-called "population control" notions, I take it? Anyway, young man, we wouldn't let *everyone* live for ever.' A feverish light glowed in Corvis's dark eyes. 'Only the few. Only the few would live at all. Consider your home city, children, full of misery and crime, people choking the streets. The lower orders go on breeding and multiplying, draining our resources, causing disease and poisonous miasmas to spread, infecting even the richer, more enter-prising elements of society. Now imagine a world where we, the few, lived and all others existed to serve us, not eating, drinking or sleeping even . . . and not increasing their numbers with wearisome regularity.'

'How can you stop people eating?' Josie shuffled closer to Alfie, away from Corvis. He trembled as he stared out into his imaginary future. 'People have to drink and sleep,' she reminded him.

'Not if they are dead.' Corvis grinned into Josie's face, making her lean even further back. He grabbed her wrist, his palm hot and sweaty. Aunt Mag clutched her hands to her heart, listening in rapture. 'The living dead, animated by the Amarant, slaves with no will but mine! They could run our factories, fight in our armies, serve in our houses with no concern for themselves, no physical needs of their own. And a small ruling elite would steer this nation to further greatness.'

'And when we have the precious plant, my lord,' Aunt Jay said, bobbing with excitement, 'we'll be able to take our rightful place at your side.'

'They're incomplete, you see,' Corvis drawled. It was as if he were talking about the poor gait of a racehorse he'd bought. 'Still prone to animal urges. No soul, either. Took a lot of blood and effort to get them to this stage. Even now they're more crow than human, despite their appearance and intellect. They need me to keep them from returning to their previous state.'

'But Lord Corvis will make us whole.' Aunt Mag grinned, her eyes wild. 'He has promised.'

'It's hideous – all those people dead.' Josie stared at Corvis, who pursed his lips and regarded his fingernails. Josie couldn't help noticing that they seemed long and pointed – more like claws than a gentleman's nails. 'I'd never tell you where the Amarant is.'

Corvis heaved an impatient sigh. 'It's important that you understand, Josie: you're signing your brother's death warrant if you refuse.' Josie stared at Alfie's pallid face. Corvis went on, 'Believe me, I will find the Amarant sooner or later. You can make it sooner and save a lot of suffering and anguish along the way. My patience isn't limitless . . . nor that of my ladies. I'm tired of waiting.' The Aunts narrowed their eyes and leered at Josie and Alfie. 'Jay, Veronica, take them to their rooms and lock them in. You have until noon tomorrow to think about it – separately – then whoever tells me will live.' Corvis's eyes burned into Josie's 'The other will die.'

NONE OF MY GOLD NOW SHALL YOU HAVE,
NOR LIKEWISE OF MY FEE;
FOR I HAVE COME TO SEE YOU HANGED,
AND HANGED YOU SHALL BE.

'MAID FREED FROM THE GALLOWS',
TRADITIONAL FOLK BALLAD

CHAPTER TWENTY ONE
THE TIGER-SKIN RUG

Kicking and howling insults, Josie threw herself at the bedroom door. The Aunts had dragged her none too gently up the stairs and pushed her into her room. She had lunged forward in panic, catching a last glimpse of Alfie before the door slammed shut. The sound of the iron bolt outside sliding home stopped her assault on the door. What was the point? She gave the solid oak a final kick.

Josie felt utterly alone. She hurled herself on to the bed. What would they tell Corvis?

Would Alfie?

Josie sat up. No, he'd never do that. He was her brother.

The afternoon inched by. Josie paced the room, trying to keep track of time. *What about this Sammy Nichols? Can we trust him?* She watched the multitudes of crows flocking together on the rooftops, nudging and shuffling along the eaves of the house. *What if Jacob changes his mind?* The room seemed to close in on Josie as the evening shadows thickened. She sat in the armchair, letting the meagre fire illuminate the room. Through the window she could see the steady glow of the light on the marsh. Where was Arabella? *What if she's changed her mind?* Josie thought.

The night darkened and the fire died. Josie dozed in the chair, jumping awake at the slightest scrape at the window or creak of the floorboards. She ran through the plan again and again. They were so dependent on others. Jacob Carr might not turn up. *Maybe the tides will change and make him late.* Josie shivered and pulled a blanket from the bed, wrapping it around her shoulders. *How long until morning?* Josie could only guess as she stared out. The windows were solid black mirrors reflecting her worried, pale face.

The cold of dawn finally seeped into her bones, waking her with a sudden start. Where was Alfie? Was he all right? Josie felt so helpless.

'I can't sit here doing nothing,' she muttered to herself and glanced round the room. She picked up a chair, swung it high over her head and brought it crashing to the floor. The crack of splintering wood sounded deafening in the quiet of the morning. *I'm not going quietly*, she thought, holding the shattered chair leg and feeling the sharp, jagged point where it had snapped off. *If I have to fight them, then I will.*

As morning crept on, Josie sized up the room for possible places to spring from and take the Aunts by surprise. She frowned. It wouldn't be easy; the room was hardly huge, nor was it cluttered with furniture.

The sound of the bolt being drawn back cut Josie's thoughts dead. She tiptoed behind the door. The handle rattled as it twisted. Josie gripped the chair leg. The hinges groaned. She pressed herself against the wall behind the door and raised the chair leg like a short spear as it swung back towards her. Seeing a dark shape through the crack, she lunged forward.

'Josie, no!' Alfie shrieked, throwing himself away from her. 'It's me and Arabella!'

Josie checked her blow just in time, but her momentum took her crashing into Alfie, tumbling him to the ground.

'What the hell d'you think you're doin'?' Arabella snapped, rushing over to Alfie and helping him to his feet. Josie sat on the floor, staring up at her.

'Sorry,' she panted. 'I thought you were one of the ladies . . .'

'Do I look like one of them old crows?' Alfie said, grinning and rubbing his head. 'And sort yerself out there – yer showin' next week's laundry! Cor, y'nearly brained me.'

Josie gave a gasp and jumped to her feet, straightening her skirts and petticoat. 'I've been so worried.'

'Not the only one,' Arabella said, brushing back her hair with a shaking hand. 'Lord Corvis wouldn't let me up here for the rest of the day. I wasn't sure if you were still alive even.'

'We nearly weren't,' Josie said. 'It was awful, Arabella. We were stuck in that horrible cellar with Lord Corvis.'

'He said he's going to kill one of us at noon,' Alfie said, wide-eyed.

Arabella put a hand to her mouth.

'So this Sammy, he can still do the delivery?' Josie said, grabbing her arm. 'He hasn't backed out? And Jacob Carr *will* be there?'

'Don't worry,' Arabella said, patting Josie's shoulder with a shaky hand. 'He'll be there. As soon as the ladies are occupied, I'll distract him and you sneak out. I'll leave the door unbolted now. It should all work. Just remember, Jacob can only stay a short time. Hurry straight to the quay or you'll miss him.'

'We'll keep an eye out for Sammy and make sure we're ready,' Alfie assured her. Arabella gave them a brave smile and left.

Josie bit her lip and poked the cold embers of the fire with the chair leg. 'I couldn't sleep for thinking last night, Alfie.'

'You an' me both,' Alfie said. 'But that Corvis has another thing comin' if 'e thinks 'e can split us up.'

Josie stabbed the fire again. 'I thought Arabella had abandoned us,' she said, dropping the chair leg into the hearth. 'I thought it'd all go wrong and we'd miss Sammy . . .'

'We won't miss him, Josie,' Alfie said and then

squinted through the window. 'In fact, 'ere he is now!'

A red-haired boy wrestled the barrow up the rough track. It was a struggle, his back bent against the weight, his feet slipping on the broken surface of the path.

'He's having trouble,' Josie said through clenched teeth. 'What if he drops it?'

The odd crow swooped at him as Josie had seen them do before and, as he drew closer, she could see fear on the boy's face. Arabella appeared on the steps below and ran out to meet him.

'Good girl, Bella. Them crows'll be countin' now, two in . . .' Alfie murmured, then turned suddenly to Josie. 'Come on. Let's get on the stairs, so we can be ready.'

They slipped into the shadowy corridor and crept to the top of the stairs. Josie poked her nose above the banister rail. She could hear the Aunts flapping and fussing with excitement. They surrounded Sammy, poking him and stroking his hair. The smell from his putrid burden filled the hall. Alfie covered his mouth and nose with his hand.

'A new boy,' Aunt Mag said, her eyes shining. 'Can you manage that load, young man?'

'You're rather late, child – been dawdling? We're hungry, you know!' added Aunt Jay.

'No Mr Carr?' Aunt Veronica croaked, stroking Sammy's arm.

Sammy stood mute and pale. Clearly the Aunts terrified him, the sack on his back wobbling as he trembled.

'Just bring it in here, boy – it's ours to deal with then.'
Aunt Jay gave him a sly wink and licked her cracked lips
with her black tongue. Arabella stood by the door to the
servants' quarters, trying to catch Sammy's eye.

'Well, go on then, boy,' Aunt Veronica cackled, slap-
ping her withered hand into Sammy's shoulders and
sending him stumbling across the hall. She turned to
Arabella. 'You can get about your duties, girl. Go on,
hurry!' Arabella pursed her lips, turned on her heel and
vanished down the corridor. Josie stared at Alfie in dismay. What would happen now?

The Aunts bundled Sammy into the side room. Josie
held her breath.

'Come on, let's make a break for it now,' Alfie hissed.

'No,' Josie replied, grabbing his sleeve. 'The Aunts
aren't settled yet. Besides, we need Arabella to detain
Sammy, to give us time to get away, remember?'

'Come on, Bella, where are yer?' Alfie whispered. They
watched the door to the servants' quarters. Nothing. The
hall lay still, only the muffled cackling of the Aunts
broke the silence.

'Where's she gone?' Josie hissed.

Sammy's voice drifted into the hall, followed by a sickening, squelching noise. 'What the . . . Oh my lord,' he
said. A high-pitched scream quickly followed. Sammy
Nichols came staggering from the side room, blood
smeared on his cheek. Raucous, crowing laughter followed him, cut short by the door slamming shut. He
paused for a second, glancing around for Arabella, then

fled through the front, not even stopping to pick up the barrow.

'Brilliant,' Alfie sighed. 'Now what do we do?'

'I don't know,' Josie muttered, creeping down the stairs and into the hall. She stared out after the disappearing figure of Sammy. She felt sick. It had all gone wrong but they had to get out *now*.

Arabella suddenly appeared from the servants' quarters. She looked pale and horrified.

'Arabella,' Josie whispered urgently, 'the plan's gone wrong. Sammy, he ran away . . .'

But Josie's words died in her throat. Arabella's face was chalk white as she shook her head. Lord Corvis stepped into view, grasping her wrist.

'What's gone wrong, young lady?' he sneered. 'Why aren't you safely locked up in your room? I wonder. Arabella? Any ideas?' The girl shook her head, her whole body trembling. Corvis raised his free hand to his mouth in a pantomime gesture of shock. 'Surely not! It couldn't be. You weren't helping them to *escape*, were you, Arabella?'

Lord Corvis grinned, savouring the children's fear. He jagged Arabella's wrist, making her cry out and stumble into him.

'I don't know what to think.' Corvis shook his head. 'My own staff turning against me.'

'It wasn't her, we tricked her . . .' Josie protested. 'It's not her fault.'

'Tricked her into unbolting your door from the

outside?' Corvis said. 'Hardly.'

'Please, your lordship . . .' Alfie began, taking a step forward. Corvis backed away, nearly tripping over the tiger-skin rug that covered the polished floor tiles. He roughly twisted Arabella's arm behind her back, making her cry out again.

'I can see that I've wasted my time. The ladies are feasting now, but . . . What are you doing?'

Corvis glared at Alfie. As Josie watched, her brother's eyes rolled back in his head and he held his shaking hands aloft. She frowned as the skin of the rug behind Corvis began to ripple and squirm.

'What's happening?' Arabella whimpered, but Josie could only stare as the head of the tiger-skin rug reared up behind Corvis and sank its inch-long fangs into his calf. He screamed in agony and threw Arabella away from him as he reached down to beat at the tiger's head.

Alfie opened his eyes and grinned weakly at Josie. 'Bit better than an army of flies,' he panted. The tiger had gone back to being nothing more than a rug, but its jaws were still locked on Corvis's lower leg. He screamed in agony and writhed on the floor. Blood smeared the tiles as he tried to prise the mouth open.

'Get it off me! Mag! Jay! Where are you?' he screamed, but the Aunts didn't respond. Josie remembered something Corvis had said about them being prone to animal urges. Perhaps they were too engrossed in the disgusting feast.

'Come on, quick!' Josie said, pulling Arabella to her feet. Almost tripping over Alfie, she turned and ran towards the open front door. But Josie paused just before they stepped outside. She grabbed Alfie's shoulder. 'Here,' she said, pulling black bonnets and cloaks from the pegs by the door. 'Put these on.'

'Yer what?' Alfie screwed his face up at the bonnets.

Josie glanced back. Corvis tried to stand but his leg gave way beneath him. It would have been comical if she wasn't so scared.

'Just do it,' she told Alfie. 'From above we may look like the Aunts going on an afternoon stroll. It may be enough to fool the crows.' The bonnets smelt rank and Josie could see lice eggs and strands of coarse black hair caught in the fabric. 'Hurry, we can't waste any time. The Aunts will realise something's wrong soon.'

'That's if they 'aven't already!' Alfie said, pulling the cloak on with a shudder.

Josie grimaced, too, trying not to think of the Aunts gorging themselves on offal. She helped Arabella tie her bonnet. The girl looked dazed. She was massaging her arm and weeping.

Josie stepped outside and hurried down the path, half running, half walking. She had to prop Arabella up as Alfie stumbled behind, the three of them trying desperately not to look too suspicious. They could hear Corvis yelling in the hall. The cloak felt heavy and the bonnet scratched Josie's head. Every scrunch of their feet on the gravel shouted out their escape. Josie could hear her breath, ragged and panting in time with Arabella's and Alfie's.

A huge, bearded black raven swooped in front of them and bounced on the scrubby lawn. It cocked its head and eyed them. They kept walking. She could hear the bird's powerful wings launch it into the air. Another crow cawed, rattling Josie's nerves. She could feel Arabella shiver with every sound as scores of black birds around them shifted and croaked uncertainly. They seemed confused but at least they stayed up on their perches on the roof and sills of Rookery Heights.

On they marched, past the wall, along the road. Josie could see the rust-red sail of Jacob's barge poking above the scrubby bushes, hazy in the distance across the marsh.

'Nearly there, look,' Josie whispered, rubbing Arabella's shoulders. 'We'll be safe once we get on the barge.'

'I'll be glad to get this stupid bonnet off,' Alfie hissed.

Arabella let out a small groan and pointed at the sail. It was moving! 'Sammy must've taken longer than we thought bringin' the sack,' she said. 'Mr Carr said he could only wait for twenty minutes or so. He's leaving.'

She broke away from Josie and began to run down the lane, stumbling on the rutted ground.

'C'mon, Josie, we can't 'ang about!' Alfie yelled, throwing the cloak and bonnet to the ground and charging after Arabella. Josie didn't move. She watched the sail glide away from them. A broad expanse of marsh – tussocks of grass interspersed with reed-filled gulleys – stood between them and the channel the boat sailed along. The most direct route to it was across the mire.

'We'll never catch it on the road,' she called after them. 'Cut across here.'

Arabella ran on, out of earshot, but Alfie skidded to a halt, looking back and forth, trying to decide whether to follow her or to join Josie.

'But the marsh is dangerous,' Alfie said, then stopped, his mouth hanging open as he stared back at the house. Rookery Heights had erupted in a cloud of black. Hundreds of crows and rooks swirled and darted in and out of each other.

'It's going to become even more dangerous here,' Josie gasped, watching the cackling thundercloud. 'We've got to get on that barge.'

She turned for the marshes and ran. She could hear Alfie following. He came alongside her and she threw off the bonnet and cloak, leaving them to lie in the long, coarse grass. Behind them, the boiling, seething swarm of birds circled and swooped, getting bigger by the second as the red sail across the marshes became smaller.

NOW THE DAY BEING DONE AND THE NIGHT COMING ON,
THOSE TWO LITTLE BABIES SAT UNDER A STONE.
THEY SOBBED AND THEY SIGHED, THEY SAT THERE AND
  CRIED,
THOSE TWO LITTLE BABIES, THEY LAY DOWN AND DIED.

PRETTY BABES IN THE WOOD, PRETTY BABES IN THE WOOD,
O, DON'T YOU REMEMBER THOSE BABES IN THE WOOD?

'BABES IN THE WOOD', TRADITIONAL FOLK SONG

CHAPTER TWENTY-TWO
LOST IN THE MIST

The sound of cackling and angry cawing grew louder as Josie and Alfie struggled through the marsh grass. Josie's legs burned with the effort of bounding through the clinging stalks that snagged and tugged at her skirts. She cursed the impractical clothing and hitched the hems up to her knees.

'Alfie, can you see the barge?' she panted. The ground undulated, making her stumble and stagger. One minute, hard tussocks met the soles of her boots; the next, soft yielding mud and thick reeds. Alfie had overtaken her, but even he struggled to move fast.

'Think so,' he gasped back. 'But it's gettin' hard to see.'

He was right. A thin grey mist began to rise from the ground, blurring the horizon and making anything distant indistinct. Josie glanced back at the thickening cloud of angry birds swirling towards them: a thousand tiny specks that conglomerated into a vengeful monster.

But some of the specks weren't so tiny. The Aunts were in among the angry swarm, screaming their bloodlust.

'What about Arabella?' she yelled.

'I don't think they're interested in her, Josie – hurry!' Alfie yelled. 'They'll be on us in a flash!'

Josie leapt from one grassy hillock to another. Her lungs felt like they would burst with the effort as she caught up with Alfie. Each step squelched and water seeped into their boots, between their toes. Running became even more difficult. The rotten smell of marsh water filled their nostrils as they plunged on, trying to ignore the insistent cackling screeches that echoed close behind them. The barge had vanished from sight, forgotten in the scramble to survive and shrouded by the thickening mist.

Josie lost her footing and collapsed on to the wet earth. The grass seemed to open up and she gasped at the cold of the marsh as it engulfed her. Brackish, soily water filled her mouth, nose and ears, deadening the screams of the crows for an instant. She pulled her head up and found herself waist deep in a gully, coughing and spluttering. Alfie grabbed her under the armpits and began to drag her out of the pit.

'No time for a bath,' he panted. 'Quick, come on . . .'

They struggled on but Josie had lost all sense of where they were heading. Cold numbed her and the water still stung her eyes. She gripped on to Alfie's coat-tails, tripping and sliding blindly as he pulled her along. Mud smeared her legs as she slipped again, dragging Alfie with her. The noise of the crows deafened them as a few birds swooped. Josie lashed out with the back of her hand, swatting the first attacker aside. Even blinded by ditch-water she couldn't miss.

A sudden chill bit into her. She rubbed her eyes and found the mist had solidified into a thick, freezing fog. Alfie was picking himself up, only a foot or so away, but he was no more than a shadow to Josie. He panted and his breath billowed into the freezing mist. Somewhere to their left, the raucous crows faded into the distance.

'Hope we've lost them,' Alfie said, his teeth chattering.

'We could lose each other in this pea-souper,' Josie said, shivering and hugging herself. Her wet clothes were no protection from the cold; they clung to her, numbing her to the bone. 'What should we do? Wait?'

'I don't think we should,' Alfie murmured, jerking his chin at something behind Josie.

She turned to see a dark figure, shadowy, some distance away, but moving towards them slowly. Josie could just see the outline of a long beak, the spiky head feathers. Frantic, she scanned right and left for a hiding place. The ground lay flat and featureless but for the murky pool of water she'd just slipped in. She grabbed Alfie and pulled him back to the pool, gasping as the cold water engulfed her again. She heard Alfie yelp as she took a deep breath. The massive crow-Aunt loomed nearer in the gloom. Josie pointed at the water, then ducked her head under, hoping that Alfie had the guts to do the same.

The freezing water hurt, making her ache in her very bones, between her eyes, in every joint, in every muscle. Her crushed lungs screamed for air and she could hear her heart drumming. Alfie gripped her shoulder, holding them both down, his cheeks puffed out and eyes screwed shut. His skin looked brown in the marshy water. Josie prayed he could stay under as long as she could. She glanced up, trying to see through the murk. A stark out-line poked up into the sky from the edge of the pool. Aunt Mag wobbled and wavered as the water rippled. The urge to draw breath became an unbearable pressure in Josie's chest and throat. She wanted to push herself skyward and suck in the sweet air above. The cold drilled into her teeth and jaws. Blackness began to seep into the fringes of her vision.

She glanced up again. The figure had gone. Josie couldn't wait any longer. With a gasp that nearly filled her lungs with water, she broke the surface and clawed her way up the slimy sides of the pool. Alfie burst up, throwing himself on to the bank, where he lay half out of the pool, gasping hoarsely for breath. Josie couldn't think, but could only breathe, drawing in lungful after lungful of air. The sound of the crows grew more distant and muffled.

'Come on,' she said through chattering teeth. She dragged Alfie right out, falling backwards in the process.

'You're about as frozen as me,' he said, his voice stammering as he grinned down at her and offered a hand.

They staggered through the marsh, unable to tell

whether it was day or night, or in which direction they were heading in the silent world of cloud. Everything lay still; only their chattering breath and the scrunch of their feet on the frozen grass disturbed the silence.

Josie stopped. 'How long have we been walking?' she said, hugging herself and shaking violently.

'D-dunno,' Alfie said. 'But I've g-got to rest soon.'

Josie didn't reply. In the distance, the strange light pulsed, faint and weak, but piercing the fog and beckoning them.

'Head that way,' she said, pointing at it, unable to tell if Alfie shivered from the cold or fear.

They stumbled on, propping each other up when they tripped. Nothing was said as they saved their energy, trying to stay conscious as the bitter cold stung their skin and threatened to overwhelm them.

The beckoning glow became all that they saw. Shadows flitted and skimmed past Josie, but still it called to her.

Slowly the mist thinned to reveal a flicker of flame. Square outlines of caravans wavered in the dancing firelight. The fog broke and Josie could make out figures huddled round a huge campfire, casting long, twisted shadows on to the grey canvas wall of a huge circus tent that loomed over them.

Josie increased her pace, pulling Alfie along. She felt almost delirious with cold but the warmth of the fire drew her. The small huddle of men, women and children stared at them as they entered the circle of heat.

One man peeled away from the group. He stood tall and looked impossibly thin, bringing images of stilt men to Josie's addled mind. His battered top hat emphasised the way he towered above everyone there. He wore a long frock coat and striped trousers. A *ringmaster*, Josie thought feverishly. The glow from the fire drew dark lines on his gaunt, skeletal face, emphasising his cheekbones and deep-set eyes. A spectacular waxed moustache sprang across either side of his face, like the hands of a clock.

'Come, children,' the ringmaster said, his voice thick with a heavy accent. 'You look tired and hungry from your journey. Sit and eat.'

Josie exchanged exhausted glances with Alfie as they slumped down on to the sea-bleached tree trunks that doubled as seats around the fire. Nobody spoke, but she didn't mind. Warmth bled back into her body, making steam rise from her clothes. She closed her eyes and sighed, revelling in the heat. Someone pushed a bowl into her hands, and soon she was gulping down lumps of meaty stew and gravy-soaked bread, oblivious of her audience. Alfie wolfed down his own food, pausing to nod and mime his thanks with a sloppy crust. The ring-master nodded back, smiling gently.

When the bowl lay clean and its heat had ebbed into Josie's hands, she looked back up at the party seated round the fire. It was a rough mix of shawled women, shaggy-haired children with grubby faces, hawk-featured men with golden earrings and missing teeth. But they all looked grey; the colour seemed washed out of their skin and their ragged, worn clothes. Josie could see that their eyes held deep sorrow, despite their smiles.

The ringmaster gestured to the shadows. 'You need sleep. I will escort you to your caravan,' he announced.

'We have a caravan?' Josie said, staggering to her feet.

'There is always room at Lorenzo's Circus,' the skinny man said, his eyes deep and sad. 'Always room for the lost.'

Nine children you have borne.
Three were buried under your bed's head,
And three under your brewing lead.
Another three on the playing green;
Count, Maid, and there be nine.

'The Maid and the Palmer', traditional folk song

CHAPTER TWENTY-THREE
HOMECOMING

Josie held her breath when she heard the name. She felt Alfie's hand grip hers. All she could hear was the crackle of the fire and her own heartbeat.

'Lorenzo's Incredible Circus,' Josie whispered. In her mind's eye she saw the poster in Scrabsnitch's shop: the ringmaster with arms extended, the lion clawing at the air and their mother, Madame Lilly.

'Forgive me.' The ringmaster bowed deeply. 'I forget my manners. I am Lorenzo, master of this circus and your host . . .'

'Then you'd know our mother, Madame Lilly,' Josie said. Suddenly she felt so alive, full of curiosity and excitement. Lorenzo's expression remained long and drawn. Josie looked around the circle; grim faces stared back at her.

'You are Lilly's children?' He sighed and shook his head.

'Yes.' Josie beamed. 'What was she like? Was she as

beautiful as we've been told? How –'

Lorenzo held up a long, slender hand. 'Child, save your questions for the morning. Let us find you a bed. You must sleep. Believe me, there will be more than enough time to talk about . . . the old days.' Lorenzo turned his back on her and started walking.

Josie shivered, fatigue seeping back once more, and glanced at Alfie, who was keeping close behind her. Away from the fire, he looked pinched with cold, and pale. They followed Lorenzo, dragging their tired bodies through the cold night. Coarse marsh grass hissed and whispered in the gentle breeze. Alfie groaned and stumbled against her.

'Are you all right?' Josie whispered, feeling his weight on her shoulder.

'I dunno,' Alfie replied. 'I feel exhausted.'

'Hardly surprising,' Josie sighed. 'We'll get some sleep soon.'

The caravans extended in a semicircle around the big tent, square shadows disappearing into the mist and dark. Lorenzo stopped at the first van and gestured.

'You can rest here,' he said. 'And then maybe tomorrow you can meet everyone.'

Josie stood in the big tent, hurling knives. Blade after blade hit its mark in a breathtaking display. The audience cheered and applauded; she thought her heart would burst with pride. Lorenzo raised a hand towards her.

'Artemis the Huntress!' he cried.

Madame Lilly stood at the entrance to the ring, clapping her bejewelled hands, her dark features full of joy.

I'm home. Josie grinned, bowing again and again. *I'm home . . .*

With a gasp, she sat bolt upright up in bed. The covers lay cast to one side. The cold of the caravan had woken her. Her breath clouded the air as she dragged the blankets back over her, desperate to cling to the pleasure of the dream. Wide awake now, she scanned the tiny caravan.

Alfie slept in the bed opposite her, so close she could have reached out and touched him. Blankets were piled on top of him, his breath puffing out from beneath them. Pots and pans hung along the wall above him and the window of a small pot-bellied stove glowed red in the corner. Josie had no recollection of getting into bed. The last thing she remembered was dragging off her wet clothes.

Muffled voices from outside drew her to the tiny frosted window that let a little moonlight into the caravan. The tall, thin figure of Lorenzo stood talking to someone Josie could not make out in the darkness.

'Will they perform?' said a gruff voice from the shadows.

'They have no choice,' Lorenzo said, his voice sad.

'They always have a choice,' replied the voice.

The two figures moved away, the rest of their conversation lost as they disappeared into the night.

Her heart leapt. There was to be a performance! The happiness of her dream still fizzed faintly within her – that warm feeling, the roar of the crowd. That would be good, wouldn't it? So why had Lorenzo sounded so despondent? Maybe he was always like that. Josie thought of Cardamom's dark moods, his forlorn loneliness offstage. And what was all that about Josie choosing not to perform? As if. She smiled to herself and sat back in bed. Performing was in her blood.

At least the old wives' tale Arabella had told them about the circus wasn't true. This was a real circus, with a tent and performers. And at least here she and Alfie would be safer from the Aunts, who didn't seem to have pursued them across the marshes.

She shook herself. She didn't have to think about them. Instead, she imagined tumbling into the ring again, the brass band striking up a lively polka as she cartwheeled across the sawdust floor. Eventually, Josie's eyelids drooped and she slipped back into a world of lights and music and cheers.

She awoke to the sound of Alfie rattling the stove as he put more logs into the firebox.

'You awake, then?' he said, dragging his trousers on and pulling his braces over his shoulders. 'The stove's just about dried these out. I hung your skirts up for a bit so it shouldn't be too bad.'

Josie dragged herself out from under the warm sheets and pulled on her torn skirts and jacket. The seams felt damp but the warmth of the stove countered the cold.

'Lorenzo's Circus, Alfie,' Josie said, excitement fluttering inside her. 'Who'd have thought it? We can find out all about Mother and perform and –'

'Yeah, right . . . Come on, let's have a look around,' Alfie said. He still looked tired, his eyes puffy and his face pale.

'Didn't you sleep very well?' Josie said, pulling her hair back and tying it up. Her ribbon was one of the few items that had dried out properly, although her hair tangled and snagged in her fingers.

'Like a log, but I still woke feelin' like bloomin' death,' Alfie said.

They stepped out into the gloom of a cold winter's day. A thin mist clung to everything, giving the caravans a ghostly quality. The horizon was invisible, the marshes lost. All that existed was this grey world. Everything huddled around the tent that loomed out of the fog like a mountain.

'Just think, Alfie, a real circus.' Josie clapped her hands. 'And they're bound to be our friends. If they knew Madame Lilly . . .'

'I'm not sure. It just looks a bit, well, dingy to me,' Alfie said, stuffing his hands in his pockets. 'Look at the state of the caravans, all peelin' paint an' cracked windows.'

'They're probably over-wintering,' Josie said. 'They'll give them a lick of paint in the spring.'

'This mist sticks to everythin'. And did you hear Lorenzo last night?' Alfie pulled a long face and put on a thick accent. 'You can *rrrest* here . . . Cor, he didn't 'ave to make it sound so permanent!'

'He was just being hospitable, that's all.' Josie frowned
at Alfie. Why was he being so negative? It wasn't good
manners to mock Lorenzo.

'And listen . . .' Alfie said, pulling a face.

'I can't hear a thing.' Josie felt a stab of irritation.

'Exactly. No birdsong,' Alfie persisted.

Josie clenched her fists. She wanted to hit him. He was
spoiling everything.

'Well, at least there aren't any crows either,' she
snapped. 'You're not thinking of Arabella's old wives'
tale, are you? It's just a circus, Alfie. If we hadn't met
them then we probably would have frozen to death by
now. They fed us and gave us a bed for the night – you
should be grateful!'

A flash of brown fur and a squeak made Josie start. A
monkey scurried across their path and up on to the ropes
of the big top nearby. An ox of a man in a baggy
chequered suit lumbered close behind. Faded white
make-up stained his unshaven face and he looked ready
to strangle the creature.

'Walnut! Come back here, you little demon,' bellowed
the man, grabbing at the monkey and sending it
corkscrewing up the ropes on to the roof of the tent.

Josie could see Alfie shaking as the figure turned to
them. She shivered, too, as the clown gave them a lop-
sided grin full of yellowed, crooked teeth.

'The babes have returned home, then, eh?' The man
beamed, tucking his thumbs into his red braces. 'I

remember you. How could Old Ulrico forget? You and your precious mother.' He spat at their feet and paced off after the monkey as it leapt from the side of the tent, scampering between the man's feet and away.

'Ulrico,' she whispered. 'From the poster – do you remember?'

'Don't think he liked us.' Alfie shivered as the shabby clown wandered into the thick fog that closed behind him like theatre curtains. 'Or the fact that we're Madame Lilly's kids.'

'Well, every show has its rough diamonds,' Josie said, pursing her lips at him. 'I can't remember a single cheerful clown back at the Erato . . .' She waited for the sarcastic retort, but none came.

'I was just sayin', that's all,' Alfie said, looking hurt.

'Well, don't . . .' Josie began, but three children came tumbling from a nearby caravan, making her jump back with a yelp – two boys, one girl, all with thick black hair, deep brown eyes and broad smiles. The eldest boy fell to his knees as the others cartwheeled over him, hands on his shoulders. As they landed, he sprang to his feet and went straight into a somersault.

'Welcome! We have been much looking forward to meeting you!' beamed the older boy. 'I'm Nicolao, this is my brother Paulo and my sister Ashena.' The other two bowed politely but they couldn't keep still, constantly shoving each other or doing handstands. Josie managed a weak smile.

'We are the Gambinis,' Ashena said, grinning. 'You

will join us for some food, no?'

Josie and Alfie nodded. But Josie was looking at the children's clothes, ragged and torn, their faces grey. They were just like everyone else they had seen in this place. She glanced over at Alfie, who raised an eyebrow. He looked no better, she thought, with the dark rings under his eyes and his haggard expression. Maybe it was living out on the marsh that did it. He swayed and stumbled drunkenly.

'Alfie, what's wrong with you?' Josie said, grabbing his elbow.

'Nuffin', just a bit tired, that's all. A bit of breakfast'll sort it, for sure.'

Inside the Gambinis' caravan a fire crackled in the stove, struggling to keep the cold morning air at bay. Josie, wrapped in an old blanket, began to relax as they shared the children's thin porridge. At least it was something warm. They sat crowded around a small table, chatting.

'I'm sorry we startled you,' Paulo said, opening the curtains and sitting by Josie. 'Tumbling is all we ever do.'

'My guardian, the Great Cardamom, taught me to tumble,' Josie said, spooning some porridge into her mouth. 'We always filled the Erato theatre.'

'Tell us more!' Ashena cried, kneeling at Josie's side. Josie forgot herself as she eagerly described Cardamom's act, Gimlet's cabinets and stage sets, and how the audience sat amazed and baffled at her guardian's tricks.

'Cardamom, he was here, with us,' Nicolao said. 'Such a happy man . . .'

'But not a great conjurer.' Paulo grinned. 'Sounds like he practises . . .'

'You knew him?' Josie said, excited.

'How's that possible?' Alfie frowned across the table at Josie, brandishing his spoon like a weapon.

'No, no . . . we . . .' Ashena said, her eyes wide. 'Yes, we hear about him, from Lorenzo, yes –'

'Anyway, tell us more. We love your stories,' Nicolao cut in, smiling.

The Gambinis listened as Josie continued, weak smiles tracing curves across their staring faces. Alfie sat opposite her, his head nodding. Josie glanced over to him every now and then. He looked like he was napping, his eyes shut, his head lolling forward. She wondered why he was so tired. *He said he slept well,* she thought. *It doesn't make sense.*

'So how long have you been performing?' Josie said, shaking herself to attention. She scanned the Gambinis' grubby faces as they huddled round her.

'All our lives,' Nicolao said, his voice sounding distant. 'It is all we know.'

'Our parents died when we were young,' Paulo added, shuffling closer. 'An accident on the trapeze.'

'They said that when they fell, the audience nearly trampled each other in an effort to see the mangled corpses,' Ashena said, gazing deep into Josie's face.

'That's terrible,' Josie said. 'Who looks after you now?'

'The circus looks after its own,' Nicolao answered.

'Even unto death,' Paulo murmured.

'Alfie, he performs, yes?' Ashena said, her voice bright and loud, breaking the sombre mood. Alfie's eyes flickered open at the mention of his name.

'No,' he mumbled and stirred his spoon around his untouched porridge. 'No. I'm an undertaker's mute.'

'A what?' asked Paulo, a puzzled smile frozen on his face.

'An undertaker's mute,' Alfie repeated. 'I help Mr Wiggins the undertaker. I help him run funerals.'

Josie felt cross with him. Why did he look so miserable? He should be glad they were safe. He just didn't like the idea of her having more in common with the circus folk. He was jealous. That's what it was.

'He is a kind of actor,' she said, narrowing her eyes at him. 'He walks behind funeral carriages looking sad, even when he doesn't know the person who died.'

'You get paid for that?' Nicolao took a mouthful of gruel and shook his head.

'It's not just that,' Alfie said, frowning. 'It's about showin' respect, doin' things right.'

'You have to do this.' Josie stood up, giggling, then did an impression of Alfie's slow, stiff funeral march. She pouted her lip and lowered her brows, swinging her head from side to side.

The caravan erupted with laughter but Alfie clattered his spoon down on the table and stood up. Sending his chair crashing to the floor, he barged out of the van, slamming the door behind him.

'YOU DUG A HOLE BENEATH THE MOON,
AND THERE YOU LAID OUR BODIES DOWN.'
'YOU COVERED THE HOLE WITH MOSSY STONES,
AND THERE YOU LEFT OUR TINY BONES.'

'THE CRUEL MOTHER', TRADITIONAL FOLK SONG

CHAPTER TWENTY-FOUR
LORENZO'S CIRCUS

The silver mist hadn't lifted as Josie stepped out into the chill morning in search of Alfie. She shouldn't have mocked him. They were both tired and far from home. *Both?* Josie wondered. What did she have back in London now? No Cardamom, no Gimlet. The folk of the Erato were kind but they weren't close. Maybe *this* could be her home now, like in her dream. Alfie still had Wiggins. He would never understand why the circus attracted her so much. She shivered. To perform again – that would be wonderful.

Lorenzo loomed out of the fog, appearing as if from nowhere. He nodded at Josie and touched the brim of his tall hat.

'You are exploring, I see,' he said. He waved a long, thin arm around the caravans. 'There isn't much to see. We are a small band of performers. Nothing too special.'

'It's special to me, Lorenzo,' Josie said, smiling and

pushing her hair behind her ear. 'It was my mother's circus.'

'Ah, your mother.' The tall ringmaster smoothed his impossibly long moustache.

'What was she like?'

'As graceful as a ballerina,' Lorenzo said. His voice softened and a gentle smile wrinkled the corners of his mouth. 'As fierce as a tigress. The most loving of mothers. She told fortunes but she danced and tumbled, too.' He raised an eyebrow at Josie. 'She even threw the odd knife. It was a tragedy that she left us and went to the city, only to return . . . dead.'

'She died of a fever,' Josie whispered. 'I know that much.'

'Cardamom brought her home.' Lorenzo's eyes looked red and moist. 'He knew she would want to rest here.'

Josie gave a start. 'She's buried here?' Would there be a grave? Somewhere she could visit?

Lorenzo shook his head slowly. 'We do not bury our dead,' he sighed. 'She lay in her caravan, surrounded by all her possessions. We burned it, a cremation, as is our custom.'

An awkward silence hung between them. A thought occurred to Josie: maybe this man knew her father, too. So little had been said about him.

'What about my father?'

Lorenzo paused, and a shadow crossed his gaunt grey face. He sighed and then reached out to touch Josie's forehead. 'His name was Necros . . . Professor Necros, he called himself.'

'The name on the poster,' Josie said, barely able to contain herself. 'I saw his name at Scrabsnitch's shop! What was he like?'

Lorenzo shrugged. 'Just another sideshow performer. He left us . . . He died . . . He wanted more than the circus could ever give him. Now, your mother.' The smile returned. 'Performing was all she ever wanted. She lived for it –'

'So do I!' Josie cut in. She hugged herself. To have so much in common with Madame Lilly!

'You are so full of life, Josie,' Lorenzo said, his eyes gleaming. 'It will be like having your mother back.'

Josie grinned. 'Can I practise throwing and tumbling with Paulo and Nicolao?'

'By all means.' An indulgent smile flickered briefly on Lorenzo's care-worn face. 'You will find all you need in the tent.' He paused and the troubled frown returned. 'Perhaps you should find your brother first. I saw him leave the caravan. He did not look happy.'

Josie sighed. 'He's so miserable,' she muttered. 'He's not excited about the circus at all.'

'He is your brother, nonetheless. You should not let bad feeling grow or it will fester for all time.' Lorenzo's eyes seemed to glow as he spoke.

Josie frowned, watching as he wandered away into the mist. *What a strange thing to say*, she thought. '*For all time.*' But he was right: things left too long became harder to repair. Alfie couldn't be far away. Perhaps he had gone back to their van. She would find him and make peace.

The entrance to the tent gaped open as Josie passed it. She couldn't help peering in. A single solid pole, as wide as a man, rose up in the centre; at its top, a circle of daylight cast down feeble rays. A shadowy twilight filled the tent. Josie could just see the circus ring, covered in sawdust, surrounding the pole. Bench seats crouched around it, giving the vast space a closed and confined feeling. A corkboard stood against the pole, next to a table with twelve silver throwing blades. They glinted in the grey light, dazzling Josie.

She hadn't thrown in weeks – not real throwing knives, not just for fun – not since that last fateful night when the Aunts arrived at her house. Josie stepped into the tent. She imagined the seats full of smiling people. Music would be playing. She picked up two of the knives and tapped them together, hearing the audience murmur, and grinned. The music would stop now, she thought – maybe there'd be a drum roll as she turned to her target. The scene became real: the expectant hush, the warmth of the gaslights hissing. Josie was back onstage at the Erato and yet in the circus, too, a strange mix of the two in her mind.

She hurled the first knife, watching it twirl and spin towards the corkboard until, with that satisfying *thunk*, it quivered in the board. She threw the second, getting it as close to the first as possible. Her imaginary audience cheered and clapped. She bowed and held up two more knives. They were beautiful, perfectly balanced. *As if they were made for me*, she thought.

Time and again she practised, lost in her dream. Lorenzo was calling her name, the Gambinis bouncing and leaping as she burst balloons, hit spinning targets and amazed the audience with her accuracy. Morning shadows shifted as the day grew older.

A shadow at the tent door broke her daydream. Alfie stood there, hands in his pockets, shoulders hunched against the chill. Josie felt a stab of guilt. She'd forgotten all about him. How long had she been in the tent? She had no idea. Alfie looked terrible – worse than before, if that were possible.

'What you playin' at?' he said, his voice sullen. Black ringed his heavy eyes. 'You been in 'ere all day?'

'I'm not playing,' Josie said, sending a knife twanging deeply into the corkboard. 'It's what I do. I'm a performer.'

'We'd be better off thinkin' of how we get back to London.' Alfie shuffled further into the tent. He stumbled, plonking himself down on to a bench before he fell.

'Alfie, what's wrong with you? You look awful and you're so miserable. We're safe here and there's going to be a performance!' Josie's heart quickened; surely he would be excited by the idea of seeing a show. 'Lorenzo wants us to take part. I heard him talking last night!'

Alfie stared at Josie, confusion in his face. 'What's wrong with me? Josie, what about the Amarant? Corvis? Have you forgotten? We've not been 'ere a day and you're prattlin' on about performin' and –'

'How dare you!' Josie hurled another blade. 'I haven't forgotten.'

But Alfie sat frozen, staring at the door. A raven, sleek-feathered and sharp-beaked, had fluttered in and landed on the benches. It waddled into the circle, cocking its head at them. Josie could see the malice in its marble eyes.

'D'you think it's one of Corvis's?' Alfie whispered, eyes wide.

'As you said before, we haven't seen any birds round here at all,' Josie whispered back. 'I'm certain it is.'

She stretched her hand out slowly, gradually reaching for one of the knives. Her movement broke the spell; it was as if the creature knew what she planned next. With a squawk, it threw itself upward, battering the musty air with powerful wings.

'It's headin' for the vent at the top,' Alfie yelled. 'If it gets away it might lead the Aunts 'ere . . .'

Josie threw the knife, aiming slightly ahead of the raven, anticipating its path. The creature's angry cawing stopped suddenly as the blade struck it squarely, sending it spiralling down to the floor with a thud. Its wings flapped feebly as it lay pinioned to the ground, until, finally, they stopped.

Pulling the knife free, Josie sighed. 'It's not fair. I just want to be my old self for once. I miss Cardamom and Gimlet.' She scrubbed out the tears with the back of her hand. 'I miss all this.' Josie waved her hand around the tent. 'Just for a moment I want it to be simple. I want to be Artemis again and throw knives, and the audience will cheer and I will bow. And there'll be no ghuls or crows or Corvis, and no Amarant.'

Alfie frowned and shook his head. 'I know, but they won't go away. And it ain't right 'ere, Josie, can't you see?'

Before Josie could reply, the Gambinis came spilling into the tent. Ashena walked in on her hands, a huge grin splitting her face.

'Lorenzo says we will perform soon,' she said, bounding to her feet.

'He says you want to practise and join us.' Nicolao bounced up and down on the spot.

'It makes us so happy.' Paulo beamed at her, gripping her hand a little too tightly.

Josie gave a thin smile back. 'It makes me happy, too, Paulo,' she said, staring defiantly over at Alfie. But her brother had slumped forward on to the ground. His eyes were rolled back in his head and his whole body shuddered.

Last night she came to me, my dead love came in;
She entered so softly that her feet made no din.
She laid a hand on me and this she did say,
'It will not be long, love, till our wedding day.'

'She Moved through the Fair', Traditional Folk Song

CHAPTER TWENTY-FIVE
THE REALITY OF ROPE

Alfie lay pale and still, wrapped in blankets. Josie leaned forward, placing a damp cloth on his brow. The heat of his skin warmed the rag. His eyes flickered and he grimaced at Josie.

'Never 'ad you down for a nursemaid,' he said, giving a weak smile.

'Can't go finding brothers and not look after them, can I?' Josie grinned at him. 'How do you feel?'

'Drained . . . like when I move the corpses.' He coughed. 'Only worse. Josie?'

'Yes?'

'Don't let's row. We got to stick together.'

Josie smiled and shook her head. 'We won't row again.' Seeing Alfie lying on the floor like that had shocked her. He was all she had left.

'I'm glad you're my sister,' Alfie said. His face relaxed and he let sleep take him.

Josie bit her lip. She was glad, too. She thought of the obnoxious boy she'd first met in the undertaker's. That wasn't really Alfie; it was just a hard shell he wore to keep out the harshness of his life. But she'd lost everyone she cared about. And now he was so fragile . . .

Lorenzo appeared at the foot of the bed, looking even taller as he stooped in the cramped caravan. Josie hadn't heard him enter.

'Some kind of seizure, I suspect,' he said. 'The poor boy.'

'He's been feeling bad since he woke up this morning,' Josie said, looking up at Lorenzo. 'Have you ever seen anything like it?'

'The marshes are full of disease,' Lorenzo said, shrugging. His long face stretched into an even longer frown. 'All we can do is make him comfortable. There will be a performance soon. It will not matter then.'

A *performance? Soon?* Josie bit her lip. She watched Lorenzo tuck the sheets round Alfie. The ringmaster looked like a huge grasshopper folded up in a matchbox. His face was so skeletal and sorrowful.

'When?' she asked.

'Tomorrow night,' the ringmaster replied slowly. 'When the tide is at its height and folk can come.'

'The tide?' Josie frowned, puzzled. What did the tide have to do with it?

'Don't you worry,' Lorenzo said. His eyes glowed again and a fierce smile lit his face. 'Just practise your throwing, sharpen your act and be ready for the performance of your life.'

He unfolded himself from Alfie's bedside and, still bent double, clambered out of the caravan. Josie turned back to Alfie, who mumbled in his sleep, sweat matting the hair on his brow.

Lorenzo's words echoed in her mind, making her stomach flutter. 'Sharpen my act,' she whispered, excitement stretching her mouth into a smile. There were other things he had said, confusing things, but all that stuck in her mind was 'the performance of your life'.

'The ropes,' Alfie whispered, tugging at her sleeve, his eyes tight shut. Josie leaned over him.

'What, Alfie? What did you say?'

'The ropes . . . look at the ropes . . .' Alfie's eyes opened a crack, then shut again as he fell back into a troubled, murmuring slumber.

Why would he want her to look at ropes? And which ones? Josie shook her head. *Must be delirious*, she thought. Dipping the rag in some cold water, she mopped his brow again.

Josie stood on a narrow platform on the centre pole near the top of the tent, her arms extended to the roof. She was so high up she could have touched it. Swings and lines dangled from beams that radiated out from where she stood. Below, the band played a merry tune and clowns cartwheeled and cavorted across the ring. In the void before her, Paulo swung to and fro, building momentum, coming closer and closer with each swing.

'The ropes, Josie, the ropes!' Alfie called distantly. She peered down into the depths of the tent. Row upon row of spectators stared back, open-mouthed. Somewhere down there in the dizzying distance, Alfie's pale, scarred face peered up, too.

Paulo swung towards her, hanging upside down on a trapeze, his hair trailing, a crazed grin on his face.

'Jump, Josie, I will catch you,' he cried, arms extended. Josie looked down again. Her mouth felt dry. The rope ladder seemed to stretch and twist down to the sawdust floor. There was no net. 'Jump,' Paulo called again.

'The ropes!'

'Just let yourself go.' Paulo's face swung nearer. His eyes looked feverish, his fingers long and claw-like. 'We will keep you safe.'

Josie grabbed the rope swing near her and recoiled at once. It felt cold and slimy, green with fine seaweed.

'Look at the ropes!' Alfie's voice called. Barnacles crusted the bar of her swing, the shells cutting into the palms of her hands. Paulo came nearer again, his eyes gaping black sockets, his face a grinning skull.

'We will take care of you,' he hissed in a voice as dry as winter leaves. His long skeletal fingers grasped at Josie, making her scream and pull away. Overbalancing, she tumbled back, her stomach lurching as she plummeted towards the ground . . .

With a gasp, she awoke, her head on Alfie's pillow. He muttered and sighed, rolling over. Josie sat up. Her heart pounded. *A horrible dream*, she thought, *yet so real*. She shuddered at the memory of Paulo's face, his hideous voice. With a groan and a stretch, Josie stood up from Alfie's bedside. He looked no better – pale and feverish, shivering and grumbling. She looked out of the small window.

Night had passed. *I must have slept right through*, Josie thought, looking back at Alfie with a twinge of guilt. Another grey, misty day. She rubbed her eyes, feeling a thrill of excitement shiver through her. A performance. Tonight. But the shocking image of Paulo reaching for her with withered hands lingered. Shaking herself, she picked up the knives and shuffled through the dewy marsh grass to the tent. Perhaps there she could practise, forget the nightmare.

The day passed quickly. Josie lost herself in rehearsal, throwing and dancing, tumbling and bowing. *Madame Lilly performed in here*, she thought. She'd never felt so close to her mother before. She imagined the glamorous gypsy woman dancing across the ring, so exotic, bewitching the locals, labourer and gentleman alike. And here Josie was, following in her footsteps, amazing audiences with her astounding skill. Madame Lilly would have been so proud of her child. Josie stopped. *Children*, she corrected herself, realisation dawning on her. *I haven't looked in on Alfie!*

In a panic, she hurried across the scrubby ground to the caravan and banged the door open. Alfie lay sleeping, his breathing deep and ragged. Josie heaved a sigh of relief and cooled his face with the damp cloth. *He seems rested,* she thought. *A bit more practice wouldn't harm.*

The light had faded a little by the time Josie made her way back to the tent again. She stopped and peered across the flat landscape and frowned. Something looked different. The mist had lifted slightly. She could just make out Rookery Heights, small and distant on its hillside. Smoke swirled around it. No, it wasn't smoke, she realised; they were crows, thousands of them, whirling and twisting in huge flocks above the house.

Another movement caught her eye, much closer this time. A black figure was stalking about the marshes, poking the gulleys with a long stick. Two more joined the first.

'The Aunts,' Josie gasped. They were still searching for them!

'Don't worry about them,' said a voice behind her. Ulrico the clown slouched, hands in pockets, regarding her with piggy eyes. 'They can't touch us – no, sir.'

'What d'you mean?' Josie asked with a frown.

'They steer clear of us, know they can't harm us.' He smirked. 'They won't come lookin' here.'

'I don't understand . . . Is it because we're so far out on the marsh?' Josie said, confused by the clown's words. She felt vulnerable and alone here, beyond the caravans with this huge man.

'Yeah, missy, that's right,' he sneered. 'Or they might think that if we've got yer, then you're not goin' anywhere anyways!' Ulrico gave a nasty chuckle which grew into full-blown laughter.

Josie covered her ears and hurried back to the caravan, the words 'you're not goin' anywhere' ringing in her head. Why did he seem to hate her so?

'Josie!' Ashena's cold hand grabbed hers and dragged her into their caravan. 'What is wrong? Why are you so upset?'

'Oh, Ashena, it's Ulrico – he said we would never leave,' Josie sobbed. 'He's so horrible.'

'He is not a nice man.' Ashena's face darkened. She clung to Josie, stroking the back of her hand. She grinned up at Josie again. 'But we are nice. We are your friends . . . We will look after you.'

Josie snatched her hand away from the clammy grip. 'I'd better see to Alfie,' she muttered. But Ashena grabbed the hems of her skirts, still grinning. She looked too gaunt, too wide-eyed . . . too desperate. Josie shuddered.

'We can be your friends for ever, Josie, yes?' Ashena whispered, staring. 'We can perform every night for the rest of time. Won't that be wonderful?'

Josie backed away, horrified by the little girl's words. 'Ashena, I have to go. I'll see you later perhaps.' Josie slammed the door behind her and ran for the caravan. Her mind tumbled and twirled like an acrobat, swinging from one thought to the next. What had come over Ashena? What did she mean, they could perform for ever? Lorenzo had said something similar. Alfie was right: there was something strange about the whole circus. Why hadn't she seen it before?

An urgent chattering startled Josie out of her thoughts. Walnut dangled above her from the ropes that held up the big tent.

'The ropes,' Josie said as the monkey swung back and forth. 'Alfie said to look at the ropes.'

For the first time, Josie noticed how green with algae they were. And the stout iron pegs at her feet were covered in dead seaweed. The tent canvas was filthy, caked in a thin layer of mud, which made it hard to work out where the ground ended and the bottom of the tent began. The monkey squeaked again. Josie felt numb. The circus hadn't moved, probably for years, she thought.

'You begin to see with real eyes.' Lorenzo appeared from behind her. 'It doesn't matter now. You are with us, where you belong. You will stay here and be safe.'

A spasm of alarm jolted through Josie. Lorenzo gazed at her. His face looked kind and gentle, but a feverish glow lit his eyes.

'We can't stay,' Josie said. 'We have to leave.'

'If only it were that simple,' Lorenzo sighed, and straightened up to his full height. 'You will understand after the performance tonight. Nobody can leave Lorenzo's Circus.'

'But we must,' Josie said again. 'I made a promise to Cardamom . . .'

'We can't always keep our promises.' Lorenzo edged forward and took Josie's hand. His fingers felt the same as Ashena's – cold, clammy and faintly disturbing. His eyes burned with the same pleading desperation. 'You are so vibrant, so beautiful, my child. So full of life. Stay here with us.'

'I can't . . . I won't.' Josie recoiled.

'You have no choice, my dear.' Lorenzo sighed again, his shoulders sagging as if with the weight of knowledge. But his eyes still burned feverishly. He extended his hand. 'Join us . . .'

Josie staggered away, shaking her head, tears stinging her face. She'd been wrong – there was something hideous and frightening about these people. Of course she and Alfie couldn't stay here for ever. She felt as if a spell had been lifted. How could she have been so blind to the dilapidation and decay? She'd been drawn in by the excitement of the circus, the glamour of performing. How could she have lost all sense of what was important so quickly? They had to find and destroy the Amarant! They'd escaped from Corvis but, she suddenly realised, even here they were still prisoners.

'FOR THE WORMS ARE MY BEDFELLOWS,
COLD CLAY IS MY SHEET,
AND WHEN THE STORMY WINDS DO BLOW,
MY BODY LIES AND SLEEPS.'

'PROUD LADY MARGARET', TRADITIONAL FOLK BALLAD

CHAPTER TWENTY-SIX
AUDIENCE OF THE DEAD

Walnut sat on the step of a dilapidated old caravan set apart from the others. Josie found herself there, having wandered, dazed, after her encounter with Lorenzo. She could see that, at one time, the caravan had been ornately painted – but not any more. Blisters of faded paint bloomed on its wood-wormed and peeling surface. She could just see the remnants of nursery-rhyme figures, laughing faces, stars and moons. Something about the van made her shiver. Josie didn't want to be here. The monkey squealed and looked at her with eyes of liquid ebony.

'Don't worry,' she said. 'I'm not stopping. I'm off to get Alfie.' She gave a squeak of surprise as she turned away. Ulrico loomed over her, blocking her path.

'You all right, missy?' he asked, grinning. Josie could see the stubble growing through the pale rolls of flesh on his chin. He still wore the remains of his make-up and looked like his caravan: faded and dilapidated. 'Walnut ain't botherin' you, is he?'

'No, no,' Josie said, backing away from the bulky clown. He edged closer, licking his lips. Tufts of hair sprouted crazily from behind his ears, but his head was quite bald.

'Sorry I startled you before, like. You aren't afraid of old Ulrico, are you?' the clown said, tilting his head and bringing his face close to Josie's. 'I've known you since you was a babe in arms. Before *he* came . . .'

'Wh-who?' Josie was backed against the wall of the caravan now, with Ulrico's rancid breath on her cheek. She turned her head to one side.

'The one who caused all our misery,' Ulrico hissed in her face. 'He loved Lilly, he did, but she'd had enough of him. He wouldn't believe us when we told him she was dead.'

'What happened?' Josie's voice trembled. His breath disgusted her, his closeness repelled her, and yet the story drew her in, kept her from fleeing. Josie edged back along the van.

'He came here, to this very spot, with his cursed magic. Begged him, we did, told him she was gone.' Ulrico's heavy, laboured breathing made Josie squeeze her eyes shut. 'But he wouldn't have it . . . Cursed us all to a living death, he did.'

'How could he curse you?' Josie asked, her eyes snapping open. 'Who was he? What was his name?'

'Professor Necros,' Ulrico hissed. 'Your father did this

to us! All because of your precious mother!'

With a scream of horror and disgust, Josie pushed Ulrico away and dashed back towards the tent.

'And you'll be joinin' us soon, missy,' Ulrico called after her. 'No one leaves the circus!'

A wet squelching from behind the vans stopped Josie in her tracks. She peered into the shadows between the silhouetted caravans and stifled a scream. Pale, shivering hands clutched the edges of the pits that dotted the marshland. Vague figures with hair plastered to their leprous skin were dragging themselves from the water, staring at Josie with dead eyes. Men, women and children, dripping from their watery graves, thronged the narrow paths between the caravans, stumbling forward, reaching out to her.

Josie glanced left and right, considered doubling back towards Ulrico, but the shuffling dead had already blocked her path. Her skin prickled as she skirted the edge of the tent, herded by the silent groping crowd. She focused on the feel of the rough canvas, desperate not to look at the slack faces that came closer and grew more numerous. Josie could smell the decay and the tang of the sea that fed the marshes and bubbled under its treacherous pits.

Nearer they crowded, pressing together, reaching and grasping. She could see torn breeches and tattered shirts. She sobbed as she fended off the cold, clammy hands. The main entrance to the big top loomed like the mouth of some giant sea monster waiting to swallow her up.

Josie had no choice but to tumble inside.

The belly of the tent smelt dank. A dull green glow illuminated the cavernous interior. Josie felt as if she were deep beneath the sea. Ropes and ladders hung from the shadows like the rigging of some sunken vessel. Josie trembled as she suddenly realised an audience was seated, watching her. They stared blankly at her, jaws slack, eyes empty.

Alfie hung limp and shivering from the corkboard in the centre of the ring. Before Josie could run to him, Lorenzo appeared beside her, thrusting the set of throwing blades into her hand. Ulrico, dressed in his ragged clown costume, paraded before the audience. He mimed laughter, pointing and jeering at Josie, his face twisted and contorted with hatred.

'Ladies and gentlemen,' Lorenzo bellowed, raising a long skeletal arm, 'from London, I bring you Artemis the Huntress and her faithful assistant, Alfie!'

'Let him down. He isn't well,' Josie said, taking a step towards Lorenzo. Why were they doing this to her brother?

'You must perform for both of you, my dear,' Lorenzo said, his voice flat, as if he was resigned to their fate. 'Or would you rather he became part of the crowd?'

Josie's gaze scanned the pitiful audience that lined the tent's benches. Pale, they stared straight ahead with their hands lifeless on their knees. The Gambinis suddenly crowded around her.

'We are cursed, Josie! Cursed to live for ever, neither alive, nor dead.' Nicolao pawed at Josie's arm, his fingertips pinching at her. His flesh began to dry and thin, crackling as it moulded to the bone beneath. Paulo tugged at her skirts, his face disintegrating, lips shrivelling to reveal a cadaverous grin. His cheek-bones protruded through the once plump skin of his face.

'Paulo!' Josie screamed and jumped back. 'No, what's happening to you?'

'We need you, Josie,' he croaked, reaching and grasping with dead dry hands. 'We crave your presence. The power of the Amarant flows freely in your veins, we can feel it. It draws us, enlivens us!'

Water began to seep up through the floor of the circus ring, trickling towards Josie's feet. She looked down with horror. This was exactly what Arabella had warned them about. They had taken a terrible risk coming to this godforsaken place.

'The tide rises. Perform for us, Josie,' Lorenzo begged, his eyes shining from the deep sockets of his skull. 'Throw your knives. Join us.'

'I promised Cardamom I would find a thing called the Amarant,' Josie cried, desperately trying to think of any way to reason with Lorenzo. She stared at the decaying ringmaster. 'The Flower of Life . . . Maybe I can help you somehow.'

'You could never help us,' Lorenzo said, shaking his grizzled head. 'As for your promise . . . as for your precious flower . . . it is lost, buried and forgotten.'

'You must join us and perform for all eternity,' hissed Ulrico.

'Stay, please stay,' Ashena whimpered, crawling through the water towards Josie's ankles. She gazed up at Josie from eyeless sockets. Josie gave a scream and staggered back.

The water swirled around her knees. She turned, aimed carefully and threw her first knife at the corkboard. The thud of the knife in the board seemed to awaken the audience. They suddenly looked up, alert. Josie tucked a second blade into the waistband of her skirts and tried to run forward, lifting her legs high to beat the frightening drag of the water on her sodden clothes. She flicked the third knife at the board as she ran. Her first had cut the bonds on Alfie's left wrist. He slumped forward as the next knife sliced the ropes on his right. Josie dived and caught him before he slipped beneath the water.

'Josie?' he murmured, half opening his eyes. 'It's them. They're drainin' the life out of me . . .'

'I know – we have to get out,' Josie said, throwing his arm over her shoulder to hoist him up.

The water lapped at their waists now, the shock of the cold reviving Alfie and making him gasp. Josie half dragged, half carried him to the centre of the tent, where the rope ladders swayed in the currents. Josie hesitated, wondering if the ladders would take their weight. A pale hand broke the surface of the water and grabbed at her, making her scream and push Alfie on to the first rung. Dazed, he pulled himself up, wheezing with the effort of each step. More hands fumbled for them as the water rose higher. Josie kicked them away with her feet.

Higher they climbed. Each rung smeared their hands with slime, making them slippery. Josie's knuckles ached and her muscles burned as she struggled to heave herself up the rope ladder, wincing each time the knife in her waistband dug into her stomach. She barely had time to jerk her head back to avoid being kicked in the face as Alfie's boot slipped. He dangled by his arms and Josie could hear his gasping sobs as he struggled to place his feet back on the ladder.

'Up there, Alfie, there's the hole at the top,' she called, hoping to encourage him. She fixed her eyes on the top of the ladder. The centre pole protruded through a wide gap edged with a metal ring, the same exit that Corvis's raven had tried to reach. Josie hoped they'd be more successful.

The incoming sea swirled around the tent now, narrowing the gap between the roof canopy and the water. It grew darker; the air felt warm and fetid. Josie could see pale bodies rising through the gloomy depths, floating upwards, arms extended. Alfie clambered up the pole and out through the hole. Josie could just see his hands clinging to the metal ring, the shadow of his body pressing into the fabric of the tent above her. He reached a hand down and she stretched hers up to meet it – but strong, bony fingers gripped her ankle and dragged her back.

The water swirled in her ears and she struggled to keep her mouth shut. She glimpsed dead eyes, pale flesh white against the green water, grasping hands. Her wet clothes pulled at her, helping the desperate hands below. She could just see the circle of light and Alfie's silhouette reaching in. With one last surge of effort, she kicked free and powered herself upwards. Alfie grabbed her upraised arms and dragged her through the hole.

The tide had almost covered the tent now. Nothing tried to break out of the top, no hands snatched at them any more. Josie kicked her feet, trying to keep above the surface as the tide rose higher. She could see Alfie struggling, too, his heavy clothes weighing him down.

Something snagged on her leg, stopping her rising with the water level. Josie glanced down, expecting another decayed fist to be gripping her. Instead, coils of green rope snaked around her calf, trailing down into the tent.

Josie blew bubbles of panic and tugged at the rope. Alfie was just a dark shape on the surface now, only a few tantalising feet away. Her lungs burned. She felt as if she would burst. She pulled again, but the rope just gave a dull twang as it tightened in the water. Josie pulled the knife from her waistband and slashed at the coils, but the rope remained stubbornly taut. Her whole body ached with cold and the effort of holding her breath in. With a final flurry of desperate hacking, she managed to cut the rope and kicked to the surface with it trailing from her leg, breaking through with a sobbing gasp.

Alfie splashed feebly over to her and they linked arms, trying to tread water. Below them, the tent became a dark, distant shape. The grisly audience was down there waiting for the two of them, waiting until they ran out of energy and succumbed to the numbing cold of the waves, waiting to welcome them back to the circus of the dead.

He is sunk in the waters, there lies asleep,
I will plunge there as well, I will kiss his cold feet,
I will kiss the white lips, once coral-like red,
And die at his side, for my true love is dead.

'The Drowned Lover', traditional folk ballad

CHAPTER TWENTY-SEVEN
THE *GALOPEDE*

Water slapped Josie's face as she kicked out, trying to keep afloat. Her clothes felt like lead weights pulling her down. She tried to tear them off, but every attempt sent her under the freezing water. Josie's legs, still entangled in the rope, ached with the effort of it. The water surged over her head, shocking her into lashing out with her arms. She broke the surface with a strangled scream.

A dark shadow filled the sky, black and rust red. Josie pulled her head up.

'A barge,' Alfie gargled, spitting out a fountain of salt-water. He panted beside her, spluttering and flailing his arms.

The huge boat was close but nobody seemed to have noticed them. Josie glimpsed a solitary figure at the stern. She could hear the swish and crack of the wind in the sails, mixed with the sea sloshing into her ears. Alfie yelled and waved his arms, sinking more than once in the process.

Kicking her legs, Josie pulled at the rope and coiled it up as best she could. Her fingers ached as she struggled to keep afloat and manipulate the rope. The waves from the barge splashed into her face as she plunged under again. She tied a loop in one end of the rope, pushing the handle of the knife through. The barge was passing rapidly – another couple of seconds and it would be gone. Josie willed her numb fingers to tighten the knot.

With a desperate scream, she sent the knife flying, then watched in despair as the rope came free and the blade flew on. Water surged over her head, filling her mouth before she could see what happened to the knife. The Amarant, Corvis – even Cardamom and Gimlet – were forgotten as Josie plunged down again, water filling her nose, mouth and ears, blotting out all sound. She felt a warmth creeping over her, a calmness; all she had to do was breathe in and sleep . . .

Something smacked on to the surface of the water above her. Instinctively, Josie grabbed hold of the floating object and felt rope criss-crossing soft cork blocks. A lifebelt! Heaving herself up on to it, she knocked heads with Alfie.

'The barge, Josie,' Alfie spat, retching up seawater and spluttering with laughter. 'We did it! We're safe!'

'Safe!' Josie coughed and pressed her forehead to Alfie's. Her legs dragged in the water as she felt herself being drawn towards the boat with rust-red sails and a black hull. The smell of tar and tobacco flooded her senses as a calloused hand gripped her under the arm.

'Welcome aboard the *Galopede*,' said a soft voice, as she was hauled over the side of the barge and dumped on to the deck. Josie knelt over and retched on to the clean wooden planks.

'Makin' a mess, chuck 'em back. Bad luck is what they is,' someone muttered angrily. A mop immediately swished under her nose, making her pull back.

'Hang on a minute, Manny,' said the voice. 'Easy with the mopping. She's 'alf the sea in her guts.'

'Threw a knife at yer from the sea,' Manny snapped. 'Bloomin' mermaid. Chuck her back.'

'Don't think the knife was aimed at me, Manny,' came the reply. 'An' she don't look like no mermaid neither . . .'

Josie's stomach heaved again, and she fell forward as whatever she had left inside her splattered over the deck. She looked up at a pair of bushy eyebrows and hard blue eyes set in a thin, angry face. The man wore a thick woollen hat pulled down over his hair. 'Mess,' he snapped and swished the mop again.

'Don't mind Manny,' said the other voice. 'He's just a touch too house proud is all.'

Josie turned to see a tall man bending down to thump Alfie's back, helping him to bring up the water he'd swallowed. Behind him, Josie glimpsed her knife buried in the woodwork, right beside the wheel.

'Darned near took me ear off,' the man chuckled. His

bearded face looked almost square, with a flat nose and squinting eyes framed by tight curls. 'Got me attention, though!'

'Mr Carr!' Josie coughed, retching seawater again.

'How in God's creation d'you know my . . . Good lord,' he said, his eyes widening. He gave Alfie a hearty slap on the back that sent him sprawling. 'The girl from Rookery Heights! Now 'ere's a tale we need to hear. But let's get you below first before you freeze to death – or there'd be no point in saving you from drownin'.'

Jacob Carr's cabin was a small box of a room, crammed with old charts and packing cases. Alfie and Josie crouched on a low pallet that acted as a bed, their clothes hanging out to dry. Rough blankets were wrapped around their slowly warming bodies. The boards of the hull creaked. The smell of pipe smoke mingled with tar and the scent of the sea.

They were safe.

'So,' said Jacob, narrowing his eyes behind his pipe, 'it's no business of mine, but Arabella left me a note to say you were in a spot of bother. I was expectin' to collect you last time I called at the quay. I must confess, I was beginnin' to think you were goners, both. What happened?'

'It all went wrong, Mr Carr,' Josie sighed. 'We did try to get away but that Sammy boy was too slow with the delivery. We ended up . . . hiding in the marshes . . .'

No need to complicate things by trying to explain about the circus, Josie thought. She shuddered at the memory of the pale, bloated shapes floating in the murky water and pulled the blanket tight around her, glad of its coarseness. She was still alive.

'An' the tide caught you, eh?' Jacob muttered. 'It's dangerous for sure out there. Land becomes sea in the twinklin' of an eye. Anyway, you bed down 'ere. We've one delivery, then on to London.' He clambered up the stepladder and out of the hold.

'So what now?' Alfie said, rocking with the movement of the barge. 'We're no nearer that Amarant or Mortlock or anythin'.'

'I know.' Josie rested her chin on her knees. 'Lorenzo said that the Amarant is buried.'

'But how would Lorenzo know? That's what I can't fathom,' Alfie said, scratching his wet head with the rough blanket.

Josie shrugged. She couldn't think straight. Her eyelids felt like stone weights. 'It's the Flower of Life, a magical thing . . .'

Alfie shook his head slowly. 'Nah. I reckon there's more to it.' He yawned and blinked. 'Just dunno what, that's all. Feels like . . .' his eyelids fluttered '. . . the more we find out . . . the less . . . we know . . . with this Amarant thing.' Alfie's eyes slid shut, the warmth and the rocking of the boat combining with his exhaustion to send him asleep on the pallet, snoring.

Josie smiled and lowered her head to the other end.

For once she *was* safe. She let her eyes close and drifted into a deep and dreamless sleep.

Screaming gulls dragged Josie from her slumber the following morning. She felt more rested than she had for days. A neat pile of clothes lay on the floor next to the bed. Josie tried her own garments on, but they still felt clammy. She held up the new clothes: a skirt, a thick woollen jumper and a blouse. Pulling them on, she wondered where Jacob had got them from. They felt dry and warm and were a comfortable fit, too.

The wind whipped at Josie's face as she popped her head out of the cabin. Alfie was chatting to Jacob, who stood square and solid at the helm of the barge. She shook her head. Yesterday, tied to the corkboard, drained by the ghostly circus folk, she wouldn't have given a ha'penny for her brother's chances. Now, far away from the circus, he had come back to life. Josie smiled, happy to have him back.

They stood at the stern of the wide vessel as it ploughed through the waves. A single mast rose up from the centre of the deck. Manny bobbed and ducked as he wrestled with a length of rope, securing it to the side of the ship. The red sails snapped in the wind. Josie grinned at Alfie. He wore a huge baggy jumper that came down to his knees and cord trousers, bundled up at the ankles. The bargeman looked straight ahead, listening with a quiet smile on his face.

'We're just making our way down the Thames, miss. Those clothes fit?' he asked Josie. 'Thought they would. They belonged to my Susan, spares for when she got wet. She doesn't come aboard these days. Married now, family of her own.'

'They're fine, Mr Carr, thank you. And I didn't thank you for saving us last night . . .' Josie said.

'Don't you worry, miss. Just glad you 'ad the sense to get our attention, however unorthodox,' Jacob replied, with an easy smile. 'Young Alfie's been tellin' me all about the funeral trade. Never knew there was so much to it.' He winked at Josie.

'No,' Josie said, hiding her grin. She looked out across the river. They weren't alone. The greys of winter were dotted with rust-red sails, barges bouncing through the choppy water towards London. In the far distance a dirty pall of smoke hung over the skyline of the city.

'We're makin' good speed. Soon be in London. You'll be glad to see this Mr Wiggins, then, I dare say?' Jacob said.

'Yeah,' Alfie cut in. 'He's my guardian. He'll be so glad to see us, Mr Carr.'

Josie remained silent, feeling the emptiness again. *Who waits for me in London?* She sighed.

'An' what about Lord Corvis?' Jacob glanced sidelong at Josie. 'Won't he wonder where you are?'

'I think we'll be fine, Mr Carr. I don't think he'll be looking for us any more,' Josie replied. The mention of Corvis made her uneasy. Could she trust Carr? He delivered to Rookery Heights, did business with Corvis after all. Maybe there was a reward out. Maybe Carr would sell them back to Corvis. Panic welled up in her chest.

'Fair enough,' Jacob said. His expression didn't change. He carried on chewing at his pipe and watching the bow of the barge. Josie shook her head. They were safe with him, she was certain. 'I won't pry. Ask no questions, as they say. You can keep those clothes, Josie. Yours will take a fair while to dry out, I reckon.'

Josie passed the morning sitting in the bow of the barge, watching it cut waves through the water. Alfie crouched with her, revelling in the sound of gulls and the hiss of the barge through the spray. The Amarant was never far from their thoughts. Each would start up a conversation, suggest an idea that would lead to a dead end or confusion.

'It's givin' me a headache,' Alfie grumbled. 'Like I said last night, the more we find out, the less we seem to know. I sometimes think it's hopeless . . .'

'Where there's a will, Alfie,' Josie said. 'We mustn't give up hope.'

'What did you say?' Alfie asked. His jaw had fallen slack.

'I said we mustn't give up hope . . .' Josie repeated.

'Nah, before that. About a will.' Alfie shook his head. 'You said somethin' about a will.'

'Not like a last will and testament, Alfie. I meant the will to do something,' Josie said. 'What are you twittering on about? I think some of that water's got into your brain.'

'No, but I *am* thinkin' about last wills and testaments.'
Alfie stood up. 'That barmy note your uncle gave you – it's
been buzzin' around my head for days now, like a tune you
can't quite remember but you're sure you know. Insisting
on being buried in Gorsefields Yard – now why would he
do that? I can't think of a dingier place to be planted.'

'Unless he wanted to lead us to something,' Josie said,
feeling her breathing quicken. 'And the way it was
written . . . You said it sounded like a riddle or puzzle.'
Josie shot a glance at her brother. 'That's it, Alfie! There
are clues hidden in that letter. There have to be.'

'But what did you do with it?' Alfie's face dropped. 'It'll
be ruined with the soakin' we've had.'

'I can remember some of it,' Josie said, drumming her
fingers on the deck. 'But we'd have to look at it closely.'
Josie's heart sank as she realised where it was. 'I left it in
the embalming room at the funeral parlour. But that was
days ago . . .'

Jacob shouted something to Manny, who scowled at
the children and then bustled past them, heaving on a
line.

'We can only hope Wiggins hasn't chucked it away,
that's all,' Alfie muttered.

Gradually, London drew nearer and the traffic on the
river grew busier. Manny leapt from job to job, tying up
sails, securing covers. All the time he never spoke, his
mouth tight and small.

'Manny's not one for conversation,' Jacob said as his
mate bustled past them. 'Saves his breath for when it's

needed. Rarely speaks on shore at all. Very particular about what he says and who he says it to.'

Red-sailed barges, bigger two- and three-masted ships, small skiffs, rowing boats – they all edged along the river, weaving in and out of each other. Josie found herself wondering at which point the river water had become so black and noxious again. She watched as the wild, marshy riverbanks gradually gave way to quays and docks, busy with men loading and unloading ships. Jacob pointed out the smaller boats that came trailing from the wharves to collect cargo from ships moored mid-river. And behind them all stood the city itself, with its domes and churches, warehouses and factories. The air became thick with smoke and the stench of the river. Jacob and Manny furled the sails and prepared to dock.

Josie and Alfie watched as the barge neared the quay. Gangs of burly men in oilskins and thick jerseys hovered, pouncing on the ropes as they were thrown out. Slowly the barge nudged the quayside. Gangways were lowered and the men swarmed into the hold of the *Galopede*.

'You can stay on the boat for a couple of nights if you need to, you know,' Jacob said, standing on the busy quayside once they had finally moored the barge. He drew on his pipe and gave them a nod. 'You're always welcome. It's nice having young folk back on deck.'

Manny rolled his eyes, but Josie thought she detected the hint of a smile play across his face.

'Thank you, Mr Carr,' she said, running her fingers through her hair. 'That's very kind of you. But I don't think Mr Wiggins will let us out of his sight after this.'

They gave a final wave and Josie led Alfie away into the crowd of dockers wheeling trolleys, carrying sacks and guiding crates being craned out of barge holds.

'Come on, Alfie,' she said, eyeing the crows and ravens that were reclaiming the skies from the river gulls. 'Let's hope that note is still in the embalming room. If it's not, we might just be sunk after all.'

Where shall I make it, my own pretty boy?
Where shall I make it, my comfort and joy?
Above in the churchyard, and dig it down deep,
Put a stone to my head and a flag to my feet,
And leave me down easy until I'll take a long sleep.

'Lord Rendall', traditional folk ballad

CHAPTER TWENTY-EIGHT
UNWELCOME NEWS

The crush of people reassured Josie as she twisted and turned between them. Each change of neighbourhood brought them nearer to Seven Dials. She just hoped and prayed that Wiggins hadn't scrapped the note. She could remember most of it, but what if there was something important that she had missed or forgotten about? Her stomach lurched.

Wharves and docks gave way to town houses and shops, the sailors and dock workers replaced by costermongers with barrows, couples linking arms, severe-looking gents marking each step with a jab of a lacquered cane and ladies clicking on the cobbles. Soon the congestion and chaos of the London streets was complete. Josie felt at home again, now that she was away from the grey marshes. Dressed in the clothes Jacob had lent them, she and Alfie looked like two river urchins, barely worth noticing. She followed her brother as he darted down ever-narrowing alleys.

Soon they found themselves at the rear of Wiggins's shop. Josie thought back to the night she'd watched Alfie in that same back room. So much had happened since then; it seemed as if years had passed.

Through the window Josie could see Mr Wiggins at one of his tables. He wasn't working. He sat with his head in his hands, staring at the tabletop. Alfie sidled up and pressed his palm to the window. Josie could see the tears in her brother's eyes.

'He thinks we're dead,' Alfie whispered, his eyes glassy. 'Poor beggar thinks we've gone.'

Alfie opened the back door next to the window and slipped inside, leaving Josie at the threshold. Alfie laid a gentle hand on his shoulder.

'Mr Wiggins?' Alfie whispered. 'You all right?'

'Alfie?' Wiggins stumbled to his feet and turned to the boy. 'Is that you?'

'Large as life, Mr W.' Alfie smiled as Wiggins wrapped his arms round him.

'I thought you were dead, what with poor Mr Gimlet . . . and the pony and trap crashed, but they said no trace of you could be found.' Wiggins patted Alfie's back. His voice barely rose above a whisper and tears trickled from beneath his thick spectacles. 'Oh, my boy, welcome back, welcome back!'

Josie watched as Alfie untangled himself from Wiggins's embrace and felt the sting of tears herself. With Cardamom and Gimlet taken, there was nobody to miss her while they'd been away, nobody to shed a tear on her return. She shuffled into the back room. Mr Wiggins coughed and dabbed his eyes with a handkerchief before giving her arm a squeeze.

'Thank the Lord you're safe,' he said. 'Both of you. Now, tell me what happened to you. Where have you been?' He lifted his lenses and peered at their rough clothing.

'Well, you'd better sit down again, Mr Wiggins,' Alfie said, 'cos it's a long story and one you'll find hard to swallow . . .'

Their tale came out jumbled and confused as Alfie and Josie took it in turns to share the details. Alfie would suddenly add something in the middle of Josie's part or she would correct some detail in his account. Mr Wiggins sat through it all, frowning and deep in thought.

'The note, Josie,' Alfie gabbled. 'We need the note.'

'Note?' Wiggins said, peering at Alfie.

'The one from my uncle,' Josie said. 'We left it here. The one about Gorsefields Yard.'

'This?' Wiggins pulled the note from his breast pocket. 'I found it on my embalming table. Doesn't make much sense, but I recognised the handwriting . . . my old friend. I kept it safe . . .'

Josie felt a glow of warmth for this old man. He cared about Cardamom – she could hear real affection for her guardian in the man's tone.

'Ah, but that's where you're wrong, Mr Wiggins.' Alfie grinned, snatching it and passing it to Josie. 'The note makes perfect sense.'

There is so much I wanted to tell you, so many regrets that will now lie buried with me. The truth is always at the end of the next sentence we never say. No one knows where the Amarant lies. Forgive my harsh words in the past, Josie, and the times I neglected you. I always loved you. Now think of my last words and don't heed the goodbye. We'll meet again. It is my last wish to be buried in Gorsefields Yard.

Take care, Josie.
Uncle Edwin, your loving guardian

'Yes, look here,' Josie said, smoothing it out. '*The truth is always at the end of the next sentence we never say.*' She jabbed a finger at Cardamom's letter. 'And at the end of the next sentence he says, *the Amarant lies.*'

Alfie looked over her shoulder. 'He was guiding you. Look: *Now think of my last words and don't heed the goodbye.* So we need to look at the last words before he says goodbye.'

Josie read breathlessly to the end of the letter. 'Here!' she cried. 'They say *buried in Gorsefields Yard.* The Amarant lies buried in Gorsefields Yard!'

Josie clapped her hands and hugged Alfie.

Wiggins sat silently for a long moment. A frown strained his brow.

'No,' he said, his voice quiet but firm.

'But, Mr Wiggins, after all we've been through . . .' Alfie said, leaping up from his seat.

'You're not going to Gorsefields Yard,' Wiggins said, gripping the side of the table.

'We have to,' Alfie said, his voice rising to a surprised squeak.

'We know it's dangerous but we must go,' Josie added, staring at Wiggins. 'After everything we've told you – don't you believe us? Why shouldn't we go?'

'Because that *is* where the Amarant lies . . . but it also happens to be the last resting place of Sebastian Mortlock!' Wiggins shouted, slamming his fist on the table. His voice dropped to a threatening whisper. 'If you uncover Mortlock's body then you might as well tell all the world that your precious Cardamom is a murderer!'

The words rang in Josie's ears like a gunshot.

'What do you mean, murderer? That's not true,' she said, trembling. 'A moment ago you said Uncle was your "old friend", and now you're accusing him of murder? I thought you cared about him? You're just jealous because he explored the world instead of grubbing around grave-yards all his life!'

Wiggins shook his head sadly. 'I only wish it weren't true,' he said, his voice falling to a low murmur. 'It was because I was Cardamom's friend that I agreed to look after you, Alfie, and because of our friendship I kept his secret safe all these years. He told me everything. How he, Corvis and Mortlock had found the Amarant. How after that he was a changed man – haunted, constantly worried that Corvis or Mortlock would go back to Africa to claim it. He kept Mortlock in sight by following

him everywhere, even joining a travelling circus with
him . . .'

'Lorenzo's Circus,' Alfie whispered.

'They wandered the land, watching each other,
becoming rivals for Madame Lilly's affections. Mortlock
won her heart, breaking Cardamom's in the process. But
it was always the Amarant that Mortlock truly loved. In
the end, he abandoned Madame Lilly for the flower.'

'None of this makes Cardamom a murderer though,'
Josie snapped.

'Mortlock returned with the Amarant,' Wiggins went
on quietly. 'Wanted to take Lilly back. But she'd found
another to love her and then the fever took her . . .
Mortlock could never accept that he'd lost her. He came
to London to kill her lover – the man he blamed for her
death . . . the Great Cardamom,' Wiggins said, polishing
his glasses with his coat-tails.

'Cardamom and Madame Lilly?' Alfie said, screwing
his face up. 'But you said she loved Mortlock?'

'But Mortlock had abandoned her; Cardamom had
always admired her. He treated her with respect and she
grew to love him. It's hard to explain but theirs was a
quiet, warm affection. He knew she still loved Mortlock
and prayed Mortlock would never return.'

'But he did,' Josie said. She thought of the letter calling Cardamom a thief. She realised for the first time that
Mortlock was accusing him of stealing Lilly, her mother.

'The two men met in Gorsefields Yard,' Wiggins murmured. 'Mortlock had even dug a grave for his old friend,

beneath the old yew tree. Cardamom told me that Mortlock began to brag – he was going to show him the full might of the Amarant by raising the dead from their graves.'

'And Cardamom killed him,' Josie whispered. 'But only to stop him from doing something terrible . . .'

'You are a loyal child,' Wiggins said with a sad smile. He hesitated. 'But misguided. Your guardian didn't kill his friend – he buried him alive. It seems they were fighting, and Cardamom grabbed a shovel and struck Mortlock with it. Mortlock fell into the grave. He was semi-conscious, but Cardamom just couldn't stop himself, and he threw shovelful after shovelful of earth down on top of his old friend. He didn't stop until Mortlock was completely buried. It must have been a kind of madness.'

'No,' Josie hissed, rising from her seat. 'It isn't true. You're making it up.'

'I'm only telling you what Cardamom told me,' Wiggins said with a sigh. 'He did what he had to do – he stopped Mortlock – but the guilt of what he'd done made it hard to live with. Mortlock's disappearance was always a mystery. It was never investigated properly. Edwin made a feeble effort to alert the police, for appearance's sake, but no one was interested. Glad to see the back of him, most folk were.' Josie thought of the letter from the police that her guardian had kept, tormenting himself with it night after night. Wiggins continued, 'If you disturb the grave now, questions will be asked. Cardamom's

good name will be dragged through the mire. His reputation will be besmirched for ever. That is why you can
never disturb Gorsefields Yard.'

Josie bit her lip. It was a terrible story – and so hard
to reconcile with everything she'd known about her
guardian. *She* didn't want to think that he had done
such a thing, so how could she live with everyone else
knowing? She thought of the smiling audiences at the
Erato, the ladies and gents who had waited to meet
the Great Cardamom. What would they say? His
final legacy would be that of a cold-blooded, brutal
murderer.

'But Cardamom asked to be buried in Gorsefields, Mr
Wiggins,' Alfie said. 'He gave us the note. He was tryin'
to point somethin' out to us.'

'Who knows how the guilty mind works, Alfie?'
Wiggins said, rubbing his eyes and pushing his spectacles
on to the top of his head. 'Maybe he felt he only deserved
to be buried at the scene of his crime.'

'Cardamom specified in his will where he wanted to be
buried and he told me to destroy the Amarant. Those
were his last words,' Josie said, folding her arms and
glaring at Wiggins. 'I know what he wanted and I'm
going to do it. Alfie?'

'Josie's right, Mr Wiggins,' Alfie said. 'Besides, when
Corvis gets his paws on it we'll all end up as living
corpses. His lordship won't rest until he has it!'

'I can't let you go, children. Let sleeping dogs lie.
Mortlock has lain there long enough and not caused any

trouble. This whole business will blow over if you let it. You watch and see.'

'If I could leave the Amarant and protect Uncle's reputation, I would. But Corvis *will* find the Amarant, Mr Wiggins. Alfie is right,' Josie said. 'And then there'll be no hope for any of us. If we can find it first and destroy it . . .'

'And how are you going to do that, Josie Chrimes?' Wiggins stared deep into her eyes.

'We'll find a way,' Josie stuttered. She couldn't hold Wiggins's gaze and glanced away. *But how?* she wondered. '*Sacrifice and a tender heart*,' Cardamom had said. What did that mean?

'No, I forbid it!' Wiggins growled. 'You will not, under any circumstances, go anywhere near Gorsefields Yard. Do I make myself clear?' Age had taken its toll on Wiggins but, looking at him, Josie remembered that he still dug graves, still walked miles after funeral processions. He could easily stop them if he wanted to.

'Sorry, Mr Wiggins,' Alfie said, snatching his guardian's glasses from his head. He walked up and down the shelves of bottles, rearranging them noisily. 'I hate to do this but if you look carefully up 'ere, then you'll find your specs in the end. Only . . . mind the arsenic!'

'Alfie, no!' Wiggins staggered to his feet but crashed into the table. Alfie grabbed a shovel and he and Josie ran, slamming the door behind them. There was nothing now that Wiggins could do to stop them.

SHE FOLLOWED HIM HIGH, SHE FOLLOWED HIM LOW,
TILL SHE CAME TO THE CHURCH-YARD;
O THERE THE GRAVE DID OPEN UP,
AND YOUNG WILLIAM HE LAY DOWN.

'SWEET WILLIAM'S GHOST', TRADITIONAL FOLK BALLAD

CHAPTER TWENTY-NINE
MORTLOCK

Josie and Alfie hovered near the gateway of Gorsefields Yard, waiting for the early night of winter. A funeral party had just broken up and the last few carriages had rattled out into the darkening lanes. One or two birds gave a subdued call as they settled down for a bitterly cold night. Josie could hear the distant bustle of the city, but here, around the yard, stillness had descended. Alfie looked cold and pinched, his face glum.

'We have to do it, Alfie,' she said, hugging herself to ease her shivering. She was saying this as much for her own sake as for his.

'I know,' Alfie murmured. 'But I didn't like doin' that to Wiggins, that's all. He deserves more respect.'

'You had no choice. He would've tried to stop us. Don't worry. Once this is all over, he'll understand.'

Now and then someone would pass by, not giving them a second glance. Alfie had hidden the shovel in a pile of old planks that someone had left leaning against the wall of the yard. 'Might look a bit odd, two youngsters hanging around a graveyard with a spade,' he'd said with a humourless grin.

The thought of what they had to do filled Josie with dread. Mortlock lay beneath the earth, a mouldering corpse, still clutching the Amarant – and they had to dig him up. She wanted to run back to Wiggins or to the *Galopede* and hide, but they couldn't shirk what had to be done. Just burying the Amarant wasn't enough – it had to be destroyed, once and for all.

Darkness settled over the city, making vague silhouettes of the dilapidated houses that huddled together around the yard. A thick layer of cloud obscured the moon. Checking there were no onlookers, they slipped in through the gates. Josie could smell the damp earth at her feet and feel the chill of night setting in. Shadows thickened, pushing their way into every corner and hollow of the cemetery. Gravestones were merging into blackness, becoming phantoms that seemed to move and quiver in the dark.

The branches of the yew hung low, groaning and creaking. Josie felt as if a lead weight lay on her shoulders and she stopped before reaching the tree, breathing deeply. Beside her, Alfie did the same. She didn't want to step beneath the yew. She didn't want to dig up a decayed body. Her heart hammered and her legs felt weak.

'Come on, Josie,' Alfie whispered, touching her elbow and steering her beneath the canopy of branches that shrouded the ancient, ridged trunk of the yew. They stood staring into each other's eyes. Josie could tell Alfie was afraid, too. His knuckles whitened as he gripped the handle of the spade. Nervously, he licked his lips and held the spade above the bare ground. With a final look at Josie and a hiss of breath, he drove the blade down into the earth.

Josie flinched. If a human voice had screamed just then, it couldn't have sounded worse than that grate of earth on metal. She glanced around at the shifting shadows of the graveyard, but not a soul moved. Alfie dumped the first pile of earth behind him and expertly slid the spade back into the ground. He flashed a grin at Josie. She hadn't realised how strong he was.

'I've watched Mr Wiggins,' he said, his voice quavering despite his brief display of confidence. 'Helped him out a few times, too.'

Josie said nothing, but stood over Alfie as he dug deeper. Slowly the hole grew. Josie knew she'd have to help him sooner or later. She couldn't stop thinking about what might lie down there. Hideous images of the circus folk and Cardamom's gutted body sprang into her mind.

Alfie paused and dragged his coat off. He was panting now and Josie noticed how he stumbled every now and then, spilling soil back into the hole.

Josie steeled herself and jumped down beside him. 'Here,' she said, grabbing the spade. 'Let me dig for a while.'

Alfie gripped the handle at first. 'Man's work –' he began.

'There's no time to argue,' Josie said, pulling the spade towards her.

Alfie resisted but she could tell the digging had weakened him. 'Just while I get me breath back, then,' he panted and scrambled out of the pit.

Josie stabbed the spade into the earth, wincing at the explosion of sound that seemed to reverberate around the yard. Each shovelful brought her closer to the body, the man who had suffocated in this rank-smelling dirt. Would he be twisted in some horrible position, as if trying to ward off the soil? Would she be able to see the expression of horror on his grimacing face? Josie gritted her teeth and slammed the spade into the bottom of the pit, throwing earth in all directions.

Alfie soon recovered and Josie gladly passed the spade back. She clambered out to keep watch as Alfie set to once more. The hole grew deeper. Josie could only see the white of his shirt as he bent to his work.

A carriage rattled past, making Josie cry out. Alfie froze. Neither of them dared breathe. They stood, Alfie up to his waist in the fresh pit, Josie towering over him, frozen like a stone monument. What if someone caught them? They could be hanged for this or thrown into prison with lunatics and murderers. Alfie waited, then slid his spade into the ground again. Every scrape, every clink of the metal blade, rang loudly in Josie's ears.

'I'm going to 'ave to rest again,' he puffed, and pulled himself out of the pit, leaning back on a pile of earth. His face was smeared with sweat and dirt and he was gasping for breath. 'You might 'ave to dig now. Don't know if I can carry on . . .'

Before Josie could say a word, a crimson glow suddenly illuminated the pit at their feet. It was faint at first but grew stronger. It pulsed like a heartbeat, casting shadows on the deep grooves of the yew tree and making the fringed leaves dance.

Josie stared, unable to speak. Alfie leaned over and peered into the pit. He gave a yelp and fell back on to the earth pile.

The light flickered around something – a shape that Josie couldn't make out. Now she could hear earth moving inside the excavated hole, dirt slipping off something, thumping to the floor. Her scalp prickled and her breath came in strangled gasps. A hand reached up from the pit, fingers stretching and trembling. In the red light, the skin looked dry and withered. Sinews snaked around the wrist and lower arm. Cracked fingernails dug into the earth as the other hand slapped on to the edge of the hole. Josie screamed as a head appeared above the side of the grave. She staggered back, covering her nose with the back of her hand, coughing on the stench that enveloped them as the rest of the living corpse heaved itself out.

'Lord above,' Alfie spluttered, staring up from the ground.

The putrefying man stood tall in the darkness, his brown skin clinging to his skeletal frame. Here and there, green putrid slime oozed from the split flesh. The corpse's hair looked patchy and matted, but long – as if it had continued to grow in the grave. His face grinned mirth-lessly. It was a death's-head smile: all teeth and no gums. Josie retched as a worm crawled from his nose cavity and plopped down on to his ridged chest. He stared at them both with brilliant white eyes. She wanted to run, to escape from the horrible sight. She closed her eyes and breathed slowly, trying to calm her leaping stomach.

'Josie, look in his body,' Alfie whispered to her. A small, red flower flickered like a tiny furnace behind his broken ribs, in the dark centre of his chest cavity.

'I am Sebastian Mortlock,' the cadaver said, his voice thick and wet. 'My children, you have come to me!'

Josie scrambled back between gravestones, tripping over Alfie as the hideous monster staggered towards her, arms outstretched.

Mortlock loomed over her.

'Do you have nothing to say to your long-lost father?'

THE GRAVE WILL DECAY YOU,
WILL TURN YOU TO DUST.
THERE IS NOT ONE IN A HUNDRED
A POOR BOY CAN TRUST.

'THE WAGONER'S LAD', TRADITIONAL FOLK SONG

CHAPTER THIRTY
TRUTH FROM THE TOMB

Mortlock stood over her. His arms fell to his sides. He tilted his head and stared at Josie.

'Am I so hideous to look upon?' he said. 'Do you not recognise your own father?'

'You're not our father,' Alfie snarled, edging round the ghastly figure to stand next to Josie. His face was pale and even in the darkness she could see he trembled violently.

'And what do you know of your father, Alfie Mortlock?'

Josie glanced at Alfie. Confusion and indecision flickered in his eyes. They knew hardly anything about their father. The subject had always been avoided. Why?

'He was a circus magician, P-Professor Necros,' Josie stuttered. 'He died . . . when we were babes . . .' Josie's voice trailed off; the pieces of the past clicked together in her mind. Cardamom had followed Mortlock to a circus.

Why hadn't she thought of that before?

'Professor Necros was my stage name. My blood runs through your veins, children. The power of the Amarant is strong within you because of me. I can sense it.' Mortlock squatted down, every sinew and joint creaking like wet leather. Flakes of flesh and chunks of bone tumbled from him as he shifted on his haunches. 'And what have they told you while I lay in my grave these last ten years, I wonder?'

'It was *you* that cursed Lorenzo's Circus,' Josie said, her voice hoarse with shock and fear. 'With the Amarant. You would have killed Cardamom, too, if he hadn't got you first.'

'Edwin Chrimes didn't lay me low, Josie,' Mortlock said. Something dripped down his cheekbone. He raised a long bony finger and pointed over her shoulder. 'He did.'

Josie swivelled round. Mr Wiggins stood frozen behind her, his mouth slack and his eyes wide with fear behind his large glasses. Somehow he must have scrabbled around until he found them. Alfie ran to his guardian.

'I had to,' Wiggins whispered, never taking his eyes off Mortlock's rotten frame. 'You would have killed Cardamom. He was my best friend . . .'

'He took Lilly from me, behind my back – brought her to this pestilential city, where she died of the fever,' Mortlock hissed. 'Chrimes was resigned to his fate until you struck me from behind . . .'

'Is it true, Mr Wiggins?' Josie said. 'You lied to us back at the shop. You said that Cardamom had buried Mortlock!'

Alfie stood speechless, staring at his guardian as if he were a stranger.

'D'you think I'm proud of it? I did what I had to do.' Wiggins's voice was low but clear. 'Cardamom was in trouble that night he came to me. He told me everything. I knew he didn't have the spine to stand up to Mortlock – he was never ruthless enough. Someone had to . . . Mortlock had the Amarant. So I followed Cardamom here.'

'Ten years I've lain pinned beneath six feet of earth, the Amarant burning into my heart, just keeping me alive,' Mortlock said, his voice thick as he struggled to swallow down the putrid liquid that seeped from the corners of his mouth. 'At first I hated them all. Cardamom, Wiggins – everyone. I cursed them as I lay in my grave. I dreamed of my revenge, the suffering I could inflict. Madness took me and I imagined laying waste to the world. But, children, my dreams were also of you as I left you, babes in your beautiful mother's arms . . .'

'But why didn't you bring our mother back to life if you had the Amarant?' Josie said, tears threatening to overwhelm her. As he'd been speaking, Mortlock's tone had softened, and now she felt bold. All her life she'd wanted her mother, dreamed of her mother – and this man, this awful festering corpse, could have done the one thing Josie had dreamed of.

'Peasants. Savages!' Mortlock's voice turned harsh again. 'The circus folk burned her in her caravan and scattered her ashes to the four winds. Were I to search for all eternity, I could never find my beloved Lilly, never return her to life.'

'You were blinded by hatred.' Wiggins trembled as he spoke and colour flooded his cheeks. 'You could never accept that Lilly cared for Cardamom. You neglected her in your lust for power and she left you.'

'No!' Mortlock shouted and took a menacing, creaking step towards Wiggins. 'Don't push me too far, old man. Remember, I have you to thank for this.' He spread his arms wide, showing them his torn body, the rags that clung to bone and strips of tattered flesh. Josie winced and turned her head away. 'You struck me down, buried me alive, and Cardamom looked on, did nothing. I never wanted power . . .'

'Then why did you want the Amarant?' Alfie murmured. He sounded sullen and looked from Wiggins to Mortlock as if he were trying to make up his mind who was the worst. Josie glanced at him. She knew the pain he was feeling – his guardian was not the man he thought he knew and loved. They had never considered their father until now, and now he turned out to be a monster. What a legacy she and her brother shared.

'Think, boy,' Mortlock said, his breath hissing from between his grinning teeth. 'A world with no death, no pain or suffering. That is my dream.'

'I told you he was mad,' Wiggins spat. 'He'd rule the world . . .'

'But it could never work,' Josie said softly, looking at

the intricate flower pressed into Mortlock's ribs. Crystal petals flashed in the gloom. She couldn't tell if it was a real plant or made of glowing stone. 'You could never fully own the Amarant. There would always be someone who would want it for themselves.'

'They would never take it from me,' Mortlock said. 'With the Amarant in my possession I am invincible. No one can equal its power.'

'You'd kill 'em,' Alfie said bluntly.

'And you said yours would be a world with no death,' Josie sighed, as sadness filled her voice. 'We must destroy the Amarant. There's no choice.'

'Only the holder of the Amarant can do that, Josie,' Mortlock said. The flower flared in his chest as he spoke. 'The Amarant is a living thing; it holds great power. The holder can wish for its death, but he will pay for its destruction with his own life.'

'I've heard enough,' Wiggins snapped and took a step forward. 'You should never have come out of that grave and I'm going to make sure you go back in – whatever the cost!'

Mortlock raised his hand. Josie screamed as the Amarant burned in his chest. An aura of blood-red light surrounded Wiggins and he fell to his knees, clutching at his heart. Alfie dashed forward.

'No! Mr Mortlock, don't, please,' Alfie shouted, tears streaming down his face. 'Not Wiggins – he's been like a father to me. Don't take 'im away from me!'

'A father?' Mortlock's eyes blazed red with the light of

the Amarant. Wiggins cried out again and doubled up in agony. 'That was all I dreamed about in the end, down there, under the cold clay. I wanted to be a father to you, to see you both again . . .'

'Then don't kill 'im, Mr Mortlock, I'm beggin' yer!' Alfie threw himself between Wiggins and Mortlock. 'For my sake!'

Mortlock lowered his hand and the deathly glow died. Wiggins gave a long rattling gasp and slumped to the floor, groaning. Josie watched as Alfie cradled him in his lap, rocking the old man like a baby and sobbing.

'I don't care what you done, Mr Wiggins,' he cried. 'I don't want you to die.'

Mortlock stood motionless, ignoring Josie, his whole attention fixed on Alfie as he held Wiggins. The Amarant's glow died to the tiniest flicker and a deep sigh, like leaves in a winter wind, blew through Mortlock's crumbling body.

'I've lost so much,' he whispered, his fingers stroking at the crimson petals blooming in his chest. 'And for what?'

'Well, if you don't want the Amarant, then why not give it to someone who can make good use of it?'

Josie turned to see the dark figure of Lord Corvis leaning against a large gravestone. He looked smaller than she remembered and more round-shouldered. His face was obscured by shadow, but its silhouette looked sharper, his nose longer. Aunt Veronica and Aunt Jay flanked him in their human form, their eyes fixed on Josie.

'You should be more careful, children. Our crows were

watching you from the moment you arrived in London. They alerted us to your presence when you left that worm-ridden barge. We've been following you ever since,' Aunt Veronica sneered.

'Corvis?' Mortlock said, and a frown clouded his mouldering face. 'Is that you?'

'In the flesh.' Corvis limped forward. Josie gaped. He'd changed almost beyond recognition. Dark, spiny feathers poked from his head, covering his face. The skin beneath had blackened to wrinkled leather. His nose had been replaced by the beginnings of a sharp beak. 'More or less.'

'Good God, man, look at you. What's happened?' Mortlock's eyes rolled away from Corvis in disgust.

'That's rich coming from you,' Corvis said, cackling and grasping another gravestone with a taloned hand. 'The Amarant hasn't been kind to either of us, I fear. My crow ladies share my life force, but I've inherited something from them, too, it seems.'

Josie glanced around. A chill shivered down the back of her neck as she looked for the third Aunt. Corvis must be distracting them, drawing their attention away while Aunt Mag crept up on them, she thought.

'I fear the Amarant's gift is not always pretty,' Corvis said quite matter-of-factly. 'But when it's in my possession, it really won't matter what I look like.'

Suddenly Josie made out a lunging shape in the darkness. She tried to scream a warning to Mortlock but it came too late. Aunt Mag appeared behind him, her eyes glinting with triumph. Mortlock's bony, putrefying body jolted and he looked down. Josie gave a despairing moan and shook her head.

Aunt Mag had punched her beak through Mortlock's corrupted flesh and grasped hold of the Amarant. With a spiteful hiss, she yanked it out through his back and, with one leap, landed at Corvis's feet, holding the flower for him to take. He grabbed it and held it up.

Mortlock swayed and crumpled to his knees. The light faded from his eyes as the energy of the Amarant seeped from his body. He stared hopelessly at Josie. She stared back, unexpected tears suddenly bursting out of her as she gazed at the wrecked face of her father. She'd feared and hated this hideous creature. Now she pitied him.

'At last!' Corvis croaked, raising the Amarant above his head. 'The power to bring order to this chaotic world.'

FOR LOVE IS STRONG AS DEATH,
PASSION FIERCE AS THE GRAVE.

THE SONG OF SOLOMON, OLD TESTAMENT

CHAPTER THIRTY-ONE

SACRIFICE AND A
TENDER HEART

Corvis stood triumphant; the Aunts knelt around him as if in worship. Their eyes flashed red as they stared greedily at the Amarant.

'The power to create more of our brothers and sisters,' cackled Aunt Mag. 'No longer to hide in the shadows, to feed on the leavings of man. We shall fill the skies and take our rightful place by your side, my lord!'

'I'm sorry,' Corvis snapped, jerking his head down to look at them. 'Do you think I would share this power with you? Eaters of offal? Scavengers from the fields of battle?'

'But you promised, my lord,' Aunt Mag hissed, scrambling to her feet and taking a step back.

'Yes, I did, didn't I?' Corvis mused. 'But then, you see, I couldn't spend another night listening to your insane cackling or watching your appalling table manners!'

He pointed his finger at Aunt Mag and the Amarant

flared into life. Its light grew and engulfed her. Josie watched as Aunt Mag writhed and screamed in agony, shrinking into herself, fluttering feebly as her shape changed. As she begged for mercy, Josie bit her lip. *She doesn't deserve this torment*, she thought. *No matter what she's done.* Smaller and smaller Aunt Mag shrunk, until her feathers vanished. All that was left was a wrinkled chick, then an egg, black and shining. Corvis shook with laughter and raised the heel of his boot over the egg.

Josie glanced down. The spade lay at her feet, blade pointing at her. She stamped her foot down, flicking the spade up and catching it. It was heavy and not designed for throwing, but instinct took over. She felt its weight, judging its centre of gravity, how to hold it and how best to throw it. With a yell, she hurled it like a spear at Corvis.

Time slowed down.

The spade's metal blade glimmered, flashing in the crimson light of the Amarant. Corvis turned, eyes wide in shock. He threw himself backwards but Josie had not aimed at his head or body – she had aimed at his arm. The spade was old; years of cutting through clay earth had sharpened it to a knife's edge. It struck Corvis's wrist. Josie winced at the shower of blood that spurted from his severed hand, which fell to the floor, still clutching the Amarant.

Corvis slumped against a gravestone, staring dumbly at the stump of his wrist pumping his lifeblood into the cold earth at his feet. He gaped at Josie, then at the two remaining Aunts, who advanced slowly towards him.

'Get back,' he said, his voice already slurring from the loss of blood. 'If you kill me then you will go back to being mere carrion crows . . .'

He tried to turn and run, but Josie could see that his feet refused to move, making him twist drunkenly and fall behind a gravestone. The Aunts fell upon him, tearing with their claws. Limbs thrashed in the air and a disgusting gargling sound forced Josie to cover her ears. For a short moment, Corvis's remaining hand gripped the top of the headstone. Josie watched, paralysed, as his blood trickled down the lettering on the stone, filling each character and spelling out the name *The Great Cardamom.*

Corvis's death scream penetrated Josie's covered ears. Then all lay still and silent. She edged forward and peered over Cardamom's gravestone, needing to be sure that Corvis was really dead. Shadows swirled like smoke in the darkness. Josie stifled a scream. Corvis lay in human form again, pale and bloated, his skin maggot white. Two crows pecked at his raw, bleeding stump, dragging at sinews and muscle. One hopped on to his shoulder and cocked its head at Josie, then plunged its beak into his eye. The other gave a raucous caw, making Josie stumble back, and both birds flapped their wings, lifting themselves into the shadows of the moonless night. Josie stared after them as they became indistinct, melting into the dark.

'Josie?' Alfie's voice snapped her out of her trance. He

still lay cradling Wiggins, who groaned every now and then.

But Alfie wasn't looking at his guardian. Instead, he stared at Mortlock, who had dragged his ravaged carcass to the fallen Amarant. He held the flower before him.

Its light grew stronger, bathing Mortlock and repairing his broken body. Brown parchment skin grew light and pink, spreading over swelling muscle. Hair sprouted from his shining scalp. His whole frame seemed to expand as organs grew and flesh returned. Soon Mortlock stood, clothed in rags from the grave, but a picture of living health.

'Maybe if you see me as I was, you will know I am not a monster,' Mortlock said with a smile. Josie nodded, taking in his broad nose and wide forehead. He reminded her of a lion with his hair swept back. Looking on him now, alive and unmarked by the grave, Josie almost forgot the terrible things he had done. Her father was alive! She turned and looked at Alfie. He shared the same wide mouth and broad nose. There was a marked family resemblance.

Wiggins let out a groan, tearing at her fantasy. Mortlock had nearly killed the old man; Mortlock had wanted to kill Cardamom. Now he was out of his grave and he would control the world.

'We can't let you keep the Amarant,' Josie said, her heart heavy. She'd lost Gimlet and Cardamom, and now Mortlock would probably kill her, Alfie and Wiggins. But this wasn't only about their lives. She had to destroy the

Amarant for everyone else who had ever loved and lost, for all the people whose lives the Amarant would pervert and ruin in the future. And for the poor cursed souls of Lorenzo's Circus.

'I can't let you take it, Josie,' Mortlock said. He already sounded resigned to the fact that he would have to destroy his own children. Then he hesitated. 'When the crow took the Amarant, you cried. Were those tears for me?'

Josie paused for a moment. 'Yes,' she said quietly. 'For the father I never had. For you, lost and powerless.'

'I am your father. Couldn't you join me in everything the Amarant will enable me to do?'

'Never.' Josie shook her head. 'You can't stop death, and you will have to kill us to keep the Amarant. Whatever you do, death will find a way to creep into your perfect world – and a living death is the most awful thing of all. The Amarant is a curse, even if it looks like something beautiful.'

'Then I shall make an end of it,' he said, raising the Amarant. Josie closed her eyes and bowed her head, waiting for the final explosion of pain that would end her life.

Nothing.

A gentle breeze blew hair across her face, and she looked up. Mortlock stood with the Amarant above his head. A trail of light corkscrewed down around his body, gradually increasing in speed. A low moaning sound came from the Amarant.

Mortlock smiled at Josie. 'The Amarant is a living

flower. I only have to command it and it will destroy itself. But the price is my own life – I told you that. Sacrifice and a tender heart, Josie . . .'

'Yes,' she said, staring up at him wonderingly, tears spilling down her face.

'I love you, Josie. Both you and Alfie,' he said gently. 'I always wanted to know you – to know what being a real father would be like. And now I've found you, seen you . . . I see that I could never keep the Amarant without killing you, my own children, and I just can't do it. Not when you are so full of life and love. And I'm tired, Josie, so tired. Now get away, quickly! Before it's too late.'

The pace of the swirling light increased, and sparks flashed from the Amarant like a miniature lightning storm. The flower's song grew to an anguished howl. Mortlock screwed his eyes shut. Alfie had clambered to his feet, and a strong wind buffeted them as they stood watching. The old yew's branches groaned and creaked as the force of the gale increased.

Alfie tugged at Josie's elbow. Wiggins leaned heavily on his shoulder. Josie glanced back to her father as he clutched the Amarant in the heart of the crimson storm. He opened his eyes and smiled, his hair blowing wildly as the Amarant howled.

'Try not to think too harshly of any of us, children,' Mortlock called above the screaming Amarant. 'Go, or it will destroy you all. Hurry!'

The noise deafened Josie now and the wind nearly blew her over. Alfie dragged her away from the blinding

halo of light that surrounded Mortlock. She shielded her
eyes as his flesh began to darken, his limbs thinned and
grew wizened. Wiggins staggered past Josie. He'd lost his
glasses again and without them he could barely see. The
wind reached hurricane force as the whirl of light around
Mortlock sought to suck everything in. Josie, Alfie and
Wiggins linked elbows and stumbled towards the gates.
Dead leaves whirled around the yard, empty bottles that
had been discarded over the graveyard wall flew past
their heads, and floral tributes from newly dug graves
smashed through the air.

Josie screamed. Skeletal fists punched through the soil.
Long-dead bodies dragged themselves from the graves of
Gorsefields Yard on decayed arms. Their empty eye sockets turned towards the Amarant as it built up to a final
explosion of power.

She could feel the force of the Amarant dragging at
them, pulling them back. Leaning their bodies into the
wind, the three of them inched nearer to the rattling
gates. With a final effort they hurled themselves forward.
The wind suddenly stopped, sending them into the street
in a tangle of arms and legs.

In the split-second stillness, Josie looked back to see
Mortlock raise a hand.

'Live, children, live!' he called, then vanished in a
blinding flash, a deafening boom. It sounded like a thous-
and cannons exploding at once.

The whole graveyard seemed to lift. Bricks and lumps
of gravestone flew out of the yard, bouncing off the

houses that surrounded it. Windows shattered. Josie heard people screaming and babies crying. Glass and debris littered the street.

Alfie lay slumped over Wiggins with his eyes closed. Josie reached for him as darkness filled her vision.

EPILOGUE

Josie sat in the parlour above Wiggins's shop. She stared out of the window at the rough and tumble of the street below. Easing herself forward, she winced and sat back. She'd never quite understood how she'd ended up back at Wiggins's, tucked up in bed. Over the following days, she'd heard broken conversations from the shop downstairs. Customers had been enquiring after Wiggins's health ever since news had got out that he'd been near the terrible gas explosion that had devastated the chapel and churchyard at Gorsefields. Wiggins was mending very well, thank you, she heard Alfie reply. He seemed to be up and about as if nothing had happened.

Josie straightened up and massaged the base of her spine with a groan.

'You still grumblin' about your aches and pains?' Alfie said as he entered the room with some cold beef and a crust of bread for her. 'I thought us Mortlocks healed quicker than most. You'd better hurry up and get better or you'll be letting the family down.'

Josie rolled her eyes. 'Is that who we are?' she muttered, not looking at Alfie. 'Mortlocks?' The idea was still new, and still painful. How would she forget that vision of her father, rotted from years in the grave? She shivered at the memory, still haunted by it every night in her sleep.

'Well, I suppose so, like it or not. You can't choose your father, can you?'

'You know what? You look like him,' Josie said. 'Much more than I do.'

'That's why Cardamom asked Wiggins to look after me, so I'm told,' Alfie said with a sniff. 'He couldn't bear to look at me once Lilly had gone. Reckons I reminded him too much of Mortlock.'

'So what about Wiggins? How could he live with you reminding him every day of Mortlock?' Josie gave Alfie a dark look. She still wondered if she could stay under the same roof as Wiggins, after all he'd done.

'He's a practical man, Josie. He did what he had to do to protect his friend and he brought me up well. Whatever you say about him, he risked everythin' to save his best friend. Not many people would do that. Where would we be – you, in particular – if he hadn't rescued Cardamom?'

'I don't know.' Josie felt the ever-present tears returning. There was so much to come to terms with, so much that was almost inexplicable in both their pasts. 'I think a lot about Cardamom. Who was he really? I thought the world of him and yet now I feel I hardly knew him at all. What was he? A charlatan? A coward who couldn't stand up to Mortlock? He never, ever told me the full truth about anything, and it's hard to forgive him for that.'

'He was an ordinary chap, Josie. But he loved you, for sure. There's good in all of us and a bit of bad, too. They were all ordinary blokes who'd grabbed hold of somethin' terrible and powerful that took them right out of their depths. That plant was too much for any man, if you ask me.'

'Yes.' Josie sighed and looked out of the window again. 'There must have been some good in Mortlock, to sacrifice himself like that. It was as if in the end he wanted a way to redeem himself. He had one last chance, and he took it.'

'Most folks ultimately want good more than evil,' Alfie said and squatted down close to her. Not for the first time Josie envied him his happy-go-lucky temperament.

'Do you suppose the curse has been lifted from Lorenzo's Circus?'

'I'd think so, now that the Amarant's destroyed,' Alfie replied. 'No plant, no power to keep the curse goin'. I'm bettin' they're all laid to rest now. An' I had word from Arabella. She's safe. Mr Carr called in at her village. She'd been pesterin' all the bargemen who moored up there, askin' if there was any news of us.'

'It's good to know she's all right,' Josie said, pulling the crust of bread apart. She was suddenly famished.

'And what about you, Josie?' Alfie said softly. 'Mr Wiggins wants you to stay here, y'know.'

'I'm not sure. I don't know what I'll do, Alfie,' Josie said, looking back out of the window.

'Well, you can stay as long as you want.' Alfie stood up. 'And if you do decide to leave, you know where we are.'

'Our father could have ruled the world,' Josie whispered, grabbing her brother's hand and staring through the window at the bustling crowds below. 'But he gave it all up for us. I keep thinking about that.'

'Then maybe we should be a little bit proud to be called Mortlock,' Alfie said, a grin lighting up his face. 'He left you with somethin' else if only you'd realise it – the most precious thing goin', I reckon.'

'What?'

Alfie held out his arms and his beaming face softened. 'Stay with us, Josie. I don't wanna lose you.'

Josie gazed at him, then, smiling for the first time in a long while, said, 'Very well, Alfie Mortlock, I'll stay. Though what you want with a bossy older sister, I can't fathom.'

Alfie laughed, stealing some of her bread. 'We're twins, how can yer be older? Bossy, yeah. Older, never . . .'

Josie jumped to her feet and put her hands on her hips. *This*, she thought, *is an argument that will go on for years.*

THERE WAS A CROW SAT ON A TREE,
AND HE WAS AS BLACK AS BLACK COULD BE.

NOW THIS OLD CROW SAID TO HIS MATE,
'LET US GO AND FIND SOMETHING TO EAT.'

THEY FLEW ACROSS THE WIDE, WILD PLAIN,
TO WHERE A FARMER HAD SOWN SOME GRAIN.

UP CAME THE FARMER WITH HIS GUN,
AND HE SHOT THEM BOTH, EXCEPTING ONE.

THE ONE THAT ESCAPED FLEW BACK TO THE TREE,
AND HE SAID, 'YOU OLD FARMER, YOU CAN'T SHOOT ME.'

'TWO OLD CROWS', TRADITIONAL FOLK SONG